HELLBOY

HELLBOY

A Novelization by Yvonne Navarro
Based on the Motion Picture Screenplay
by Guillermo Del Toro

POCKET STAR BOOKS
New York   London   Toronto   Sydney

This book is a work of fiction. Names, characters, places and incidents are
products of the author's imagination or are used fictitiously. Any resemblance to actual events or locales or persons, living or dead, is entirely
coincidental.

An *Original* Publication of POCKET BOOKS

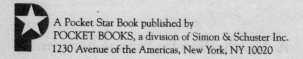

A Pocket Star Book published by
POCKET BOOKS, a division of Simon & Schuster Inc.
1230 Avenue of the Americas, New York, NY 10020

Copyright © 2004 by Revolution Studios Distribution Company, LLC.
All Rights Reserved.

ISBN: 0-7434-9289-7

First Pocket Books printing March 2004

10 9 8 7 6 5 4 3 2 1

POCKET STAR BOOKS and colophon are registered
trademarks of Simon & Schuster Inc.

Manufactured in the United States of America

For information regarding special discounts for bulk purchases,
please contact Simon & Schuster Special Sales at 1-800-456-6798
or business@simonandschuster.com

For my friend,
Christopher Golden

Thank you to:
Christopher Golden
Mike Mignola
Guillermo del Toro
Margaret Clark
Weston Ochse
Martin Cochran
Shira Kozak
Keith Guin
Marty Meadows
Alda Ward Smith
Atomic Comics in Mesa, Arizona

Prologue

MEMORIES.

There's something conducive about the darkness and what it does to the files inside an old man's mind. If daylight had a texture, it would be abrasive, always filled with stops and starts and the pitfalls of distraction. But darkness? Darkness is different. It's like . . . *oil*, smooth and warm, sliding into the cracks and crevices made by decades of hard living, leveling out the mental paths so that the steps of recollection can be made without stumbling. Add the color red to light the way and a man can find just enough illumination to reveal a thousand things that might or might not have been better left hidden. . . .

The darkroom had always been a comforting place for George Matlin. It was the place to which he retreated when the world and all the strange things in it became too overwhelming, when they had to be put down on photo paper to prove, even to himself, that such things really *did* exist. Now that he'd gotten on in years, he found himself there more and more often, although he wasn't sure why. It wasn't like he could hide from the things he'd experienced, from all the knowledge packed into his brain's memory cells. So many of his friends had succumbed to senility or, worse, Alzheimer's disease; he couldn't decide if the fact that his mind hadn't sought refuge in that foggy veil of incapacity was a blessing or a curse.

Before he got started, Matlin spent a little time walking around and touching the well-used things. The majority of what was in here was outdated or overworn. The optical enlargers, the battered porcelain trays, the timers—they were all long past the time when they should have been replaced by . . . what would one of the young people say? Of course—newer, better, bigger. But again, these things, these *old* things, like the stills hanging out to dry and awaiting inspection, gave him a sense of contentment and place, showed him that he still belonged in this small, solitary room.

Matlin rubbed the back of his neck, feeling and accepting the extra flesh beneath his fingertips before he reached up and pushed his glasses more firmly against the bridge of his nose. He'd definitely picked up a few pounds since his military days, but then so had most of his comrades. When his deployments as a combat photographer and the daily PT drills had came to a halt, nature had moved quickly in to claim her spaces in his body.

Nearsighted or not, he still caught the small movement out of the corner of his eye—the technician, waiting for him to start, his expression both curious and disbelieving. Matlin had seen that expression a hundred . . . no, a thousand times during his life. The interesting thing was that it had usually been in the mirror.

"Is he real?" he said to the technician. "Oh yeah—absolutely." Matlin rubbed the back of his stiff neck again. He might accept it, but he hated being old. "I haven't talked about it for years, you know?" He glanced at the camera, then smiled as he reached down and hefted a box full of old negatives. "Everyone called me crazy," he said as he pawed through it, "but I have the negative."

Matlin glanced up again but the technician had already slipped outside the darkroom. An instant later the red lightbulb above the door winked on, bathing the small room in eerie, scarlet light. Matlin heard the tech's voice, sounding tinny over the small intercom.

"Get ready. Three, two, one—roll tape."

Matlin took a deep breath and willed his voice to be strong and steady, no shaking allowed. He refused to sound like a decrepit elderly has-been while he made this recording—it was too important. He closed his eyes briefly and let the images flow back into his mind; when he opened his eyes, his gaze was as bright and clear as his voice.

"It all started back in forty-four. I was a Corps photographer aboard an Allied submarine off the coast of Scotland. It was a classified mission, and I was only twenty-one. . . ."

1

HOT AND HUMID AND CROWDED, ALL AWASH IN RED— the inside of the submarine was like some sort of devil's festival on a southern Alabama night at the height of summer. Add a few mosquitoes and the illusion might have been complete . . . well, except for the clanking of the pipes and the hiss of steam, the constant low sound of metal groaning under untold pounds of water pressure. Matlin had three 35mm cameras hung around his neck, and he would have added another—a good photographer can never have enough equipment—except it would have made the narrow pathways even more impossible to navigate. His cameras were already taking a beating every time someone squeezed by him in the passageway.

As if they'd been reading his mind, a squad of Special Ops soldiers hustled past him as they loaded their weapons, oblivious to the thumps and bumps they layered on the young photographer and certainly paying no attention to his equipment or the seamen who ran the sub and watched them suspiciously as they passed. But Matlin wasn't complaining as he shrank back, even though a duo of pipes dug painfully into his spine. He'd be a happy man if he could just keep the box of negatives he'd been going through from getting knocked out of his hand.

Matlin pulled the cardboard crate closer to his chest as he saw Sergeant Whitman bringing up the rear. He looked aggravated—well, he always looked that way—and his uniform was soaked in sweat. Matlin wondered whether he'd been working his men or if it was the stress that was making the man heat up; Whitman was a tough-as-nails career military guy who'd already worried himself out of most of his iron gray hair, so it was hard to tell. Matlin had a moment to wonder where the sergeant was going, then he remembered that they had a civilian on board, an English guy who wasn't much older than Matlin himself but who already had the ear of President Roosevelt. Pretty high profile for a young guy, and it was a sure bet Whitman was headed down to talk to him.

Whitman marched past, jaw jutting out and an unlit cigar clenched tightly between his teeth. Matlin fell into step behind him, still thinking about the Englishman he hadn't yet met. Already a professor, Trevor Bruttenholm—"Broom" for short—was supposed to be the "paranormal adviser." To Matlin, who believed in what he could see and always had a camera around

to prove it, this wasn't just incredible, it was *unbelievable*. Add to it Bruttenholm's proximity to the president himself, and it was enough to make Matlin think the whole world had gone insane.

Sergeant Whitman continued down the narrow, uncomfortable passageway to a small stateroom, then pushed in the door. Over Whitman's shoulder, Matlin got his first glimpse of the so-called paranormal adviser, Broom. He looked a bit older than Matlin had heard, but not by much, and perhaps his appearance was a by-product of the tension they were all under. Maybe twenty-nine, Broom was a tall, gaunt young man with olive-toned skin that looked unhealthy in the poor lighting of the room. With his oxfords, dress slacks, and a shirt topped by a wool vest, Bruttenholm looked out of place on the submarine, among all the men dressed in various military uniforms. Matlin had to grin to himself when he realized the professor was even wearing cuff links. Alone in the room, he was seated at a small table on which he'd placed an ancient-looking set of tarot cards.

"Broom," snapped Whitman. "Topside—*now*."

Without bothering to look at Sergeant Whitman, Broom turned the top two cards faceup.

The Fool.

The Moon.

"The sooner we're done, the better," Whitman growled.

Broom nodded and stood, then turned and grabbed an open wooden box whose antique sides were worn smooth. Over Whitman's shoulder, Matlin got a glimpse of its contents: old books just as worn as the box itself, a dozen different amulets and odd-looking paraphernalia. Bolted from one end to the other was a leather strap that let the man carry it like a carpenter's box. The professor hefted it over his shoulder, then gave the sergeant a heavy-lidded look. "This is an important mission, Sergeant Whitman. I hope you realize that."

Whitman only stared back at him, barely concealing his animosity. "Oh, you don't wanna know what I think. Topside *now*."

Changing his mind, Broom slid the big box off his shoulder and rummaged quickly through it until he found a smaller box, along with a couple of specific amulets. He started after Whitman, then paused at the table. With a troubled expression, he reached down and flipped the next card faceup. It flicked against the tabletop with a soft *snap*.

The Devil.

The north of Scotland in October wasn't the most pleasant place in the world to be. It was cold, raining like God himself had turned the celestial shower on to Cold and forgotten to shut it down, and the pall of the war hung over everything. The

tunnel they were in masked the sound of the rain, but it was chilly and humid in here, oppressive. The few flashlights Whitman's men had seemed dim and were aimed at the floor to provide only the bare minimum of light, just enough to ensure they didn't step over some edge and fall into an abyss. The mountain pressed down on them, making the tunnel carved into it seem flimsy, a fool's pathway through something that could crush them in barely the blink of an eternal eye.

Sergeant Whitman's face was rigid, his cheekbones edged sharply by the sparse light, his eyes recessed pits of darkness as he motioned to the soldiers to spread out. He would have passed Broom and gone to the front of the group, but the younger man reached out and snagged his arm. His voice was an insistent half-whisper. "Sergeant Whitman? Sergeant Whitman, may I have a word?"

The sergeant tugged his sleeve out of Broom's grip and looked at him impatiently. "What is it?"

Broom glanced around and saw several of the men watching them. "In private, if you don't mind."

The tunnel had widened into a larger room that was apparently a small, ancient chapel, and the professor led Whitman off to the side, out of earshot of anyone else. Whitman had a flashlight but he was keeping it at low power; when Broom pulled something out of one of the deep pockets of his coat, the sergeant had to shine the weak beam on it to see what Broom was offering him.

"Your men," Broom said urgently. He held up his wooden box, then lifted the lid. His fingers dug around until he could pull out one of the items, and he lifted it so Whitman could see the wooden rosary. "They'll need these."

Whitman's mouth fell open in amazement, then he scowled. "You're a Catholic?"

Broom swallowed and his gaze flicked around the chapel carved out of the mountainous rock, its ceiling long ago fallen in. Above them the sky boiled with storm clouds, and hanging from the stone walls overhead and slightly to his rear was a larger-than-life carving of Christ. The darkly stained wood was cracked with age and dripping with mold from the humidity, and the image was anything but comforting. "Among other things, yes. But that's hardly the point."

Whitman snorted, then brought out an automatic. He shoved a magazine into the stock and loaded the first round, then offered it to Broom. "Here. *You'll* need this."

But the professor shook his head. "I abhor violence." The sergeant shrugged and turned, shoving the weapon back into a holster at his belt. His firm stride had already taken him six feet away when Broom called after him. "Sergeant Whitman, I hope you don't think me mad—"

Whitman didn't pause. "Three days too late for that one . . . *Professor*."

Broom exhaled in defeat, then dared to again look up at the wooden carving of Christ.

It had no eyes.

Cameras and straps tangling around his neck, Matlin struggled with his tripod and a camera bag as he finally caught up with Whitman and his troop. Damn, but it was going to be hard to get any kind of a decent photograph in here. There was next to nothing for light, and no way could he set up one of his shooters and leave it be for the amount of exposure time he'd need to get a semidecent photograph.

Still, this was as exciting as any assignment he'd ever been on, and he was going to try his best. With that in mind, Matlin managed to work his way up to the front by the time the tunnel widened into some kind of room and that Bruttenholm guy—Broom, as they were all calling him—came hustling out of the darkness at one side of it. He made a beeline for Sergeant Whitman, and when the older man turned to meet Broom, it was obvious he was ticked off. If the word making the rounds on the sub were true, Whitman would have just as soon thrown Broom overboard as looked at him.

"You're wasting our time," he growled out in a low voice, thrusting his big-jawed face forward until it was only an inch from Broom's. "There's nothing on this island but sheep and rocks."

But Broom didn't back down. "Ruins," he pointed out quietly as he scanned the area around them, "not rocks. The remains of Trondham Abbey. Built on an intersection of Ley Lines, the boundaries between our world and the other—"

"What a load of *crap*," Whitman interrupted. "Hell, a week ago, I hadn't even heard the word parabnormal—"

"Paranormal," corrected Broom, but the sergeant had already turned away, as if he were ready to instruct his men to leave. "But you read the transmission."

Whitman stopped and spun back, glowering at the younger man. "*Half* transmission. Nonsense—German ghost stories."

Broom regarded the man solemnly. "I have seen ghosts, Sergeant."

"Oh, I'll bet you have," Whitman sneered at him.

While he'd wisely stayed out of it, Matlin hadn't missed a word of the two men's argument. The soldiers had slowed, sensing their sergeant might tell them to turn back; Matlin had ended up in the lead and now, just about to crest a small slope, he set his tripod down with a grunt of relief. He glanced over his shoulder at Whitman and Broom, then stretched forward, trying to see over the rise and if it were worth it to go any farther. The first thing he saw were the lights. Then he gasped.

Thirty feet below was an impressive Romanesque ruin. Strands of work lights were spread around a cavernous space, illuminating tall, heavy archways and crumbling statues. Dozens of Nazi soldiers scurried around the space, making it look like an ant farm encircled by thick stone walls.

Matlin heard Sergeant Whitman's sharp intake of breath as he and Broom clambered up next to him and peered over the rise. When he glanced sideways, he saw one corner of Broom's mouth turn up, but Matlin wasn't sure if the professor was smiling or showing how displeased he was at the display of manpower and equipment below. When Broom spoke, his tone was bland, but his words had an unmistakable bite.

"They must be here for the sheep."

All the flashlights had been extinguished, and now the few people who were authorized to talk were careful to do so only in hoarse whispers. Broom huddled between Sergeant Whitman and that photographer, Matlin; he hoped to God their heads didn't show over the edge of their hiding place, that some razor-sighted Nazi didn't happen to glance their way and see something—a glint of light off a metal fastener, the shine of a rifle barrel where the blackening had worn away—that would cause the whole operation to come crashing down on their heads.

German soldiers still rushed back and forth below, but the thing that interested Whitman the most was a little farther to the back, in an area off to itself. In that spot, about a dozen soldiers worked swiftly to assemble some kind of a large, steel machine. Overseeing it all and barking orders every few seconds was a spindly Nazi dressed in black leather. Although everyone else seemed to be dressed normally, this man's face was covered by something that looked like a modified gas mask. That was a puzzle all to itself, because there didn't appear to be any reason for something like that.

Whitman nudged Broom a little too hard, sending the point of his elbow painfully into the muscle of the professor's upper left arm. "The freak in the gas mask?"

Broom pulled away and massaged the spot with his right hand, his eyes squeezed against the viewfinder of his binoculars. He had a good bead on the men scrambling around below, and . . . yes, there he was. He'd been afraid of that. "Karl Ruprecht Kroenen, one of the Reich's top scientists. Head of the Thule Occult Society." Broom grimaced and passed the binoculars back to Whitman. "If he's here, this is worse than I thought."

Whitman jammed the binoculars against his eyes hard enough to leave impressions in his skin. After a few seconds, he lowered them and turned to the radio man on his left. "Air and sea backup. What's closest?"

The guy cranked a transmitter to life, then mumbled quietly into it. A few seconds later, he got a response. "Londonderry, sir. Forty minutes away."

Sergeant Whitman balled his fist and swung his head around, staring down at the Nazis. There was a knot of dread in his gut. "We don't *have* forty minutes."

2

SAFE BEHIND HIS MASK, KARL KROENEN GAVE A WIDE, dark grin, then wrapped one dry-skinned hand around a lever in front of him. He ran his tongue over the inside of his teeth for good measure, then threw the stiff switch on the huge machine.

An untold number of gears churned to life and steam pistons thrust bright copper rails upright. As two metal rings were lifted high into the air and gyroscoped outward, Kroenen signaled excitedly for more lights.

Illumination flooded the expanse of an ancient sacristy lined with eroded stone saints. Their dark, eyeless faces gazed blankly at a tall, gaunt, and nearly naked man with his arms fully extended who was standing in the center of the room. He stared hard at a woman coming toward him, and when he spoke, his voice was stern and his breath plumed outward in a freezing temperature that seemed to have no effect on him.

"No matter what happens to me, Ilsa, you must carry on with the work."

Beneath tightly drawn blond hair, there was no smile on Ilsa's coldly beautiful face, no warmth in her ageless, Aryan expression. "I will not leave you, Grigori," she said matter-of-factly. In a rare show of emotion, the look on her face changed, turning to near-reverence as she draped a richly embroidered robe over Grigori's shoulders, hiding his jutting collarbones beneath the scarlet fabric.

Grigori scowled. "Yes, you will," he said harshly. "Leave me. *Deny* me."

She shook her head, her face melting back into a perfect picture of detachment. "Never."

He sighed, then reached into a hidden pocket within the robe's folds and pulled out a small, leather-bound book. He flipped through the pages quickly, checking to see that the notes and hand-drawn illustrations were still complete and free from damage. He held it out to her. "This will guide you back to me."

She nodded and accepted the book, then he pulled her close to him. Face-to-face, the clouds of their breath mingled on the chill drafts easing through the underground church. Her stubborn, icy countenance finally gave way and twin tracks of tears slowly made their way down her flawless cheeks. He inhaled, using Ilsa's own breath to speak. "I grant you everlasting life," he said quietly. "And youth, and the power to serve me."

Next to him was a small table. Grigori reached to

the side and dipped his fingers into a wooden bowl filled with blood, and Ilsa didn't pull away as half in ritual, half in consolation, he wiped her tears away with a crimson-covered thumb.

"It's time."

The moment broken, both of them glanced at the speaker. Von Krupt was an acrid German general who liked to hide his eyes behind lenses the color of dried blood. He pulled a pocket watch out with a meaty, leather-gloved hand and held it up to show them the time; it spun in his grip, flashing first the clock face, then a gold swastika, then the clock face again. After a long, last glance, Ilsa and Grigori nodded and stepped apart.

With his thin back ramrod straight and his head held high, Grigori walked toward the colossal machine. Ilsa followed closely behind him, holding an umbrella over his head to protect him from the rain now pouring through the open ceiling. The machine's steel and copper clockworks gleamed in the floodlights, and a hundred metal tubes twisted and shimmered amid countless wires.

As if he couldn't resist it, Von Krupt strode alongside them, like a mother haranguing a wayward child. "Five years of research and construction, Grigori! Five *years!*" His voice was climbing toward strident. "The Führer doesn't look kindly on failure!"

Grigori didn't bother to glance at him. "There will

be no failure, General. I promised Herr Hitler a miracle. I'll deliver one."

Kroenen, decked out in a full Nazi officer's uniform, was waiting for Grigori, already muttering excitedly behind his mask and nearly twitching with anticipation. He ran a tightly gloved hand over a polished oak box on a panel in front of him, then opened it to reveal a massive gold and copper *mecha*-glove, a monstrously sized thing from which trailed half a dozen cables and hoses. He picked it up with meticulous care and gazed at it reverently before turning to Grigori. The nearly naked man extended one hand as if making a great sacrifice, and Kroenen carefully fit the *mecha*-glove over it.

Turning away from Kroenen and the panel, Grigori walked regally to the top of the waiting altar. He paid no mind to the cables trailing behind him, trusting that Kroenen or someone else would keep them from tangling. His gaze was misty and faraway. "Tonight," he said in a hollow voice that still carried easily to everyone in the room, "we will open a portal and awaken the Ogdru Jahad—the Seven Gods of Chaos." His inky gaze cleared for a moment as he surveyed the men listening to him. They could see the pride etched into Grigori's face. "Our enemies will be destroyed. In an instant, all impurity in this world will be razed and from the ashes a new Eden will arise!"

With a dark smile, Grigori refocused his gaze on the machine in front of him. "*Ragnarok,*" he whispered. "*Anung Ia Anung.*"

A flex of his fingers, ever so slight. And in response—

The two huge metal rings overhead swung to life around the machine's central axis.

TCHINK!

WHIRRR!

Steam shot from tens of pipes and ducts as an invisible blast of energy doused Grigori with enough strength to make him sway.

Ilsa grinned almost maniacally and signaled sharply at two of the Führer's scientists who were positioned at one of the numerous control panels. This was the moment! "More power!" she shrieked. "Don't let the power drop!"

The one closest to her gave a curt nod, then fought to heft a twenty-inch, solid-gold cylinder from a holder above the console. There were three openings directly in front of him, and the man grunted with the effort of inserting the cylinder into the first of them.

As soon as the round chunk of metal dropped into place, a beam of light cut through the air above Grigori. On each side of it, strange symbols began flickering in and out of view, twisting around and dripping red like living fire writing on an invisible surface. Then the beam of light widened, spreading until it was a growing slash in the very fabric of the universe. The edges of the split sizzled with color, and something . . . alien, otherworldly, *unknown*, sparkled on the other side. The slash widened again and the wind in the sacristy rose to a howl, tearing free one of the six-foot work lights. Before anyone could blink, the strand of heavy lights flew through the air and went into the cosmic split.

The people below craned their necks to see, then gasped. Something *moved* within the gash in the air—the massive being Grigori had called Ogdru Jahad, the seven egglike monoliths of unholy origin. As they stared, trying to see more, wondering if they should believe what their own eyes declared was true, the egg shapes began to pulse. Whatever horrible creatures had been slumbering within the translucent walls of the elongated shapes started to awaken as the light swept past; one by one, the giant creatures opened their filmy eyes and began to move lazy, fleshy tentacles within their crystalline prisons.

Beyond the altar's control panel, Grigori screamed as his body began to rise. Veins swelled in his neck as his face contorted with ecstasy . . . or was it pain? It was probably a combination of both.

Somehow, below all the screaming and the wind and the impossible that was happening right before his disbelieving eyes, Sergeant Whitman heard it.

Click.

He whirled and glared at Matlin. The photographer had forgotten himself, where he was, his *sanity*. He was not only standing in full view of anyone who might turn around, he had one of his camera view pieces pressed against his eye and was snapping pictures as fast as he could. Furious, Whitman yanked the younger man down, hard, then pulled out a long bayonet. "Listen to me, you moron," he hissed as the bruised Matlin blinked at him. "You do that again, I'll carve you a new—"

Too late.

The second of the Nazi scientists at the control panel suddenly stood up straight and stared right at the part of the rise that was concealing them, then scowled as he realized what he'd heard had to be intruders. Whitman cursed under his breath, but before he could do anything more, Broom crab-walked next to him on the ground and clutched at his sleeve. "Listen to me!" he whispered fiercely. Despite the chilly temperature, Broom's youthful face shone with fear sweat. "The portal is *open!* You *have* to stop them!"

Whitman yanked his arm free and peered over the rise, but the scientist had apparently dismissed them as unimportant in the grander scheme of the game. That was both a blessing and a curse; had the man raised an alarm, Whitman and his men would have been knee-deep in trouble . . . but at least it would have stopped—maybe—their ritual from going any further. Instead, they were going to have to take action. And they were also going to have to be quick about it.

The guy now had a matching gold cylinder in his hand; without being told to, he turned it upright and positioned it so that he could shove it home into the next compartment in the control panel.

Something bumped against the side of his foot, and he automatically looked down. It took one puzzled moment too long for him to register exactly what it was—

Grenade!

—and then the explosion blew his leg into bloody pieces.

"*Go!*" screamed Sergeant Whitman, and the Allied soldiers stormed the ancient stone chapel.

The gunfire was deafening, the firepower deadly in all directions. In the onslaught, a dozen Nazis fell immediately; others took longer, stubbornly returning the fight, determined to hold their little piece of the underground so that they could continue whatever diabolical ceremony this had been. As the Nazis' machine-gun nest fell beneath a fusillade of bullets, Von Krupt snatched up one of his fallen soldier's rifles and began firing wildly; the young Professor Broom paid for being in the wrong place at the wrong time with a bullet in the leg. As he went down, clutching at the wound and nearly breathless with the intensity of the pain, Whitman retaliated by sending a volley of bullets straight into the old Nazi's chest.

A half dozen grim-faced Allied soldiers had managed to back Kroenen into a corner. Instead of surrendering, the masked Nazi went into a crouch, then snapped his arms forward—

Tchkkk!!!

Two gleaming metal blades slid free from twin steel bands hidden below the cuffs of his uniform. Guns were not always the answer to everything, and the soldiers' overconfidence in their weapons exacted a heavy price; as they moved toward Kroenen, certain that the Nazi would give up his knives in the face of their rifles, he went through them like the four-bladed propeller of a P-51-D. Incredibly, his steel cut right through their weapons with barely a hitch each time, then continued through flesh and bone like it wasn't even there. Blood and water ran together and tinted the muddy ground a dirty brownish pink.

The hand-to-hand fight was one thing, but they couldn't forget the bigger picture, the bigger *danger*. Wheezing with agony, Broom dragged himself along the ground until he made it to the body of a dead GI. He yanked one of the man's grenades from his belt, pulled the pin out with his teeth, then threw it as hard as he could, straight at the generator. Broom grinned wildly through the pain as he saw the grenade wedge between two moving tie rods. Now it would only be a matter of seconds.

At the end of his wet work, Kroenen must have glimpsed the small missile sailing over his head. The Nazi shrieked and retracted his blades, soaking his jacket cuffs with blood as he lunged after the grenade. The gyrating rails of the machine sliced into his jacket, but Kroenen didn't notice. Just as his fingers reached the grenade—

BAAAAMMMM!

—it exploded.

Kroenen didn't even have time to scream, and the blast deadened his eardrums instantly. The concussion sent him soaring through the air and slammed him into a jagged stone wall; before he could slide down to the ground, dual pieces of shrapnel, ends sharp and long yet strong enough to puncture stone, pinned the Nazi in place like an insect.

Still crouched on the other side of the rise, praying first that his cameras wouldn't get damaged and second that he wouldn't get shot, Matlin moved to the left to try to get a better view, then nearly screamed when a third piece of shrapnel, javelin-long and thin, plunged into the ground—

Fffffffft!

—precisely where he'd just been hunkered down.

Ilsa's panicked shriek rose above everything else in the chamber.

"*Grigooooori!*"

He was still hanging overhead, floating in front of the maw of the open portal. His screaming had stopped but his face was distorted, pulled and stretched like ectoplasmic taffy; his body was bending in places it shouldn't, contorting and breaking in others, twisting in still more. Before Ilsa could scream again, before even the next burst of gunfire—

The portal imploded.

Nothing was left behind but a few burned rails and Grigori's strange metal glove, empty and sending a plume of smoke into the mist-soaked air.

Matlin looked around frantically, but Ilsa and Grigori were gone. Sucked into the portal? There was no way to tell for sure. Even Kroenen had managed to escape, the only mark of his exit two blood-covered shards of metal embedded firmly in the stone wall. Behind him, backup had finally arrived and another flood of Allied soldiers was pouring into the abbey ruins; certain of the impending victory, Matlin scuttled over the rise and made his way to where Broom lay clutching his bleeding leg. The photographer grabbed a strap off the weapon of a fallen Nazi and quickly fastened a tourniquet. "It's almost over!" His voice was a shout, but he could still barely hear himself above all the noise.

But Broom only shook his head. "No, it's *not*." As Sergeant Whitman staggered up to them, Broom stretched until he reached the outer rings of the smoking machine. He dug his fingers into a puddle of white, viscous goo and held them up, then shook his hand to make sure they turned their attention on him. "Cordon off the area," he told Whitman. "Something came through."

Whitman stared at him, incredulous. "From *where?*"

Broom glanced at the wall fifteen feet away, his gaze raking the thirteenth-century fresco depicting Heaven and Hell. Whitman followed his gaze, then looked back at him questioningly . . .

. . . but Broom simply didn't have an answer for him.

It was strange to be inside an ancient chapel, yet still have the cold rain pouring through what little was left of the roof, drenching the uniforms until they hung uncomfortably against the soldiers' skin and sunk the cold into their joints. Now that all the men had pulled their flashlights out, watery halos bobbed through the downpour like disconnected headlights at night, lighting the way for the heavy rifles the men held at the ready. A rosary had been tied to each dark barrel and the beaded strands swung in front of the flashlights, making little flickers of unpleasant black shadows.

Grinding his teeth, Broom rummaged through the med kit someone had thrown at him until he found a clean roll of gauze. Like everything else, it was soaked with rain the instant he brought it out, but at least he could use it to wrap his leg in place of Matlin's tourniquet and, hopefully, stop the bleeding. The pain was bad, but less than he'd expected; strong enough to be dangerously distracting, not so much that he was debilitated. More of a danger was blood loss and all the complications that could arise, but he didn't have time to worry about that right now. A few feet away, the photographer, Matlin, and Sergeant Whitman roamed through the debris, poking at bodies to make sure they were dead and peering into the more shadowy places. Neither was sure what they were looking for, but both were certain they'd know it when they found it.

Matlin wandered over to where Broom was tying off his hastily constructed bandage. The gauze was already full of dirt and water, an open invitation to infection. He watched for a long moment, then asked, "Do you believe in Hell?"

Broom didn't answer right away, but he finally looked up and sighed. "There is a place . . . a dark place where evil slumbers and awaits to return. From there it infects our dreams. Our thoughts. Grigori gave us a glance at it tonight."

Matlin chewed his lip thoughtfully. " 'Grigori.' That's Russian, right?" When Broom nodded, he said, "I thought they were on our side."

"Grigori Yefimovich Rasputin," Broom said, very softly.

Matlin's eyes widened. "Come on—*Rasputin?*"

"Spiritual adviser to the Romanovs." The professor struggled to his feet, wincing as he put weight on his injured leg but stubbornly doing it anyway. The bullet was still in there, grinding away at his flesh and making the muscle burn like it was on fire, but getting it out would have to wait until they got back on the sub. "In 1916, at a dinner in his honor, he was poisoned, shot, stabbed, clubbed, drowned, and castrated."

Matlin snorted in disbelief. "Nineteen-sixteen? That would make him more than seventy—"

A sound cut off his words, a sort of rustling from somewhere in the shadows against the far wall. Matlin spun and pulled his pistol as Broom brought up his flashlight and played the beam over the dark, dripping stones. The light was weak and ineffective at this distance, but they still thought they saw something move in the darkness. Matlin swallowed and snapped off the gun's safety; with Broom's words about Hell nibbling at the edge of his mind, he tried not to shake as he crept toward the closest of the crumbling statues.

Something small and red screeched and leaped into the air. Matlin nearly screamed himself as he brought the pistol up and instinctively fired at it. The thing leaped again, going from arch to arch, trying to flee as more soldiers ran forward and joined in trying to bring

it down. In a matter of seconds the chapel was filled
with the roar of gunfire and bullet holes pocked the
already crumbling stonework as they tracked the creature's overhead hops.

Out of ammunition, Matlin lowered his pistol.
"What the hell was that?" he demanded amid the gunshots. "An ape?"

Broom squinted overhead, struggling to see past the
muzzle flashes. "No—it was red. *Bright* red."

Whitman, his face flushed and dripping, hobbled
over to where they stood, his head jerking every time
he thought he saw something move overhead. "What
are you two talking about?" he demanded.

Matlin's mouth twisted. "A red ape."

Broom scowled at the photographer as the gunfire
died abruptly—the soldiers had lost track of their prey.
"It's *not* an ape—" He broke off suddenly, straining to
hear above the ringing of his own ears. Was that
breathing he was hearing?

"There," Matlin said suddenly. He pointed at the
blackness between side-by-side statues of a gargoyle
and a saint. In the overhead space, something moved
slightly. "It's got a big stone in its hand."

The professor shook his head and strained to see,
then took a cautious step forward. "I think that *is*
its hand." Another step, and the creature hissed at
him.

The sergeant thrust his jaw out and aimed his rifle

upward, but Broom reached out a hand and pushed the barrel down. "Wait."

In the pause that followed, the waiting men saw . . . *Eyes*.

Bright golden, veined with streaks of burnt sienna, and set in a face colored crimson, they stared from the shadows and waited.

It was just a hunch, but Broom thought it was worth a try. Moving slowly so he didn't spook it, he stepped a little closer, then fished a battered Baby Ruth candy bar out of his jacket pocket. The candy was smashed and gooey, but he was betting it wouldn't make a difference. Peeling back the wrapper, Broom waved the candy bar back and forth. Too fast—the creature shrank back, afraid.

Broom waited for a few moments, then brought the candy bar up to his mouth and took a bite. He chewed, making as much noise as possible, smacking his lips. The little golden eyes appeared again, blinking curiously, trying to see. Broom extended his hand and offered the candy bar again.

A moment's hesitation, then a small, red face pushed its way out of the darkness, followed immediately by a right arm. The arm was the same color as its face except it was, incredibly, made of solid *stone*. Tiny runes were engraved around its thick, round wrist, and four perfectly articulated stone fingers wiggled and reached for the chocolate. Except for the stone hand,

the creature looked like a miniature version of one of
the demon statues scattered around the chapel, all the
way from the curving horns protruding from its head
to the long tail that trailed from its small, muscular
body.

"Jesus," said one of the young soldiers in amazement. "Would ya look at the size of that whammer!"

Broom ignored him and moved a little closer, holding out the candy bar as bait. The creature peeked
nervously at the other men staring at it, but when
Broom looked at it and reached upward—

The little red demon slid down from the statue and
climbed into his arms.

Broom remembered seeing a thin blanket in the
med pack. Still holding the creature, he walked over
and plucked it from the ground, then draped it over
the back of the thing he was holding. From beneath
the blanket, the stubby little red fingers snatched the
candy out of his hand.

Broom grinned and looked at the stunned faces of
Whitman, Matlin, and the other men. "It's a boy," he announced. He actually sounded proud. "Just a baby boy."

With their curiosity overcoming their fear, the soldiers clustered around to see it, gradually losing their
jumpiness as they realized it wasn't going to bite or attack. Always ready to take advantage of a good oppor-
tunity, Matlin quickly began directing them until he
had what he wanted: a group shot, with Broom hold-

ing the demon baby like a proud new father and patting his back.

Broom smiled at the little red creature held snug in his arms. He didn't know if it understood him, but it blinked its bright golden eyes trustingly and twitched its tail like a big, happy cat.

"Best photo of my career," Matlin said dreamily. The red bulb was still lit over the doorway, and he liked the way it bathed the room in red, bringing back the busier days of his photography career as well as reinforcing the memories he was recounting. "And no one has ever seen it since," he added. There was no disguising the disappointment in his voice. "They keep saying he's not real, but I want to set the record straight before I go."

On one of the work counters was an old portfolio. The leather was cracked from use, battered by years of being out in the weather of a hundred different assignments and countries. He'd never considered replacing it—the portfolio was like the lucky underwear that the star pitcher has to wear to the play-offs or else. Matlin pulled it over and unzipped it, fighting with the sticky, heavy-duty zipper to get it to let go. When he finally got it open, the photographer pulled an old eight-by-ten from the pile of pictures inside. He smiled at the next batch of memories unfolding in his mind.

"Here," he said, holding it up. "The *real* picture, not the retouched one that appeared in *Life* magazine." His finger was shaking as he pointed to it. "This is him. The very same night we found him—the night Broom gave him that name." Matlin hesitated. "Can I say it on TV?

"He called him Hellboy."

3

SITTING ON AN EXTREMELY UNCOMFORTABLE CHAIR ON the wide stage, Tom Manning told himself for the tenth time that he was on national television, he would *not* lose patience, nor would he insult the over-made-up host of this so-called television talk show. From his position, Manning couldn't see much beyond the lights focused at him and the host; megawattage spotlights that were so bright he was vaguely surprised that the people who had to stare into them day after day didn't go blind—it was like looking into a dozen suns all at the same time. He'd always loved being on television, but these things were *hot*; he'd gotten out his best Armani suit for this fiasco, and all he'd ended up feeling like was a bacon-wrapped hot dog under a broiler.

The show's host gave him a bright, plasticized smile that was obviously phony, then gestured for Manning to turn and look over his shoulder. When he did so, a screen behind them flashed to bright life. A cascade of tabloid covers and news clippings rolled across it, all, of course, artfully arranged for the best—i.e., most shocking—effect:

"Hellboy Sighting in Reno! Government Denial!"

And another one, complete with color footage of a fistfight in progress, that Manning decided on the spot would be his personal, secret favorite:

"Jerry Springer's Next Show: I Was Hellboy's Bride!"

Manning started to turn back to the audience, but the host impatiently motioned for him to keep watching. He glanced back just in time to see a line of grainy footage depicting a blurred image that was supposedly Hellboy crossing an alley. To Manning, it was nothing but a ludicrous modern-day imitation of Bigfoot in the woods.

Unable to keep quiet any longer, Manning pointed to the screen. "Look at that," he said in mock disgust. "That's a costume! These people amaze me." He ran a careful hand over his tinted black hair before continuing, hoping his bald spot didn't show through under all these overly bright lights. "With their conveniently blurry footage of their beloved 'Hellboy.' And they claim that he works for the FBI?" He snorted.

The host gave him another overly toothy smile. It reminded Manning of a shark outfitted with fake chompers, circling a seal from below and looking for the perfect angle of attack. "Mr. Manning," he said in a butter-smooth voice, "as the head of the Special Operations Division at the FBI, you've seen dozens of pictures like this!"

Manning nodded, then leaned forward, going for the sincerity perspective. "Exactly!" he exclaimed. He sent a token glance toward the film footage that was frozen on the screen. "So why is it that they're all out of focus? Come on—God knows, people manage to get good pictures at a wedding!" He pointed at yet another blurry picture being displayed on the monitor. "That's the alleged best man?"

Amid a roomful of laughter, the delighted audience broke into applause.

BIRGAU PASS, MOLDOVA

In the Kishinev Mountains, the snow whipped along on a vicious wind, picking up speed as it slid down the high slopes on either side and battering the three figures struggling to climb the ice-slick steps of a massive rock formation. When the passageway narrowed to where it was barely wide enough to let them through, the wind only intensified; more than frigid, the subzero temperatures had long ago numbed what little skin was exposed on the travelers' faces and tinged their hands and feet with the first shadows of frostbite.

They struggled on through the knee-deep snow until the shoulder-width pass finally dead-ended.

With a heavily gloved hand, one of the group reached out and dug into the snow until a small section of the rocky ground was cleared. After a few seconds, a symbol chiseled into the stone emerged through the whiteness, and the figure pulled out the leather-bound book that had once belonged to Grigori Yefimovich Rasputin. Flipping through it quickly revealed a matching illustration.

In front of them was a wall of ice, rising above them until it melded into the snow swirling through the pass and made it impossible to tell where the ice ended and the mountain began. Shuddering with cold, the first figure took out a heavy steel hammer, hefted it, then swung it hard.

CRAAAAAACK!

Another hit—

CRAAAAAACK!

And a dozen more after that, and finally the cloudy wall of ice shattered and fell at their feet.

The last of the figures pulled a homespun woolen scarf aside, revealing the craggy, weatherbeaten face of an aging peasant. "I will guide you no further," he said, managing English but with a thick Romanian accent.

The second figure, smaller than the other two, nodded and pulled something from his pocket. He offered it out to the peasant and the man grinned, showing poorly cared-for teeth; pleased, he greedily snatched his pay—two small gold ingots, each bearing a deeply engraved swastika on it—from the leather-covered palm.

Beyond the remains of the curtain of ice was a rough-walled corridor. The only light was what now spilled through the entranceway, except for something small at the far end—

A firefly.

Odd to see such a thing in these mountains and at the height of the brutal winter, but it let them know without a doubt that they were on the right path.

The first two figures moved into the stone passageway without hesitation, and after a few seconds their peasant guide reluctantly followed. Not far into it, the corridor turned right slightly, then straightened again and opened into a cathedral-like vault, easily large enough to hold a stadium. From an opening too far above to actually see, an eerie blue light streamed down, illuminating a magnificent labyrinth. Here and there, more fireflies speckled the air, their luminescent bodies winking on and off.

Everything in here was indescribably huge. Cyclopean statues guarded architecture that could only be called inhuman, twisting monoliths of darkly colored, carved stone. Dozens of walkways and ramparts split the space, dwarfing the humans and making them seem tiny and insignificant. They walked until they were finally at the center of the complex, where the stone floor was covered in grooves that radiated from a shallow stone basin.

The peasant guide pulled his hat off as though he feared he was standing in a hallowed place, a church, and would be accused of showing disrespect. Then he tugged at his scarf uncomfortably and glanced around. When he spoke, fear made him lapse into his native Romanian. *"Noi nu ar trebui sa fim aici."*

We should not be here.

The two other people exchanged glances, then the first one withdrew another two gold pieces from a hidden pocket, tossing them at the feet of the guide. The gold surfaces glittered around the engraved swastikas.

The peasant looked from them to the two ingots thoughtfully, then glanced around the cavernous space in which they stood. Making his decision, he shrugged and knelt to scoop them up. Before his fingers could actually close around the gold—

TCHKKK!

The sharp end of a long blade burst through the front of his chest. He blinked twice and opened his mouth as though he wanted to protest, then slowly tilted forward and fell. From behind him, the second person withdrew the bloodied blade and watched impassively as the peasant twitched and died at their feet. After a moment, he tugged the layers of woolen scarves aside, revealing his signature mask. Karl Kroenen calmly cleaned his blade in the snow as the other figure shed her clothing—Ilsa, cold and lovely and not looking a day older than she had more than a half century earlier.

Sheathing the blade, Kroenen bent and retrieved the gold, then pulled the other two pieces from the dead guide's pocket—one should not waste. Finally he used a booted foot to turn the man's body on its back, nudging it into place so that the blood, steaming and smelling heavily of copper in the frigid air, traced a glyph in the stone grooves and quickly filled the small center basin.

A long beat later, and a ripple formed in the puddle of blood, vibrating and reshaping itself into the image of a man's head. It began to rise, pulling itself into shape as it grew in height. Finally, it stood there, naked and haloed by the bright, shimmering fireflies.

Ilsa stared at it, then found her voice. "Your eyes . . . What did they do to your *eyes?*"

In the darkened X-ray lab, four white-coated doctors studied the line of X-rays clipped to the long light box in front of them. Every now and then one of them would punch a button and split the silence in the room with the quiet *whirrr* of the conveyor as it moved one to the left or to the right and put a different film at center stage. Hospitals always had a certain sense of grayness about them when the overhead fluorescents were turned off, but there was no comfort in the shadows that moved in to fill the spaces abandoned by the light. The air was always a little too chilly, the quiet a little too disconcerting, the smell a little too sanitized.

Another X-ray slid forward and the group of physicians peered at it momentarily, then exchanged somber glances. The windows were covered with light-blocking miniblinds, but they could still hear the rain splattering the outside of the glass, driven by the unseasonably cold wind.

Finally the doctor on the far left cleared his throat and looked at the others. "Have you told him yet?"

The man next to him, taller and with distinguished-looking salt-and-pepper hair, didn't answer. Instead, he glanced to the side of the light box, where he could see through a small window of one-way glass into the adjacent examining room. As he watched, Trevor Bruttenholm, now in his eighties, carefully buttoned his shirt. From his wrist dangled his ever-present rosary.

The doctor sighed and straightened the tie beneath his white lab coat, then left the others and went to join Professor Bruttenholm, or Broom, as the old man had insisted he be called. On the surface, he looked to be in good shape, up in his years but lean and fit. But anyone with a trained eye would catch the slightly sallow tint to his color, the telltale sign of loosening skin that signaled a weight loss that had happened a bit too quickly. Worse was the shakiness that showed up while doing everyday things, *little* things, the occasional grimace of pain, and now and then, the under-current of exhaustion clearly visible.

Broom looked up as he entered and the doctor could tell immediately that the old man had read the news on his face: He was an excellent physician, but after all these years, he still hadn't mastered the art of completely masking his feelings when he had the worst kind of news to give to a patient, especially one he liked.

Broom didn't say anything, just waited.

The doctor pressed his lips together tightly, then forced himself to form the words. "Malignant sarcoma. In the lungs, the spine, the liver."

Broom looked from the doctor, then down to the tarot cards he held in his hands. Finally, he asked, "Approximately how long?"

"Maybe . . . six weeks."

Broom nodded, thinking.

"I can arrange for hospitalization," the physician offered. Saying these things was always difficult, and you never knew how the patient was going to react. He had people tell him he was wrong and to go to hell, once a woman had even thrown her purse at him. He kept going. "Pain management to make the time more bearable."

But Broom, always the quiet one, only shook his head as he aimlessly shuffled his deck of tarot cards. "I'd rather stay home. You know, I'll be making arrangements." He paused before adding, "For my son."

The doctor nodded, then folded his hands. There were things he was obligated to say, although he knew the futility of it. "You can always get a second opinion."

Broom slipped the top card off the deck and looked at it stoically.

Death.

"That won't be necessary."

Halloween in Manhattan, fall in the air. Dried leaves skittered along the pavement, slipping along the curbs and into the street, where they mingled with bits of trash and were occasionally swept into little whirlwinds. The storefronts were filled with blinking black and orange lights, strands of tiny pumpkins with bright, winking eyes that bobbed along the tops of the displays. Below the lights, pumpkin bowls and containers were painted with both friendly and scary faces and contained candy of every imaginable size and color, with candy corn always the frontrunner of the season.

Broom made his way out of the building, leaning heavily on his cane, smiling a bit as two kids dressed as skeletons and carrying little orange jack-o'-lantern candy buckets ran in front of him. Agent Lime had Broom's limo, a black Mercedes, waiting at the curb, but Broom paused before climbing inside, then went back to a newsstand and bought a dozen Baby Ruth bars. Before he could return to the limo, his gaze was caught by a wall display of televisions in an electronics store. They were all tuned to the same station, and as Broom watched, a blurry red shape blinked onto all the screens—Hellboy.

"Son," Broom whispered.

As he stared at the display, it changed to a smiling talk show host, some Regis Philbin knockoff with nearly the same name and dental work sitting behind a rounded oak desk. Typical daytime television—teeth too big, eyes too wide, shining hair too stiff and perfect. "Mr. Manning," he said brightly, *"what about the 'Bureau for Paranormal Research and Defense?' The FBI has been known to conceal—"*

"That word," interrupted Tom Manning, *"conceal—"*

"—from the American public—"

Broom frowned as he watched, but Manning held up his hand to stop the host's spiel. *"Phil— Phil. Hold your little green horses. Let me tell you and the American public one thing. This bureau for . . . what was it?"*

The multi-screen host blinked. *"Paranormal Research and—"*

"Defense," Manning finished for him. *"Right. Well, I'm here to clear this up once and for all."* Manning put on his own professionally made-for-television grin— he did so love to be on the big screen—and looked square at the camera. *"There. Is. No. Such. Thing."*

Broom smiled and headed back to the limo.

4

BUREAU FOR PARANORMAL RESEARCH AND
DEFENSE, NEWARK, NEW JERSEY

SITUATED HIGH ON A THICKLY WOODED HILL AT THE
edge of a bluff, the building complex was low-slung
and very high-tech. As if the forest wasn't enough, it
was camouflaged by colors that blended perfectly with
its surroundings—even the building foundations
seemed fused with the very rock on which they'd been
constructed. That same camouflage coloration was
etched onto the seven-foot walls that ran around the
entire compound, and if that weren't enough, triple
rounds of ultrathin razor wire, visible only if one were
specifically looking for it, ensured that not even the
birds would land on the wall. A massive gate, closed
tightly against the outside world, guaranteed that
nothing passed through the entrance without advance
scrutiny.

John Myers brought his flashy red moped to a stop
with the front tire just about touching the barrier.
He'd thought it was wood, but on closer inspection,

he realized it was metal—colored steel crisscrossed with heavy reinforcing bars. He'd been driving in the rain for hours, and when he climbed off the seat, he shuddered at the way his pants, soaked through to the skin, pulled away from the leather seat. He hated to think about what all this water was doing to the stuff he'd crammed into the two cheap suitcases precariously tied to the back of the moped. One of these days he was going to buy some new luggage.

On one side of the gate was a buzzer, and Myers grinned a little to himself as he pressed it, noting the fake Waste Management sign above the bell. He wondered if that actually fooled anyone, then decided it probably did—he sure wasn't seeing any reporters hanging around out here in the downpour and snapping pictures.

"Yes?"

He jumped at the sound of the voice, surprisingly loud through a speaker so well hidden that he couldn't spot it. The cold was making him shiver, eroding his attention. "John Myers. FBI transfer from Quantico."

For a long moment, nothing happened, then he jumped again as a piece of the stone pillar, something else he hadn't noticed, folded down on hidden hydraulics. Another beat and a hooded eyepiece and LCD screen scanner slid forward from the opening.

"Look at the birdie, son."

Myers pressed his face obediently up to the eyepiece, willing himself not to flinch because he knew what was coming. Suddenly a violet-colored light scanned his retina, moving back and forth in an instant. A millisecond later his identification and badge numbers flashed on the small screen, an instant after that and the heavy gate gave a *clank* as it slid open. Myers climbed back on his moped and pushed it through the entrance; when the gate closed solidly behind him, he felt a little bit like he'd disappeared into a strange part of the world that no one else knew about. As he restarted the bike and headed up the road toward the buildings, Myers knew instinctively that this was probably very true in a lot of ways.

The meandering road led Myers to what he assumed was the main building in the complex. Nondescript from the outside, covered in the same camouflage paint and surrounded by trees that doubtlessly made it look like part of the forest from above, he discovered that the inside was an entirely different story. Lots of marble and mirrors, behind which Myers knew without a doubt lurked security cameras. The thick green plants at the juncture of floor and walls probably hid everything from microphones to gas valves that could be used in a lockdown or other extreme emergency. In the center of the lobby was a massive circular desk made of high-tech, polished metal; behind that waited a solitary guard who watched Myers impassively as he approached. There was no name tag or identifying logo on his gray jumpsuit; in fact, it looked very much like the uniform that a garbage-truck driver might wear.

Myers put on a pleasant smile as he stepped up to the desk and set down his old suitcases. The reception counter had a high-cut edge that made him feel like a five-year-old in a room full of adult-sized furniture. He resisted the urge to hang his fingers from it—that was way too much like Kilroy Was Here. "Hello. I'm—"

"Late," the guard cut in. "Five minutes late."

Myers blinked. "Yes, I—"

"Section fifty-one," the guard interrupted again. He looked down at something in front of him that Myers couldn't see. "Step back."

Myers stared at him, confused. "Pardon?"

The guard's voice was completely emotionless. "Ten steps back, please."

Confused, Myers bent and picked up his suitcases, then complied. When he looked at the floor as he backed up, he saw for the first time that he was moving to the center of a giant Bureau for Paranormal Research and Defense symbol. The colors below his feet formed the logo, a small triangle superimposed on a fist holding a sword. The initials B.P. were on the left, with R.D. in a matching position on the right.

"Watch your hands and elbows," the guard instructed him.

With a mild lurch, the floor beneath Myers's feet began to sink and he realized he was on the platform of a small elevator. He grinned. He just loved this high-tech secret stuff—hidden cameras, microphones, shoe phones like in the old *Get Smart* episodes (he'd tried to build one of those once). Standing on the platform, Myers was still smiling as he sank past floor level and the panel overhead slid shut and let a row of safety lights wink on around the edge of his circle. There were no sides to the elevator and he had to fight a sense of vertigo when he saw that his elevator was just one of a number of others, moving up and down in a vast underground area. The effect was very much like being on a floating disk in the middle of space.

A cool draft that smelled vaguely like metal and oil kissed the skin of his face, and what he could see of the dimly lit and quiet area—no Muzak here—showed him only more elevators interspersed with the huge support pillars holding up the building above him. His own platform just kept dropping until the light around him blacked out and it finally settled to a stop in a narrow, dark space; an instant later, a band of fluorescent lights buzzed to life, showing Myers that he was inside a cramped circular chamber. On the wall in front of him, painted in huge strokes, was the number 51. To the right of that, recessed into the chamber walls, was a magnificently carved oak door. Not knowing what else to do, Myers gave the door a firm knock.

No answer.

There was nothing else to do—no Up button for him to push to go back to the main floor and question the guard—so finally he reached out, turned the knob, and went through the door.

He found himself walking into someone's office, or maybe it was a library. There were books everywhere—in fact, the walls were almost *made* of them, floor to ceiling, on three sides. The soft glow of several reading lamps, the library kind with the soothing green glass shades, bathed everything in an intimate, warm light. In the far corner was a spiral staircase, the old-fashioned style made of wrought iron; it led up into the shadows, probably to an area filled with more books. The machinery smell of the elevator was gone, replaced by the sweeter scents of old paper and leather, tinged somewhere with cedar.

One wall, however, was different. This one was made entirely of a thick pane of glass—apparently a fish tank. There was clearly water up to the top of it, but it must have been some kind of strange, special glass; none of the reflection came through, no swimming pool-like glimmering or twisting water shadows.

"Turn the pages, please."

Myers hadn't noticed the speaker and now he jumped at the voice that crackled through an intercom next to the tank. Curious, he moved closer to the glass. He thought he'd seen something in there, a shadow moving, something large.

"Over here, if you don't mind."

A long, sleek form with a face glided past, then disappeared into the dark depths of the water.

"Jesus Christ!" Myers exclaimed and stumbled backward. He steadied himself, then noticed the four book stands facing the glass, each with an open volume on it. Steeling himself, he leaned close to the tank's window, wanting to see. Down at the corner, he saw a small sign, barely noticeable: Abe Sapien.

As if the creature inside knew he wanted to see it, it swam obligingly up to the glass. It wasn't a fish as Myers had first thought, but a man . . . with *gills*. Slender and smooth-skinned, he was dolphin-gray with darker bluish patterns streaking his soft-looking surface. Bright blue eyes shone with intelligence as they regarded Myers, and behind his thick-lipped mouth, slightly darker gills pulsed bubbles into the water. His limbs were long and graceful, moving effortlessly through the water.

Myers swallowed, then pointed at the books. "These? You're reading these?"

The fish man—Abe—nodded, so Myers did the only thing he could: he turned the pages for him. Before Abe Sapien could say anything else, Myers turned in response to a noise behind him. Another man, bent with age and leaning heavily on a cane, came slowly into the room, then smiled at Myers and motioned to the tank. "Four books at once," he said proudly. "Every day . . . as long as I'm here to turn the pages." The old man's smile widened. "My name's Broom. Professor Trevor Broom."

Myers offered his hand. "Sir. I'm—"

Myers jerked and spun back to the tank as Abe slapped a webbed hand against the glass behind him, startling him enough to leave his hand hanging in the air while he never finished his sentence.

"*Agent John T. Myers, Kansas City. Seventy-six, 'T' stands for Thaddeus, mother's oldest brother.*" Abe's blue eyes blinked once, then he continued. "*Scar on your chin happened when you were ten. You still wonder if it's ever going to fade away.*"

Myers lowered his hand and gaped at the fish man. "How did it—"

"He," Broom said patiently. "Not 'it.' Abraham Sapien, discovered alive in a secret chamber at St. Trinian's Foundling Hospital in Washington." He raised an age-spotted hand and pointed at the wall, where a small piece of antique paper was sealed inside an expensive frame. "They took his name from this little inscription that was stuck on his tank."

Myers walked close enough to see the writing. "Ichthyo Sapiens," he read aloud. "April 14, 1865."

Broom nodded. "The day Abraham Lincoln died. Hence 'Abe' Sapien." The professor made his way back to the tank, then uncovered a tray on a small table next to it. On the tray were four greenish eggs; the stench that wafted from them made Myers gag and reel backward. Broom shot him an apologetic glance. "Rotten eggs—a delicacy. Abe loves them."

Broom lifted the tray carefully overhead and slid them into the water through an open hatch. In the tank Abe smiled and executed a smooth, subaquatic bow, then effortlessly nabbed the eggs as they floated through the water.

Myers watched him, fascinated. "How does he know so much about me?" he finally asked.

Broom put the tray aside and slid one hand into his pocket as he leaned gratefully against one of the heavy leather visitor's chairs in front of his desk. "Abe possesses a unique frontal lobe," he answered. He paused long enough to let this sink in, then continued. "Unique—that's a word you'll hear quite a bit around here."

Myers nodded. "And where am I exactly, sir?"

A corner of Broom's mouth turned up. "As you entered the lobby, there was an inscription—"

"On the desk, yes. In Latin."

"Impressive," Broom said, unperturbed by the interruption. "Do you remember what it said?"

Myers rubbed his face and concentrated for a moment, then nodded. *"In absentia luci, tenebrae vinciunt."*

Broom looked pleased. " 'In the absence of light,

darkness prevails.' " He raised one eyebrow and looked steadily at Myers. "For there *are* things that go bump in the night, Agent Myers." Despite the faint smile that crossed his features, Broom's expression suddenly turned quite dark. "We are the ones who bump back."

The corridor Broom was leading Myers down was, he'd been told, "Freak Corridor A." There wasn't much in the way of overhead lighting; instead, the glass-fronted cases that lined the walls were lit from within; the illumination not only allowed Myers to see their contents but cast enough light to fill the hallway.

Despite its rather flamboyant title, Myers wasn't looking at anything that far out of the ordinary. He'd seen weird occult artifacts in a dozen wax museums and carnivals, not to mention the ever-present horror movies. Still, he dutifully scanned the cases as Professor Broom led him past each one. Inside one case was a mummified hand, still showing decaying strings of the fabric, now brown and filthy, in which it had once been wrapped. Past that was a clay golem, one of his favorite creatures in the realm of the supernatural. This one was slightly undersized and clearly dried up; still, if what Myers had read about golems was even remotely accurate, alive—if it ever had been—the golem would have been a fearsome opponent, nearly unstoppable.

Next to that was a pagan altar, quite lavishly appointed with a pair of obviously solid silver and gold daggers, the heavy handles of which were encrusted with precious stones and deeply carved with lewd figurines. Half-spent candles in red and black flanked the daggers, while tiny golden bowls of unidentified items—possibly herbs and other rather unsavory things—were arranged between the daggers and below the candles in the shape of a pentagram. Myers glanced at the display a final time as he passed, then blinked as he realized that both daggers were stained with the unmistakable residue of dried blood. Very creepy. Concentrating on that, he jumped as Broom began to speak.

"In 1937, Hitler joined 'The Thule Society,' a group of German aristocrats obsessed with the occult," the professor told him. The old man pointed at the next display, which contained an ancient, broken lance. Myers peered at it, then paused to look more closely. There was something about the artifact that demanded more than a perfunctory glance, and it wasn't long before he found out.

"In 1938," Broom continued, "he acquired the Spear of Longinus, which pierced the body of Christ. He who holds it becomes invincible." Myers said nothing as he tried to process this piece of information. Invincible? Myers found that notion doubtful, but Professor Bloom sounded as though he truly believed this. Then again, Myers had to admit that he would have never believed a man could live underwater, yet he'd seen just that only a few minutes earlier. Broom's next words made the old professor's thoughts on the matter crystal clear and sent a shiver down Myers's spine.

"Hitler's power increased tenfold."

They were at the end of the corridor now, entering and exiting through a series of brushed silver pneumatic doors that made quiet *shsssh shsssh* sounds as they operated. One would open when they stepped up to it, then close behind them before the next would open, extra security and air purification to protect the relics. When the two men had gone through another set, Broom spoke again. "In 1943, President Roosevelt decided to fight back. Thus the Bureau for Paranormal Research and Defense was born."

Myers started to comment, then found himself instead staring at the next two doors. Half a dozen workmen were sweating and grunting as they struggled to replace two of them; there was no need to ask why, but the what of it definitely raised questions. Across the heavy surface were deep, oversized dents, most of which were substantial enough to deform the two-inch-thick metal plates.

Broom's voice was pensive as he paused for a moment to watch the workmen. "In 1958, the occult war finally ended when Adolf Hitler died."

Myers blinked, then frowned and pulled his gaze away from the new doors being manhandled into position. His mind immediately popped up with a correction. "1945, you mean. Hitler died in forty-five."

Broom gave him an enigmatic smile. "Did he now?"

Myers had always thought he had, but now Broom's words and his surroundings were suddenly broadening his mind, opening it up to a number of more interesting possibilities. Moving carefully past the workers, at last Myers and Broom reached the final door. It was stainless steel and massive, like a bank vault's, and Myers had visions of something contaminated and quarantined . . . and really, *really* strong . . . on the other side. Feeding his overworking imagination was a cart on which had been piled a stack of beef and mashed potatoes at least four feet high. It was enough to feed a roomful of soldiers, but they usually wouldn't all eat off the same plate. Waiting patiently next to the cart was a burly guy in a suit; Myers had seen the type a thousand times before, definitely government, definitely no-nonsense to the general public.

Broom dug into his vest pocket and pulled out two Baby Ruth bars, then handed them to Myers. "Agent Myers, this is Agent Clay. Follow his lead."

Myers stared uncomprehendingly from the two candy bars in his hand to Broom's retreating back. "You're not coming?"

Broom didn't bother turning around as he gave a

small, dismissive wave. "I handpicked you from a roster of over seventy Academy graduates. Make me proud."

Before Myers could say anything else, Broom stepped through the closest pneumatic door and it slid shut behind him.

Shsssssh.

He turned helplessly to face Agent Clay, but the bigger man only shrugged. "They're not speaking. Professor Broom had him grounded."

Now Myers was totally confused. "Grounded? *Who's* grounded?"

A corner of Clay's mouth turned up as he realized how little Myers actually knew about what he was getting into. "Okay. You saw the fish man, right?" When Myers nodded, Clay's small smile turned into an outright grin. "Well, come on in and meet the rest of the family." He pulled an odd-shaped electronic key from his jacket pocket and used it to unlock the door. A turn, a *clank*, then three solenoid locks revolved before a couple of steel vertical pistons lifted. When the vaultlike door finally opened, Agent Clay pushed the food-laden cart through the entrance and gestured at Myers to come in after him.

Myers followed, eager to learn more. On the other side of the entryway was a solid concrete bunker. There were no windows, and the decorating would have been austere except for a few seemingly out of place samurai suits of armor and weapons. Even stranger were the cats—there were dozens of them wandering around and curled up on the furniture. On the inanimate side were the Zippo lighters; like the cats, there wasn't anywhere Myers looked that he didn't see one—new, old, dull, shiny, from every era.

In the center of the large room was a sofa that looked like the kind of urban design project seen on the more ridiculous reality TV shows. It was huge, made from the bed of a pickup truck, and stuffed with cushions, blankets, and comic books. There was junk everywhere—books, comics, odds and ends; all in all, it was like the world's biggest bachelor pad—big, messy, and poorly lit.

Agent Clay folded his arms. "He gets fed six times a day," he said matter-of-factly. "He's got a thing for cats. You'll be his nanny, his keeper, his best friend. He never goes out unsupervised."

Myers was still gaping at the "apartment" spread out in front of him. "Who?"

Clay gave him a look full of exaggerated patience, then pointed at a torn comic book tossed on an end table.

HELLBOY: THE UNCANNY

Myers picked it up automatically, then focused on the cover. He frowned, trying to understand the image. It showed that Hellboy character the media was always squawking about, this time on top of a building, locked in battle with a monstrous ape. It was like watching a demon go up against King Kong.

Out of the corner of his eye, Myers caught movement. He looked toward it instinctively, then felt his jaw drop as a tail, long and red, waved in and out of a pool of light about ten feet away. One of the cats mewled and leaped at it, trying to play; the tail moved away from the cat, then back, obviously teasing.

Something clicked in Myers's brain and he jerked his head back toward Agent Clay. "You're kidding!"

"Those comics," someone rumbled. "They never got the eyes right." The voice was deeper than any human voice Myers had ever heard, chesty and powerful.

The comic tumbled from Myers's hand. "Oh, *Jesus!*" he breathed. "Hellboy . . . is *real?*"

Agent Clay looked like he was enjoying himself immensely. "Yup. Sixty years old by our count." Although he was keeping his expression professionally bland, Clay's dark eyes were shining with laughter. "But he doesn't age like we do. Think dog years—he's barely out of his teens."

Myers gasped as he finally focused on what was in the shadows. It was a monument-sized figure, sitting in total relaxation while it used a massive arm to easily curl what had to be a three-hundred-pound, stainless-steel dumbbell. The novice agent could see biceps the size of cooked hams working in the crimson-fleshed arm. His heart was pounding in surprise but Myers strained to see despite himself; he was rewarded with a glimpse of an unlit cigar stub held tightly in a stark, straight mouth.

"What's with the hair, Clay?" the voice rumbled again. "Finally got those implants?"

A dim part of him knew his mouth was still open, but Myers seemed powerless to close it as he watched Clay flush with embarrassment and self-consciously run a hand front to back across his scalp. "It'll fill in. Where do you want your dinner, Red? By the couch?"

Finally Myers managed to close his mouth with an annoyingly audible *click*. He watched Clay push the cart until just to the start of a pile of junked television sets. Trashed or not, they all still worked; they must have been wired together, because on the screens the same footage, a loop of Fleischer cartoons and home movies, cycled endlessly. One image, that of an attractive young woman with raven black hair and china-pale skin, steadily reappeared.

"Who's the squirt?" demanded Hellboy. He already sounded unhappy enough to make Myers fight the urge to shake. If he was supposed to be taking care of this . . . uh, of Hellboy, then he needed to stand his ground and be confident.

"Agent Myers is your new liaison," Clay said calmly.

There was an uncomfortable pause, then Hellboy asked in a softer voice. "Got tired of me?"

Clay grinned. "Nah. I'll be around, Red. Just back in the field."

BANG!

Hellboy dropped the dumbbell. The sound of it hitting the carpeted concrete floor was enough to make Myers jump. So much for acting confident.

"I don't want him."

Clay shrugged. "Manning says I'm too soft on you." He nudged Myers hard with his elbow. "The candy," he said under his breath. "Give him the candy."

Myers blinked, then remembered the two candy bars he was holding. Give him the candy? This was a three-hundred-fifty-pound creature, not a four-year-old. "Oh—uh, hello," he heard himself manage. "I . . . I have these. For you." He held up the Baby Ruth bars.

When he saw them, Hellboy sat up straighter in the shadows. "Father's back?" When Clay nodded, Hellboy asked a little more carefully, "Still angry?"

Clay lifted his chin and gave Hellboy a stern look. "Well, you *did* break out—"

"I wanted to see her," Hellboy grumbled. "It's nobody's business," he added in a voice that sounded as though he were talking only to himself.

But Clay shook his head. "It *is*. You got yourself on TV again."

Hellboy didn't respond, just sat sulking in the shadows. Finally, he said in a resigned voice, "Myers, huh? You have a first name?"

Myers swallowed, but before he could answer, Agent Clay nudged him again. "Try not to stare," he said quietly. "He hates when people stare."

Myers gave a little nod. "Uh . . . oh. John," he finally remembered to tell Hellboy. Out of the corner of his mouth, he semiwhispered. "Stare at what?"

"His horns," Clay said in a quiet, bland voice, as though he were telling Myers nothing more important than last weekend's football scores. "He files 'em. To fit in."

Myers's eyes widened. "His *what*?"

There was movement a few feet away, and Hellboy finally rose to his full height and strolled into the better lit part of the room where Myers could get his first good look. He was quite the awe-inspiring image, with his patterned scarlet skin bulging with exaggerated muscle, his chiseled features housing deep-set, clear, golden eyes. Myers had seen the image a hundred times, no, a *thousand*, on television and in the news rags—especially the so-called "scandal sheets"—but to have that image made flesh, right here and now, in *person* . . . He could no more have stopped his involuntary recoil than he could have kept the sun from rising in the east.

And in spite of himself, he couldn't help staring at the horn stumps.

"Whatcha looking at, John?" Hellboy's voice was a mildly dangerous growl.

"O-oh," Myers stuttered. "N-n-no. I—"

His useless denial was mercifully cut short when a shrill alarm suddenly screamed from a small speaker overhead. On the wall to the right, a light he hadn't noticed previously came to life, blinking a sudden, furious red. His denial forgotten, Myers looked around, bewildered.

Hellboy glided forward, the movement of his huge body surprisingly smooth and quick. "Hey, hey, hey!" he chortled in Clay's direction. "They're playing our song!"

Clay, however, was suddenly all business. "We're on the move," he barked and gestured brusquely at both Hellboy and Myers.

Hellboy looked at Myers and gave him what Myers thought might, once he got used to seeing it, actually be a grin. "C'mon, champ—Happy Halloween!" The expression widened, showing blocky bottom teeth along a massive underbite.

"You're taking me for a walk!"

5

THE MACHEN LIBRARY, MANHATTAN

THE MACHEN LIBRARY WAS AN IMPOSING, FOUR-STORY structure comprised of mortared-together massive stone blocks and held up by pillars and pediments on all sides. Suspended from four wires across its grand entrance was a long banner, oversized and gaudy in the orange-and-black colors of the season—

MAGICK: THE ANCIENT POWER

Peering through the one-way glass, Hellboy could see the entrance and the overabundance of people crammed into the area in front of it. Halloween or not, it should have been nothing more than a normal afternoon filled with college students, tourists, folks grabbing a quick tour of the new exhibition on their lunch breaks. Instead, outside was complete chaos; in addition to the people who, willingly or unwillingly, had gotten trapped in the melee, there were policemen, television reporters, even mounted police. The numbers were too great to count, the noise solid enough to make it through the glass and into Hellboy's ears.

Dozens of reporters protested as the cops crowded them backward so they could wave a line of black sedans through. Not too far from where they were driving past, a blond reporter held a microphone close to her mouth and gave her waiting cameraman her best and brightest smile. "The NYPD has yet to issue a statement," she said around a mouthful of capped, impeccably white teeth. "We've got SWAT vans, paramedics, you name it. And now here's a garbage truck." Her wide eyes and big smile faltered and she looked away from the camera for a moment, bewilderment etching into her pretty features as she tracked the vehicle. On the side of it, Hellboy knew she was reading Squeaky Clean, Inc. Waste Management Services. "A garbage truck?"

In the front cab, Agent Clay, his face as impassive and plain as the workman's clothes in which he'd rapidly changed, carefully steered the clunky-looking truck through the crowd while Myers, redressed in the same gray uniform, sat nervously on the passenger side, trying to take it all in. He'd thought he'd have a little time to get acclimated to his new transfer position, meet the boss—Broom—and the other hierarchy before getting tossed into field work. Obviously not.

The media crews outside were being held back by the security forces and when the people milling about looked up and saw the garbage truck bearing down on them, they parted like the Red Sea for Moses. Hellboy could see dozens of faces through the heavy, one-way glass that masqueraded as a mirrored logo on the outside of the truck; only inches away, a mounted policeman worked his horse carefully through the people and slowly passed their vehicle. Hellboy grinned to himself and wondered what the horse would do if it saw him.

He shifted uncomfortably on the side bench, wishing he could stand up, stretch his legs, his arms, stretch *something*. It was always like this in the undercover vehicles; even the oversized ones like this—and he had to admit a garbage truck was someone's pretty good idea—could barely handle his massive frame. He couldn't move around much, and they were always telling him to be careful about the expensive equipment surrounding him. Break this and it cost this much; break that, and there was a bill for some other amount. Blah blah blah. Sure, he could appreciate the getup—fully equipped mobile crime labs didn't come cheap—but the powers that be ought to try riding for hours while stuck in a hunched-over position, see how *their* backs felt when they tried to straighten out. Every time he moved he had to remember that the thing was crammed with high-tech gear and low-tech talismans; everything in here was equally important in the *Do Not Break!* realm.

And, of course, Hellboy was sharing the space, which made things all the more crowded. Sitting across from him, Abe Sapien had been out of the water for about as long as he could manage without help; now he carefully fitted a respirator over his smooth-skinned face. It was a strange contraption that looked like a modified Elizabethan collar. The valves around the bottom of it bubbled and hissed as Abe inhaled liquid through his mouth and expelled it through his gills. For all of its bulkiness, the respirator must've done some wonderful things, because Abe visibly relaxed after a few inhalations.

"Look at them ugly suckers, Blue." Hellboy gestured at the crowd shambling around the outside of the truck. "One sheet of glass between them and us."

Abe's voice was tinny through the respirator. "Story of my life."

Hellboy grinned as he looked away from the glass and studied the scarred, knobby knuckles of his red-skinned hand. "I break it, they see us—Happy Halloween. No more hiding." He looked pensively back at the glass. "I could be outside."

Abe folded his hands and regarded him dispassionately. "You mean outside with *her*."

Hellboy shot him a glance, then reached over and plucked a huge utility belt from a shelf. It was laden heavily with amulets, rosaries, horseshoes, and other out-of-the-ordinary gear. After strapping it on, he grabbed a handful of stogie stubs from an ashtray off to the side; he lit one, then dropped the rest of the cigar bits into a pouch hanging from the belt. Finally he said, "Don't get psychic on me, Abe."

Abe gave a graceful lift of one shoulder. "Nothing psychic about it. You're easy."

Hellboy pulled a key from a smaller pocket on the belt and unlocked a steel box at his feet. The inscription stenciled on its lid always made him grin appreciatively—The Good Samaritan. Flipping it open, he pulled out a mean-looking, custom-built handgun. Double-barreled with a clean, blue finish, it was a veritable handheld cannon. But this was one of those rare days when even the Good Samaritan couldn't make him switch into good-mood mode. He held up the gun and looked at it glumly. "How am I ever gonna get a girl?" he lamented. "I drive around in a garbage truck!"

Abe shook his head, making the air bubbles in his collar shimmer. "Liz left us, Red. Take the hint."

Hellboy hefted the gun again and scowled at it. "We don't take hints," he growled.

Up front, Clay steered the garbage truck into an interior courtyard, then let it coast slowly forward as heavy iron gates were readied behind them. He could see the FBI and B.P.R.D. teams outside, spreading out and ordering the uniformed cops to leave as they secured the area for themselves. The resentful glares from the local police did nothing to change the situation. That done, three B.P.R.D. agents, Quarry, Stone, and Moss, quickly closed the gates and had the entire area sealed off.

The radio in Agent Clay's left hand crackled to life as Stone told him, *"All areas secured."*

Clay craned his neck so he could look at the roof of the building in front of them. From the rooftop, Agent Lime gave him the all-clear signal. Clay lifted the radio to his mouth. "Seal the doors. Red and Blue are coming in." He hit the brakes and the truck shuddered to a stop, then he pulled hard on a lever on the dashboard. In the back, the Dumpster loader unfolded on its hinges, dropping like a drawbridge to reveal Hellboy and Abe.

Clay turned back and looked at them. "Okay, boys. Let's sync up our locators."

Abe and Hellboy flipped a switch on their belts at the same time Agents Clay and Myers flipped theirs. Tiny lights blinked to life and each made a barely perceptible *beep*. Satisfied, Hellboy clambered out of the garbage truck and headed toward the library. Abe, Clay, and Myers were right on his heels.

The inside of the building was spacious and full of massive stone pillars and expansive marble panels. Display cases lined the walls on either side of the lobby area, but the various trinkets inside obviously hadn't interested anyone. All the cases were intact— not a single piece of broken glass dared mar the immaculately swept floor. A couple more banners advertising the library's magic exhibition flanked the wide marble staircase where they could be best viewed by visitors, not that anyone could've missed the huge one hanging outside.

Agent Clay pulled a report from a pocket hidden inside his coverall. He unfolded it and read the summary out loud. "At 1900 an alarm tripped. Breaking and entering, robbery. Six guards dead."

Hellboy's eyes widened. "Hold on, hold on," he interrupted. "I thought we checked this place. Fakes and reproductions."

"Apparently not everything was fake," said a familiar voice.

Hellboy jerked at the sound of Professor Broom's voice. "Father?" When Broom didn't say anything, Hellboy sheepishly averted his gaze from the steadier one of the fragile old man and stared at the floor. He looked like some kind of childish Goliath, chastised and sullen, about to start toeing the ground at any moment.

After an awkward pause, Agent Clay cleared his throat and motioned for the group to follow him down the main corridor. The sun had fully set, pulling away the light of the day and leaving the museum's high ceilings shadowed in the checkerboard light-and-dark pattern cast by the faraway hanging lights. At the end of the corridor was a double set of eight-foot-tall brass doors, brightly polished and impressive. They were closed, and while there was no indication that they should do so, Myers found himself slowing as he approached them, some secret instinct making him more cautious than appearances said he had to be. Then again, appearances could be *very* deceiving.

Abe stepped to the front, then held up his leather-gloved hands. With a *snap*, he pulled one free, then slapped his hand against the door, spread his webbed fingers, and concentrated. His bright blue eyes fluttered and closed as two agents hurried up, dragging a rolling munitions case. Myers watched from the sidelines, his gaze flicking from the concentrating Abe Sapien to Hellboy as the red-skinned demon opened the case and looked over a potpourri of bullets.

Professor Broom spoke for the first time since the group had stopped at the doors. "A sixteenth-century statue was destroyed," he said quietly. He gave Hellboy a meaningful look. "Saint Dionysius the Aeropagite."

Hellboy tilted his massive head to one side and considered this. "Who wards off demons."

"Smuggled into this country by an overzealous curator," Broom continued impassively. "The statue, however, was hollow."

"Ah." Hellboy nodded. "A reliquary."

"A *prison*," Broom corrected. "The Vatican deemed its contents dangerous enough to include it on the List of Avignon . . . of which we hold a copy."

Hellboy looked again into the munitions case. There were shells of all sizes and shapes, and he dug a big hand into the contents, then selected a full clip of bullets and a speed loader. "Would you look at these babies?" His straight line of a mouth widened into a ferocious grin. "Made 'em myself," he said proudly. "Holy water, silver shavings, white oak. The works."

In front of him, Abe shuddered and pulled his hand away from the door. In a low voice, he said, "Behind this door . . . a dark entity. Evil, ancient. *Hungry.*" Abe turned back, then spotted a few leather-bound volumes of ancient magic that another agent had brought on Broom's orders.

Hellboy shrugged carelessly. "Oh well. Lemme go in and say hi."

He wrapped his big fingers around both door handles and pulled, then stepped into an unexpected, flickering, amber glow on the other side.

In here was a whole different world.

It had been easy to forget the mission on the far side of the doors Hellboy had closed behind him. Out there was a normal world, the same sun-soaked one always filled with people and cops and media, the constant danger of discovery and public exposure that made him always have to hide. The one in here? It was unnaturally dark, tinted mostly by the blue emergency lamps that had powered on to take the place of the regular light fixtures that had been destroyed. The exhibits cases were all crushed, their contents interspersed with the shattered glass and twisted pieces of metal strewn throughout the room; here and there, small piles of what had once been featured items crackled as they burned at floor level, like small campfires lit by hellish Boy Scouts.

Everything was in shadow but thanks to the fires, nothing was still. The darkness flickered and moved, making inanimate objects like the larger carvings and statues seem like living, twitching things—more than a few times Hellboy jumped as he thought he saw movement out of the corner of his eye. So far, though, it was turning out to be nothing more than fire-fed shadow patterns. The whole thing would have seemed like the temper tantrum of someone . . . okay, some*thing*, the same size as Hellboy, except for a few minor details, like the blood-filled, half-chewed guard boots on the floor, the leather belts with the teeth marks in them, the tattered remains of scarlet-stained uniforms and hats.

Hellboy eyed them, then wrinkled his nose. He lifted the radio to his mouth and thumbed on the speaker. "Blue," he whispered into it, "it stinks in here. Like finely aged roadkill."

Before Abe could come back with a reply, Hellboy stopped and listened carefully. Was he hearing what he thought he was hearing? Oh yeah—there it was, the sickening sound of snapping bones and hearty chewing. The smell increased and Hellboy scowled and reluctantly sniffed. Stronger—*yuck*. He sniffed again, then tilted his head up as he finally realized the noise and noshing were coming from overhead.

A huge, pale creature hung from the ceiling. The thing had powerful arms and hind legs riddled with muscles and thick veins, along with a wicked-looking head covered in tentacles. Its face was mostly hidden in the shadows so Hellboy couldn't see everything, but he could hear it, all right. There was no mistaking the sound of slow chewing, and he could just see the bottom of the sharp-angled jaws that were shiny with blood.

Hellboy made a face. "Hey, Stinky," he called "Kitchen's closed."

The thing overhead seemed like it turned its head toward the sound of Hellboy's voice, but it wasn't going to be bothered with him until it was through with its meal. It just kept munching, hanging there without any effort at all.

"Whatcha having?" Hellboy asked casually. "Six library guards, raw? Plus belts and boots?" He shook his head, trying to sound nonchalant to disguise the fact that he was carefully scoping out what was very shortly going to be the battle zone. "Man, you're gonna need some *heavy* fiber to move that out."

Abe's bubbly voice suddenly vibrated through the

tiny speaker tucked behind Hellboy's ear. *"Red, I found something."* There was a pause, then Abe continued. *"I found a small medieval engraving in one of these books. There's not much here, but the entity's name is Sammael, the desolate one, son of Nergal."*

Hellboy listened to Abe's voice, never taking his eyes off the creature clinging to the ceiling. As if it had heard its name, Sammael abruptly released his hold and dropped nimbly to the floor a few feet in front of him. Now that the creature was on the same level, Hellboy got treated to a better view of it, including part of its exposed neck. It looked vaguely like a big dog, and Hellboy's mouth twisted in disgust at the sight of white, slimy skin, cracked like old marble and crisscrossed with blue veins.

"Hold it," Hellboy said, although he wasn't sure if he was talking to Abe or the Sammael beast in front of him. "Hey, Sammy," he said loudly. "What do you say we work this out peacefully? I'm not a great shot." Even so, Hellboy raised his gun. "But the Samaritan here uses really big bullets." He waited, but nothing happened. Did the thing have brain power in there? He tried repeating himself. "So what do you say we work this out?"

Without warning, Sammael raised to his hind legs, then suddenly he turned . . . or the top part of him did. The bottom part stayed still while his upper half went *craaaackkkk!* and did a startling three-hundred-

and-sixty-degree turn. Then he screeched and leaped away.

Hellboy squeezed the Good Samaritan's trigger.

The high-caliber ammo ripped through two columns before it finally connected with Sammael. The bullet kept going, blasting right through it and destroying a statue and the large window on the other side of its body. Sammael gave a piercing squeal, loud enough to annoy even Hellboy's ears, then fell over on one side. It gave a final rattling cough, then was still.

"That's all for you, Sammy," Hellboy said with satisfaction. He watched the body for a couple of seconds, just to be sure, then backed up.

Abe's voice trilled in his ear again. This time there was a worried tone to it. *"Red, you need to hear the rest of the information!"*

Hellboy turned away and jammed his pistol into the holster on his utility belt with a flourish, like a gunslinger. "Nah, he's taken care of."

But Abe was insistent. *"No! Listen to this— Sammael, the desolate one, lord of the shadows, son of Nergal, hound of resurrection."*

Hellboy grimaced. Resurrection? Seldom a good word. "See?" he said. "I don't like that."

"Hound of resurrection," Abe repeated.

Hellboy turned back around. The corpse was gone, but he wasn't a bit surprised.

"*Harbinger of pestilence, seed of destruction,*" Abe continued hurriedly.

Hellboy glanced around warily. "Skip to end, will you? How do I kill it?"

There was a beat of silence before Abe finally answered. "*It doesn't say.*"

6

HELLBOY FOUND OUT FOR SURE THAT SAMMAEL WAS still alive when the hound-creature hit him so hard that he sailed through the air and crashed into the brass doors.

As the thick metal doors bulged and cracked, he wasn't so stunned that he couldn't imagine Abe and Father backpedaling, as well they should. If that new guy, Myers, had any salt in him, he'd please Father by pulling out his piece and trying to find a way in to help Hellboy . . . not that his fragile human frame could take the kind of pummeling it was clear Hellboy was going to get. As if to attest to that, before Hellboy could find his way upright again, Sammael was back, lashing out with another massive and extremely painful punch.

Hellboy went up and up and up, taking out at least six of the surrounding glass cabinets before he hit one of the big reinforced windows. Some reinforcement—he crashed through it and kept going—

falling

—a full two stories through the darkness outside

the building, the extra high stories that only hundred-year-old government buildings and museums can lay claim to. He landed hard on his side in some kind of industrial garbage bin. Blood dripped from his mouth, and as he fought to stay conscious and drag his bruised body out of the metal box, Hellboy thought he saw someone through his pain-slitted eyes.

"*Child . . .*"

He blinked and scrubbed at his face, succeeding only in smearing his own blood into his eyes, tinting everything red to go along with the black-and-yellow sparkles of unconsciousness that were trying to horn in on his action. Now who was this? Squinting up, straining to focus, Hellboy finally saw a man in a black suit and overcoat standing in front of him like a phantom; his eyes were shielded by pitch-black sunglasses.

"All grown up, I see," said the figure in a low voice.

Hellboy squeezed his eyes shut, then forced them open again. He was feeling better already. A man had to appreciate supernatural healing powers. Still, something wasn't right. Something about *this* guy. "That voice," he muttered. "It's . . ."

"I sang the first lullaby you ever heard, my child," the man said in a voice as smooth and chilling as cold, black oil. "I ushered you into this world." He paused, giving Hellboy time to consider this. "I alone know your true calling. Your true *name*."

Knew his name? If the old stories were true, that

meant the spook standing in front of him was none other than Grigori. Hellboy already didn't like him.

"Don't tell me," Hellboy said testily. "It's Zeppo." Tired of the wordplay, his quickly sharpening vision found the Good Samaritan, lying at the edge of a puddle about ten feet away. He rolled to his knees, then tensed his muscles for a leap. But before it could happen, something blurred before his eyes and the ground vibrated. When his vision stopped shaking, Hellboy realized that Sammael had dropped into the space between him and the gun, his landing a hell of a lot easier than Hellboy's own.

The black-clad Grigori sighed. "I can see that you're still young and don't know your place." He cast a sideways glance at Sammael, and when Grigori spoke again, his voice was soft and deadly. "*Teach him.*"

Hellboy lunged for the gun, but before his hand could close around it, a yellow tongue, as thick as an arm and seven feet long, whipped out from Sammael's mouth. Butter-colored sacs billowed out from the tongue's fleshy length, expanding and contracting. Hellboy grunted and fell beneath more agony than he'd *ever* felt, writhing as the thing squeezed and pulled on his arm, grinding his teeth as smoke began seeping from the area where Sammael's flesh was cooking his arm. He tried to pull away but Sammael's hold only tightened, like a boa constrictor locking in closer with every exhalation of its prey. In another few seconds, Hellboy was going to start screaming, and he didn't want to do that, not here and now, and specifically not in front of this Grigori creep.

BAM BAM BAM!

Muzzle flashes cut through the alley's darkness and around the pain; Hellboy realized Myers was suddenly there, the barrel of his revolver dribbling smoke as he emptied his rounds at the demon attacking Hellboy. Amber liquid—Sammael's blood—exploded from half a dozen holes in his tongue, and with a squeal the hound-creature released Hellboy and snapped his tongue back into his mouth.

The pain was nearly smothering, but Hellboy managed to roll away, combat-crawling until he could take cover behind the Dumpster. Out of one swollen eye, he saw Myers dive for the Good Samaritan; a snatch and a grab, then the gun was in Myers's hand. The agent then plunged behind the container to where Hellboy lay, trying to recover, willing his body to mend itself and be damned quick about it.

"What do you think you're doing?" Hellboy demanded. He might be howling inside, but at least on the outside he could still sound belligerent.

Myers proudly held up the Good Samaritan. "Helping you," he announced. "I just—"

"No one *ever* helps me," Hellboy said angrily. "It's *my* job!" He yanked his weapon out of Myers's hand

and tried to reload it, then grunted as fresh pain swelled through his arm. Nope—it was hurting him too much. "Damn," he growled. "Okay—here." Myers took the gun when Hellboy offered it along with a fresh clip from his utility belt. After a second's pause, Hellboy reached into one of the smaller utility pockets and pulled out a vacuum-sealed packet. He tossed it to Myers. "Then load this."

Myers obediently tore open the packet, revealing a single, shining bullet. At his questioning look, Hellboy nodded. "It's a tracking bullet. Crack the pin and load it."

KLANG!

Myers jumped and almost dropped the tracer as Sammael's tongue literally *punched* through the steel-sided Dumpster.

KLANG! KLANG!

Their luck was holding—for now—and each time the demon's tongue barely missed them. But how much longer could they hold out? His nerves were screaming, but at last Myers was coolheaded enough to crack the safety pin on the bullet; the head of it lit up with chemical fire as he got the gun loaded and tossed it to Hellboy. As he did, his gaze fell on Hellboy's arm. The flesh was still smoking, and inside an ugly bloody gash was a large, gleaming, black stinger. "Jeez," he exclaimed, and pointed. "What the hell is *that?*"

Hellboy grimaced and yanked it out, then dropped it on the ground. One of his heavy feet shot out and crushed it. The sound it made was ugly, like an over-ripe grape popping.

Despite his badly injured arm, Hellboy was again churning with energy. "Let me go ask." Good Samaritan in hand, Hellboy boldly stepped out from behind the Dumpster.

Sammael's dark yellow tongue instantly wrapped around the gun's muzzle. Always aiming to be cooperative, Hellboy fired.

Bam! Bam! Bam!

Suddenly the harsh, white lines of its face were lit with a nuclear green glow as the tracking bullet slid into position inside the Good Samaritan.

BAM!

Sammael was still clinging to the wall overhead when the bullet traced a pattern straight to his chest and exploded. Bright green goo saturated the creature's muscle-covered chest. Startled, it shrieked and released its hold, then did another one of those weird body-twists and took off—up and over the wall separating the library's private alley from the rest of the city, and then it was gone.

With Hellboy right behind it.

Now Hellboy knew he was going to have to be a little more careful about things.

He could hear Father's constant admonitions running through his head about being seen in public— there had been *so* many—but at the same time, he needed to find this ugly sucker and step on him, *hard*. Hellboy crouched and glanced around warily, but so far, so good; he was in a loading alley, nice and empty at this late hour. And there was the trail he wanted, a line of glowing green goop like radiation-soaked breadcrumbs left by Hansel and Gretel.

There was a thump behind Hellboy as Myers clambered awkwardly over the wall after him and dropped to the ground. The agent hissed—something hurt— and cradled his arm, then chased after Hellboy as he hit full stride. "Wait!" Myers called frantically. "No— what are you doing?"

Hellboy paid no attention to the newbie. Sammael was close—Hellboy could *smell* him. Another few steps and bingo—he got a glimpse of the fleeing creature's backside. He grinned in triumph and upped his pace, running at full speed now, registering dimly but not yet fully understanding the meaning of the bright and blinking lights farther ahead, beyond the end of the alley.

A shrill backup alarm suddenly went off—*beep! beep! beep!*—and something big abruptly backed across the alley, cutting all of them off from the world beyond. A ten-wheeler truck, rear doors open, carefully positioned itself against a waiting loading dock.

As he barreled toward it, Hellboy saw workers and crates of pumpkins—the whole Halloween-Thanksgiving thing, of course. But when life throws you pumpkins, go around 'em—he *had* to grab that hound-demon before it got away and went into the dinner buffet that was the rest of mankind.

Sammael never even slowed down. He leaped and landed on top of the trailer, giving it a nice, heavy dent before he jumped off the other side and plunged into the midst of the crowd milling around the neighborhood's fall carnival.

One of the workers jerked and turned, trying to follow Sammael's streaking progress. "What the hell is *that?*" he demanded, pulling on the arm of a coworker. His friend gaped upward, his attention caught by the rapid movement, but he was too slow and he'd missed it.

Then Hellboy bounded up and landed on the roof of the truck's cab. The steel top buckled and dropped inward, shattering the windshield and the safety glass on both sides; inside, the driver screamed and scrunched down as the sharp-edged bits of glass pelted him.

Now three of the workers had run onto the loading dock and were rubbernecking at the destruction . . . and Hellboy. "Whoa," gasped one of the men. "Whoa—whoa!" He seemed incapable of saying anything else.

Hellboy glanced down at what was left of the front of the truck. "Oops," he said, and catapulted away.

The carnival area wasn't that big, and it began no more than twenty feet from the other side of the truck. At the start of it, to the left, was a small carousel and refreshment stand flanking a small pumpkin patch. A sign out front announced "Any Size $5 As Long As You Can Carry It!" A few people, mostly parents humoring their young kids, milled around the lumpy piles of bright orange, poking and prodding and trying to find the best and biggest in the bunch. Here and there a small boy or girl staggered beneath the weight of a pumpkin they could barely lift.

Hellboy could see Sammael already at the far end. As he trained his eyes on the demon, he saw the hound-creature stop and curiously examine a small trick-or-treater dressed as a golden dragon. Rumbling under his breath, hoping the beast wouldn't decide that the little polyester-covered dragon would make a nice little snack, Hellboy started for him.

Back at the truck, Myers was squeezing himself between the loading dock and the back of the truck, speaking urgently into his headset. "We'll hit the street in a minute! We're heading toward civilians!" A half dozen dockworkers ran toward him, yelling and pointing, while others pulled at the driver's door of the truck and tried to free their buddy. Myers dodged past and waved them away. "Yeah, yeah—crazy costume, huh?" Already leaving them behind with stunned expressions, he added over his shoulder as he rushed after Hellboy, "Trick or treat!"

Up ahead, Sammael dismissed the little dragon and bounded on, splattering more of the green tracking goop with every step. He paid no attention to any more of the trick-or-treaters or their parents as he darted past, heading straight into the street and the heavy evening traffic. Brakes squealed as the drivers tried to stop; the kids screamed in surprise and delight as Sammael leaped again and landed on the opposite sidewalk.

Hellboy was right on his heels, as unconcerned with the traffic as Sammael was. And following closely behind was Myers, who should have been paying a little more attention to the cars and trucks, particularly the oversized four-by-four with the high, off-road tires that was heading straight at him.

It was too late to go back, and there wasn't enough time to get the hell out of the way. Myers froze, staring at the oncoming headlights like a proverbial deer getting shined by a poacher on a country road. A glance back gave Hellboy the whole picture—the four-by-four being driven too fast by the reckless teenager, and Myers, a very breakable human smack in its path. He thought he saw Myers close his eyes in surrender.

Not acceptable.

Hellboy's next step was a powerful half turn that propelled him back in the direction he'd come from and somersaulted him high over the parents and costumed kids in his way. He came down with a ground-shaking *thud* that was hard enough to spiderweb the roadway, right next to where Agent Myers had no choice but to wait for his end. Hellboy's stone hand shot forward and met the front of the truck where in another instant it would have had Myers's face imprinted on its grille.

Yep. He could still find plenty of uses for the ol' Right Hand of Doom.

The impact flipped the car clear over Hellboy and Myers. It landed behind them with an ear-splitting crash that deployed both air bags and smothered the astonished screams of the kid driving it. A double spin and the screech of twisting metal, and the vehicle finally came to rest smack in the middle of the street. The smell of burning rubber filled the air along with blaring horns as the other cars on the road slammed on their brakes and the traffic ground to a stop, hopelessly snarled.

Next to Hellboy, Myers inhaled and finally opened his eyes.

"Are you okay?" Hellboy asked. When Agent

Myers nodded, Hellboy looked satisfied. "Good. Stay here."

And before Myers could protest, Hellboy was off again, bounding into the lights of the carnival amid the delighted squeals of a hundred trick-or-treaters who never fully understood what they were really seeing.

7

HELLBOY SAW THAT SAMMAEL PUT THE LITTLE CARNI-val into the been-there, done-that category quickly, and he was grateful for this. Still, the hound creature was leaving a bright green trail. He didn't need more wrist-slapping from Father for being seen and making the Bureau have to come up with yet another denial . . . in addition to the Halloween stories they were going to have to make up to cover tonight's fiasco. The trail led him quickly into an adjacent alley, poorly lit and full of overflowing trash bins, half-crushed boxes, and old tires. The roadway was cracked and crumbling with disuse, poked with holes worn into it by thousands of cars and trucks. Way down at the end, Hellboy could see the twisted remains of a metal grate; when he got there, he found it'd been ripped free from the front of a large, round opening in the ground. The smell wafting upward was one of dampness and dark, undercut by mildew and, of course, Sammael's meaty slaughter-house scent. From somewhere far away, Hellboy could hear a heavy rumbling. He thought of sewers and water reclamation centers, and decided it could be worse.

Always one for an adventure, he dropped into the opening.

It wasn't too far down. He landed with a *thud*, then paused and looked around curiously. Subway tunnel— he should have realized. That didn't surprise him as much as seeing Sammael a few yards away. The demon looked like he was just sitting there, expecting Hellboy, maybe gonna invite him to tea.

Okay. Hellboy could deal.

"Waiting for me, Sammy?" he asked. He wasn't sure Sammael actually *could* talk or understand him, so Hellboy didn't bother listening for an answer before he started toward the beast. He'd taken all of two big steps, gun drawn and ready, when something very, *very* loud blared from not far away.

Hellboy grinned and put away the Good Samaritan when he saw the headlights barreling down the tracks toward them. "Uh oh," he told Sammael with deceptive mildness. "Between a rock and a hard place."

But Sammael only gave him a tooth-filled grin, turned, and sprinted right for the front of the approaching train.

"Aw, *crap!*" Hellboy exclaimed as he saw the demon unhinge a long, scythelike bone from its forearm. The front car was only a few feet away when

Sammael leaped at the front car and smashed right through the leading glass and steel door.

Sparks showered onto the tracks and Hellboy's ears caught the sound of screaming people and crunching metal—he could imagine the razor-whip that was Sammael's tongue punching easily through all the car doors until the demon could flee out the rear of the train and onto the tracks behind it.

And, of course, here was the train, hurtling right at Hellboy.

He grimaced, but by the time he leaped, he already knew he'd waited too long to clear the top of it.

HUMPF!

The train hit him hard and his legs rattled over the tracks as he punched a hole through the bottom of the train with his stone hand and grabbed hold of anything that might carry his immense weight. Steam exploded from the rupture and surrounded him with heat and sparks; bouncing wildly, he looked up just in time to see the train engineer, a panicked expression on his face, yank a fire extinguisher off the wall of his cab. Another second and he was leaning down and slamming Hellboy on the head with it.

"Ow—hey!" Hellboy protested, trying to ward off the blows. "*Hey!* I'm on *your* side—"

Another whack and he lost his grip and clattered under the train, bumping and thumping painfully down the center of the tracks until he could figure out how to more or less flatten himself enough to let the train whiz by overhead. The undercarriage grazed his horn stumps, heating them up until they smoked; no amount of trying would make his head get any smaller and out of the way.

Finally, the train was gone. Hellboy stood up and rubbed the smoking nubs of his horns irritably, think that this whole Sammael thing was getting to be a real pain in more than one bodily area. He glanced around, but the tunnel was dark, damp, and totally empty. Sammael was gone . . . but then Hellboy grinned. There it was, that handy trail of green glop, nicely leading the way. There was just nothing like pounding the crap out of monsters and he marched after it, ready to fight again, gaze trained on the un-folding tunnel.

Abruptly the trail ended.

What the hell? Glowering, Hellboy turned first in one direction, then the other. There was nothing but the darkness, cut by the occasional dim safety lights. The rounded tunnel was filthy and stained, feeding moisture into long puddles that ran beneath the rails at the bottom. And as before, it was also completely empty.

Something wet and gooey dripped onto his hand.

He looked down and started to shake off the water, then realized it wasn't water at all. His eyes widened at the sight of the glowing chartreuse droplet hanging on to one knuckle. He craned his neck and looked up. "Aw, I forgot—"

Hanging overhead like a pallid, deformed bat, Sammael dropped heavily onto him, wrapping its muscular arms and legs around Hellboy and squeezing him in a lung-crushing bear hug. With a grunt, Hellboy twisted as hard as he could, then got his hands up and around Sammael's jaw; a vicious pull, and the bones parted with a shuddering *crack!*

Sammael released Hellboy and staggered backward, his clawed hands pawing at his face. Hellboy started to move in for the kill, then jerked back as the demon shoved the bones of his face back in place and they snapped together; another instant and there was a faint *shsssssssk* sound as the flesh literally knit itself back into one piece in front of Hellboy's eyes.

Nice trick, Hellboy thought, but before he could formulate his next move, Sammael swept the bone-scythe in his arm forward. It caught Hellboy painfully across the ankles and knocked him off his feet. He landed heavily between the center rails, then Sammael was on top on him and—

tchaaaaaaak!

—the creature sunk the scythe deep into the meat of Hellboy's left shoulder.

He roared in pain and tried to buck Sammael off, but he was pinned by the protrusion from Sammael's arm. Every movement doubled the agony, and already Sammael's mouth was opening and his evil, yellow tongue was rearing back to strike.

Hellboy jerked his head away instinctively, then out of the corner of his eye he caught a glimpse of something only a couple of feet away. He gave Sammael a toothy grin as he stretched out his stone right hand. *"Screw you!"*

And latched on to the third rail.

Lightning and fire filled his vision and the smell of burning flesh shot up his nose. There was heat—a lot of it—but Hellboy being what he was, that just wasn't such a big deal. He held on for a count of three, then released the rail; when his vision cleared he could see the smoke rising from his hand and the rest of his body; on top of him was Sammael, convulsing and crispy in a cloud of black vapor. When Hellboy swatted the demon, he fell over with a *thud*, the bone spur that had been embedded in Hellboy's shoulder collapsed in a pile of dark ash.

Hellboy pulled himself to a crouch, then stood and flexed his shoulder. It hurt, but he'd survive. One arm still had a little bit of flame running along it, so he pulled one of the cigars out of his belt pouch and lit it, then shook his arm until the fire went out—gonna have to get his coat repaired again. He looked down at Sammael's body. "I'm fireproof," he told the corpse as he puffed on the cigar. He exhaled thick smoke, then gave the dead body a final kick and turned away.

"You weren't."

Traffic was tied up completely now, made worse by the oversized tow truck dragging the totaled four-by-four onto its bed and the requisite fire truck and ambulance. Adding to that were the ever-present television reporters and their crews, shoving microphones into the faces of anyone who looked promising; they'd given up on the kid early on when it was obvious he'd dropped into trauma nonmemory. Myers had told the cops to keep the press away from him and so far they'd done a good job of it; he was putting his signature on the latest pile of police forms when his radio beeped. The sound made him jerk and sent a nasty little spasm of pain through his freshly bandaged arm.

"Myers? How's your arm?"

The police officer took the clipboard from him and Myers turned away so he could talk. "My arm is fine," he told Hellboy tersely. "Where are you?" He made sure again that no one was close enough to hear, then repeated himself. "Where *are* you?"

When Hellboy answered, his radio voice was static-filled and hollow, like he was fast on the move. *"I just fried Stinky,"* he said. *"Tell Father I'll be home. He shouldn't wait up."*

Myers's eyes widened. "Wait," he said urgently into the mouthpiece of his headset. "Wait—you can't go anywhere! I have to go with you—"

There was a long enough pause where Myers thought he'd lost the transmission, then Hellboy finally answered. *"No, no, no,"* he said. *"It's fine. I do my job, I take a break."*

Myers was pacing now, walking in a tight, frantic circle on the sidewalk. His only focus was this conversation. *"No,"* he said sharply. *"Stop. Don't do this! Listen to me—tell me where you are."*

"Myers?"

Agent Myers repositioned the microphone nervously. Maybe Hellboy was having problems hearing him. "Yes?"

"Good-bye."

In the subway tunnel, Hellboy imagined Myers's face and grinned to himself. Poor guy—this was just his first taste of what it was going to be like as Hellboy's babysitter. With a flick of one oversized finger, Hellboy turned off his belt locator and moved away into the darkness.

Never noticing that behind him, the charred remains of Sammael's body began to leak a pale, poisonous black light.

Standing in the abandoned baths, Kroenen carefully adjusted the volume on his old phonograph. The strident sounds of Wagner filled the room, echoing off the dirty white tile, sinks, and stalls surrounding him, Grigori, and Ilsa with majestic music.

Off to one side, Ilsa stood behind Grigori with a wickedly sharp straight razor in her hand. The wet blade glinted in the low light as she ran it lovingly over Grigori's scalp, carefully following the bumps and curves, never missing or nicking. When that was done, she put down the razor and dried his skin, then soaped and rinsed her hands thoroughly before lifting two glass eyes from a sterile container on one of the counters. A gentle push positioned one in each of Grigori's empty eye sockets; as he turned his head, they automatically slid into the correct position.

Grigori smiled at her and Kroenen. "Sammael has fulfilled his destiny," he told them. He held up his closed hand, then unfolded the fingers. On his palm, rolled into a foul-looking ball, was the light that had escaped from Sammael's scorched form. "Die in peace," he said softly. "And be reborn again . . . and again." He closed his fist and looked at the others.

Ilsa nodded in agreement. "Only seven more days to the eclipse, Griska."

Rasputin—Grigori—stood and Ilsa stared at him, fascinated and, as always, in adoration. He was an awe-inspiring sight as his neck and shoulders swelled and rose, shifting and rolling beneath his human skin.

"The child will be there," Grigori said dreamily. "And so will we all. Won't we?"

Grigori turned and looked behind him, where a tunnel branched off of the main baths. A silhouette appeared in the darkened entrance, and then another. Even in the shadows, the twin shapes were unmistakable.

Sammael.

8

THE LIBRARY WAS A MESS.

Professor Broom walked slowly through the rubble, looking for anything and everything that might help them get to the bottom of this attack. When Dr. Manning came striding up behind him—no doubt he'd made his grand entrance in his usual slick black limousine—Broom made it a point *not* to jump. He just would not give the younger, already power-drunk man the satisfaction. Crews with classified-level clearances were cleaning up all around him, sweeping up the debris, picking through the imitation artifacts, carrying out what pieces remained of the bodies and partially-eaten clothing worn by the guards.

"Every time the media gets a look at him," Manning said in an overly loud voice from directly behind Broom's shoulder, "they come to *me*. I'm running out of lies, Trevor."

Broom turned around to face him and raised one eyebrow, fighting not to aim a sarcastic smile toward him. "I thought you liked being on TV."

"I do," Manning said. He looked like he wanted to

talk about his latest appearance; he frowned and paused for a moment, forcing himself to get back on track. "How many escapes?" he demanded. "This year alone—five!"

Broom shoved his hands into his jacket pocket and looked at Manning sharply. "Tom, he's our *guest*, not a prisoner."

"Your 'guest' happens to be six-foot-nine, bright red, and is government funded," Manning reminded him. He crossed his arms and regarded Broom stoically.

The professor sighed. "He's just going through a phase."

Manning swung one hand into the breast pocket of his jacket and removed a thin, expensive cigar, then lit it using a kitchen match. "A phase?" His voice was filled with acid. "What do you think this is, *The Brady Bunch?* These *freaks*—" He choked off his sentence when he realized Abe Sapien was looking at him and listening to every word. Ears attuned, Abe was prowling the exhibit hall, palm open and ready to pick up on anything he could. "These *freaks*, Trevor," Manning continued in a lower voice, "they give me the creeps. And I'm not the only one." He glared at Professor Broom. "You're up for review. You *and* your petting zoo."

Broom rubbed his forehead wearily. "I know where to find him. I'll get him back."

Manning scowled but didn't say anything, then focused on Abe Sapien as he noticed something embedded in the floor, a long, sharp dagger. He reached for it. "Hey, fish stick," Manning said sharply. "Don't touch anything!"

But Abe only waved away Manning's instruction. "I need to touch it to see."

"See *what?*" Manning demanded, moving toward him.

Abe regarded him calmly. "The past, the future . . . whatever this object holds."

Manning gaped at him, then turned on Professor Broom. "Is he serious?"

"Don't worry about fingerprints," Abe said. "I never had any." Before Manning could stop him, Abe reached down and picked up the dagger, then blinked thoughtfully and turned to Broom. "They were over here, Professor."

Manning rolled his eyes, then added a fluttering motion in the air with his fingers. "Oooooh! Who was here? Nixon? Houdini? Do you mind sharing your mystic insights?"

Broom ignored him and examined the dagger Abe offered him. When he turned it over, he saw the Ragnarok symbol that crowned its hilt. A dragon and a swastika.

"Show me, Abe," Broom said softly. He reached out one age-spotted hand and met Abe's eyes. "Show me."

And Abe did.

The Magick Exhibit Hall was dark and quiet, deserted. At the far end, a lone guard checked one of the alarm monitoring stations. Everything on the console looked good, but he frowned as something odd caught his attention—a ticking sound. Pulling a flashlight from his belt, he walked the perimeter of the room, shining the light into the corners and under the furniture. There was nothing to see, so the security guard shrugged and moved into the next room.

From the last corner that he checked, that he missed, a spidery form rose from the pool of shadows on the floor.

Kroenen, his body encased in shiny black latex from head to toe, checked the close-fitting harness on his chest; its carefully maintained gears ticked softly, in perfect working order. With the guard gone, he moved out of the corner and stepped up to a nearby glass case that stood about four feet tall. Inside was an ancient wooden statue of one of the Eastern Orthodox saints, exquisitely painted. He glanced around and sneered to himself; all these things were fakes, useless pieces of wood carefully worked over so that they would deceive the foolish, unsuspecting public. And yet this one, the most important one, had been overlooked.

Fools.

Kroenen saw movement on the glass surface—the lovely Ilsa, stepping up silently behind him.

"Move," she ordered.

Obediently Kroenen stepped aside. Ilsa looked at the glass, measuring it with her eyes, looking for the best place to strike. She chose a spot low and to the right, then swung her hammer at it; the glass disintegrated, falling like sharp water. The library's alarm shrieked instantly to life along with the generator-driven emergency lights hung every two yards at the juncture of the ceiling and walls.

Neither Kroenen nor Ilsa moved. When the last of the glass had hit the ground, Kroenen yanked an evil-looking doubled-edged sword from a sheath at his belt; he twirled it overhead, then arced it across the statue at shoulder height.

For a moment, nothing happened. Then, with a sound like a window splitting in extreme temperatures, a diagonal crack appeared in the richly painted wood. A second later, the upper part of the statue toppled off.

As Kroenen carefully rewound a small crank in the center of the gear structure on his chest, Ilsa moved past him and reached into the hollow center of the statue with both hands. Grunting, she lifted out the object inside, a large reliquary jar. The top slid aside momentarily, revealing shimmering golden sand.

"You—don't move! Hands up!"

Ilsa and Kroenen looked back. Guards were filing through the nearest door, six in all. Armed with guns and flashlights, they looked anything but happy to find intruders.

Body shaking with enough force to mimic a seizure, Kroenen pulled a second blade from his belt and stepped up to face the guards.

One of the guards decided not to wait for the unauthorized and quite well-armed visitor to attack. He squeezed the trigger of his gun—

BAM!

—and the bullet tore into Kroenen's arm. Kroenen didn't cry out or fall—he didn't even seem to notice. The guard gaped at the small explosion of dust that appeared in the hole where his bullet had struck—not torn flesh, not spurting blood, but dust. Fear overrode his training and he fired again and again; a split second after his second shot, his panicking coworkers added their own bullets to the flurry.

But Kroenen wasn't about to be hit again. He swung his circular blades up and over, twisting and turning until they were little more than a blur in front of his body. Sparks flashed in the dimly lit hallway as the shots ricocheted wildly, pinging through the shadows; three of the guards grunted and fell, struck by their own returning bullets. By that time, two of the others were practically on top of Kroenen, but he made short work of them, too, this time using his blades, letting their blood wash the floor beneath his feet and sweep away where the dust from his body had fallen. Finally it was just one last guard.

"Don't," the man said. Kroenen was too far away to reach him with his knives and the guard raised his weapon threateningly . . . then screamed as something he couldn't see grabbed his wrist and twisted. The bone broke with a snap, then the flesh of his neck pushed upward under his chin, as though a ghost had wrapped invisible hands *around his neck. Gagging, he flailed and kicked as his body was lifted into the air, and it wasn't until the red-and-yellow bubble lights of the police cars arriving outside shone through the windows that Kroenen and Ilsa could see what held the man. It was Grigori, his arm muscles twitching and shifting beneath his skin as he gained more strength with each breath. A quick and brutal twist sent the top and bottom parts of the hapless guard's body in different directions. The man went limp in Grigori's hold, and he carelessly tossed aside the dead body.*

He turned to look at Ilsa. "Ready the welcome, my love."

Nodding, Ilsa leaned over the reliquary jar and opened it, then picked it up and poured a slow circle of fine, pale powder onto the floor.

Looking down at the circle, Grigori smiled. "Salt," he said. "Gathered from the tears of a thousand martyrs. Restraining the essence of Sammael, the hellhound, the seed of destruction." He sliced through the air with his open hand, drawing glyphs in the emptiness. Then he held out one hand and a small, black flame sprang to life in the very center of it, dancing on his open palm. He pulled his hand away and the flame stayed where it was in the air, suspended over the center of the circle. After a moment, the tiny spot of fire slowly descended to just above the golden-colored salt.

The heap of sand below the flame began to move, churning and flowing like hot mercury. It spread outward as its lines fused into more of a heap, melting and bub-

bling, foaming as the circle grew larger and larger. Bones began to take shape, tendons and ligaments and muscles stretched themselves outward and connected, slick skin knitting over the whole and pulling up and up and up, until finally . . . Sammael.

And the hellhound stood fully upright and roared with the joy of its own existence.

Abe let go of Professor Broom's hand and stepped back, then jerked as he realized Broom was pale and shaking. Was it because of the intensity of the vision? Watching him, he saw Broom wince and grab at his side; Abe reached for the older man's arm automatically, offering his support, momentarily feeling what Broom felt—a bolt of pain, sharp enough to pull his breath away. He steadied Broom, then raised his webbed hand and tested the air a few inches away from the professor's back.

Abe's eyes widened. "Professor," he said softly. "You are very sick."

The old man blinked at him and said, too quietly for anyone else to hear, "I don't want Hellboy to know." He gently pushed Abe's hand away. "Sixty years ago, Abe, they tried to destroy the world. And they're back—in *my* lifetime!" For a moment, the professor looked absolutely stunned. "They're back . . . to finish the job."

9

TONIGHT, CENTRAL PARK WAS AN OKAY PLACE TO BE.

Hellboy knew that normally folks would stay away from the place, wisely avoiding the muggers, rapists, and murderers that often prowled there after dark. It was only on special occasions, such as the warmer weather and the little Halloween celebration currently set up, that New Yorkers were free to enjoy—within reason—the greenery and outside area without fearing for their lives. Right now, there was plenty of light to help keep things livable; lines of tiny, sparkling orange lights, Halloween cousins of Christmas decorations, crisscrossed from tree to tree, waving cheerfully in the mild October breeze along with abundant paper lanterns.

The weather was perfect—no rain, cool enough for snuggling but not so cold that people ended up shivering instead of enjoying the festivities. Children ran and teased one another, making comically scary faces around their rubber masks, their high-pitched laughter winding through the small crowd milling about. Even the smells were good—hot and buttery corn on the cob, warm pumpkin pie, mulled cider with cinnamon.

Slightly out of the flow of traffic but still close enough to the rest of the people for safety's sake, a young couple sat on the bench and listened to the bluesy music floating through the small fair. Laughing, the guy brought up a brown paper bag and pulled out a six-pack of beer, cold enough to make the sides of the cans sweat. He set it on the bench at his side, and when his girlfriend giggled and whispered something in his ear, he pushed it off to the side, then grabbed her and gave her a long, hearty kiss.

With his eyes closed, the young man missed the bright red tail that slid around the side of the bench and deftly snatched away his evening's liquid refreshment.

Hellboy grinned, pleased with his little larceny. Okay, so maybe he shouldn't have swiped it, but he might be doing that couple back in the park a favor— they were probably too young to be drinking anyway, and there was always the don't-drink-and-drive thing. He was just protecting them from themselves.

The lights of the Halloween festival were a long way gone now. This street was darker, quieter, *safer* for someone like him, who didn't want to be seen by the everyday eye. The trees were evenly spaced on each side of the avenue in this older neighborhood, and so heavily leafed that their crowns nearly met overhead, deepening the shadows and making the pools of illumination thrown by the streetlights seem like solitary islands. The dried leaves flying up in little whirlwinds of cool air only added to the sense of loneliness.

As Hellboy walked on, carefully keeping himself in the darkness, several emergency vehicles roared past, their lights and sirens grinding through the silence of the otherwise deserted street. When they were gone and the street fell back into silence, Hellboy stepped up his pace until, finally, his destination came into view.

Bellamie Mental Hospital had been built in the 1940s, when funding from the local government had been a little more plentiful. Later decades had seen the Feds pump more than a little cash into the facility, said cash specifically being earmarked to support particular areas that were kept out of the general public eye . . . and even out of range of most of its own medical staff. Six stories of dark brick rose up behind a high wall topped with barbed wire, a security feature designed as much to keep people out as it was to keep the patients in.

The scene beyond the wall was a little more cheerful; while all the windows were covered in dark steel mesh, Hellboy could see colorful jack-o'-lanterns and funny-faced paper skeletons taped to the windows, along with the expected assortment of seasonable bats, spiders, and cartoon cauldrons. Between the wall and the building was a lush topiary garden, and the sight always made Hellboy shake his big head in amazement. What rocket scientist, architect, or hospital administrator had thought it was a good idea to put something like that outside a building full of people with mental problems? He hoped they weren't surprised when half of their patients complained about how the shapely green rabbits and various other animals moved or chased them. Jeez.

It took all of two seconds for Hellboy to get on top of the wall, choose his spot, and flatten the wire until he had himself a nice place to sit and wait and, of course, watch the second-floor windows. The cold beer cans felt good against his hot skin, so he kept his tail-hold on the six-pack, swinging it idly but also being gentle about it; it wasn't good to have the beer can blow up in your face when you popped the top. The part of his arm where Sammael had grabbed him was aching badly and bleeding, and Hellboy glanced at it irritably. The sleeve of his overcoat was soaked in blood; he'd have to get that looked at, but later. He had other things to look forward to right now, and like always, he knew it would only be a matter of time.

The second floor hallway was twenty-six-year-old Liz Sherman's haven, her own chosen place of peace and quiet. The patients were good—fairly stable and well-behaved, and she'd worked hard to get placement down here and away from the more volatile wards of the upper floors. Her own behavior was good enough so that one of her regular duties was to carry the evening meds tray for the nightly rounds. The evening psychiatrist in charge, Dr. Marsh, was an older woman nearly as tall and lithe as Liz herself, except with regal white hair kept in an impeccable and expensive style. In that respect, she could have been Liz's opposite, her tanned complexion and light hair contrasting sharply with Liz's own longer, raven black hair and piercing dark eyes, the pale skin of her face marred by the scar that crossed her forehead. Where Liz wore the expected patient's gown, Dr. Marsh sported a white lab jacket over an expensive designer business suit and was always sure not to have any pens or other sharp objects in the jacket's pockets.

They were almost at the end of the patient line when Kenny, one of the more vocal Down's Syndrome patients, cocked his head slightly and turned toward the window. He looked, then abandoned the medicine line and pressed his face against the reinforced glass. "There's a big red guy down there!" he burbled.

Dr. Marsh glanced at him and raised one impeccably groomed eyebrow. Then she went back to checking off little boxes on her clipboard against the medicine cups on the tray Liz was holding for her. "That's fine, darling. Santa's not here for another month."

But Kenny shook his head. "Not Santa—big. And *red*." He switched from shaking his head to nodding vigorously, trying to make his point. "With gold eyes . . . and he has beer!"

Liz looked at Kenny sharply, but of course the boy didn't notice her glance and wouldn't have understood if he had. Dr. Marsh was through dispensing the medications, so Liz tucked the tray under one arm and briefly closed her eyes, then tugged on one of the wide, heavy rubber bands around each of her wrists. She pulled it out and let it go, wincing as it snapped hard against her skin. After giving the tray back to the desk nurse and watching Dr. Marsh move farther down the hall, Liz wandered over to one of the windows, moving as though she had nothing better in the world to do than gaze out at the stars struggling to peek out from between the October clouds and the city smog. But there was nothing—the gardens below were empty.

Sure they were.

The thing about the second floor ward of Bellamie was that it was low security—many of the second-floor patients, Liz included, were allowed to go in and out of the gardens at will, so long as it was at a reasonable hour. She was pushing the envelope here a little, since it was after dark on a rapidly cooling October evening (and Halloween night to boot—the staff at the hospital were *very* aware of that seemingly minor detail), but she thought she had maybe ten or fifteen minutes before the guard at the topiary door outright refused. She'd also dressed sensibly for the outing, as there was nothing like a vacant-eyed patient wearing only a thin hospital gown and wanting to go outside to tip off security that all was not copacetic in someone's mental la-la land. The truth? Please; the *last* thing Liz Sherman would *ever* need was a sweater to keep her warm. It also helped that she had an old Polaroid camera swinging from a strap around her neck; that was so much a familiar sight to the hospital personnel that for her to leave it behind would have been worse. Human beings, even mentally unstable ones, always followed routines, and the professional folks here always looked suspiciously at anything that deviated from the normal pattern of things.

Even so, Liz kept on her overly warm sweater as she went outside, knowing the sharp-eyed man was watching her through the security glass, maybe a little too closely. *Down, boy,* she thought and smiled a little to herself. *You don't want to get singed.* Outside, the sunset had taken the last of the day's heat with it and the air was cool and on its way to crisp. She thought it felt wonderful and, had she been going to stay out here, would have welcomed the ongoing cold night-time air. But there was no time to think about such things now; instead, she focused on the trail of blood, a splash here, a splotch over there, that finally led around to the back of a large, thorn-studded bush.

Yeah, she thought so.

Liz took a deep breath. "Back so soon?"

Something rustled, then moved deeper within the branches. She waited, then saw a leg and part of the familiar overcoat slip into view. Another second and Hellboy's tail poked out from beyond the leaves; its end was curled around a dripping six-pack of some kind of foreign brew.

"Uh . . . I brought beer."

In spite of herself, a corner of Liz's mouth turned up at the hopeful note in the big guy's voice. She lifted the camera to one eye, found the frame she wanted, and pushed the button. "To wash down my Lithium pills?" She peered into the bushes but couldn't quite get a view of him. "I may get a few perks, H.B., but I'm still a patient."

The rustling in the branches grew louder, and he finally climbed out, looking at the ground, at the bushes, the building—anywhere but directly at her. She always thought it was funny that Hellboy was so strong and rock 'em, sock 'em, but so helplessly shy around her. She started to say something about this, then forgot those words as her gaze stopped on his arm. Even thought it was night and the dark color of his overcoat camouflaged it, she could see the fabric was soaked with enough blood to make it drip. She frowned. "You better have that looked at."

Hellboy blinked, then glanced down at his arm and shrugged. "Just a scratch." He paused awkwardly. "I . . . wanted to see you."

Liz sighed, then motioned for him to follow her to a bench that was around the corner and about as far away from the door she'd come out of as possible. Hellboy would hear the guard the instant he opened the door, and the distance would give them time to say good-bye. They settled on the bench and she watched him for a few minutes while neither of them said anything. He was so big, and so completely . . . out of place in the real world.

He was a lot like her.

Finally, Hellboy spoke. "We miss you at the Bureau," he said hesitantly. "Abe's crazier every day. And Father's still mad at me." He saw her smile and took it as a sign of encouragement. He rushed on. "Come back, Liz. Come back. I—"

"No," she broke in. "Not this time, H.B. It's been months since I've had an episode. And you know what?" Her gaze bored into his. "I'm learning to *control* it."

He said nothing, just watched as she looked down at her own right hand. Another beat and a faint blue aura of fire bloomed around it, crawling over her fingers like a pale, velvet haze. She stared at it for a moment, then flexed the fingers thoughtfully. "I'm learn-ing where it comes from," she said at last. Then she added in a softer voice, "And for once in my life, I'm not afraid." Without warning, Liz clenched her fist and put out the flame. When she looked at Hellboy again, her gaze had cleared of the introspection. She raised a finger and pointed. "Looks like your ride is here."

Hellboy followed her gesture and his shoulders slumped. When the wall turned in on itself and sur-rounded the main area, it went from solid to tall and stately wrought iron. It was through this metal barrier that Hellboy and Liz could see the well-known garbage truck and a couple of black sedans as they steered onto the hospital grounds. "Great," Hellboy grumbled. "The Nanny Squad."

As though on cue, at least a dozen agents clam-bered out of the three vehicles, with Clay and Myers at the forefront. Another second and Broom pushed out of one of the sedans, his movements oddly slow and clunky. They weren't making any effort to be quiet, and Liz and Hellboy could hear them easily from here.

"Sir?" Myers asked. "May I go first?"

Myers started their way, but Clay stopped him. "Not so fast," the older agent protested. He turned to Broom. "He barely knows him."

Liz saw Hellboy chuckle beneath his breath at Professor Broom's reply. "Then he should make it his business to change that." Always the no-nonsense approach.

It would be only a few seconds before Myers got here, so Liz stood and put a hand on Hellboy's shoulder. "Listen, H.B.," she said. She tried to make her voice half firm, half pleading, but in reality, what were the chances either would work? So much of the time he just did what he wanted. "I've got a chance out here. If you truly care about me . . . *don't come back anymore.*"

For a long, painful moment, Hellboy said nothing, just sat there staring unhappily at the ground. She was already walking away when he tried unsuccessfully to smile. "Good night, then."

"Good night," Liz said, but her voice was already faint, as though her mind were anywhere but here or on Hellboy.

She didn't turn around.

10

HELLBOY WATCHED LIZ WALK AWAY . . . AGAIN.

There was a lump in his throat the size of the Brooklyn Bridge, but he'd be damned if he'd be left standing here like some moke who'd just been dumped, even if that *was* pretty much what had just happened. Every self-respecting guy knew that the least he could do was try to get the last word in.

Hellboy cleared his throat, but his voice still sounded like driveway gravel when he spoke. "Yeah," Hellboy said, a little too loudly. "I gotta go, too. Lots to do."

His head was spinning a little—funny how being around Liz could do that to him—but he stood up anyway. He registered a sort of *splooshing* sound and felt the fabric of his overcoat drag, like he'd been standing in the rain; when he looked down at the bench, he was vaguely surprised to see an actual puddle of blood on the bench, enough so that it was dripping down the front of the stone seat into a pool at his feet.

Hellboy ignored it and looked up as Agent Myers tentatively approached. "What took you so long?"

Myers glanced at the scarlet circle on the ground and concern flashed over his features. "Come on," he said. "Time to go home." He inclined his head toward the oozing wound in Hellboy's arm. "Tape you up."

Hellboy tried to scowl at him, but the light-headedness creeping up on him made it difficult. His mouth and jaw felt numb and vaguely uncooperative. "What are you, a Boy Scout?"

Myers shook his head. "No. I never was."

Hellboy felt behind him for the bench. Maybe he'd sit down again for a bit. "Could've fooled me," he managed to retort. He waved a hand in the air. "Go away." He meant it to sound like a command, but even he had to admit it came across as pretty damned weak when his legs wobbled and instead of sinking back onto the bench, he went down to his knees.

Like worker ants surrounding a big, tasty bug, Agents Clay, Quarry, and Moss were on him in an instant, right alongside the new and determined to be ever-present Myers. Hellboy wanted to push them away as they pulled him back onto his feet, but he didn't have the strength.

Agent Clay's big hand was firm around Hellboy's elbow. "Come on, champ. You look a little woozy there."

Hellboy tried to shoulder him off, but he couldn't. His head just wouldn't clear up and his ears were ringing. Even so, he snorted and glanced at the gash on his arm. "This? This is nothing. You know what'll kill me?" Hellboy stabbed a finger toward a doorway across the garden; Liz stood silhouetted in it, backlit by the hospital fluorescents. "*Her.*"

His legs jittered and he keeled over with a grunt, then tried unsuccessfully to help the agents as they struggled to get him back to the garbage truck.

When that was finally done, Myers wiped his brow and glanced back at the hospital. The woman Hellboy had been talking to—Liz—was still standing in the doorway and watching them. His gaze caught hers and they stared curiously at each other. Before Myers could think about it further, the woman turned and disappeared into the building, pulling the door firmly shut behind her.

Overbright white lights, white walls, lots of gleaming stainless steel and antiseptic-bathed counters and cabinets, sterile air that smelled like alcohol and clean cotton. The stainless steel table on which Hellboy was lying was built more for efficiency than comfort, but at least it was cool against Hellboy's perpetually hot skin, always a good thing. Still, they ought to think more of the patient—he'd bet that when Liz sat down to talk to her psychiatrists, she had a nice, comfy couch or a recliner to sit on, maybe made of good leather that was cool against her skin.

He wondered what she was doing right now.

Probably not thinking about him.

Hellboy gave himself a mental shake and refocused on Father, who was sitting on a stool beside the table and studying him with those sad eyes of his. On the other side of the table, Abe bent over Hellboy's injured arm, peering into the ugly wound with a magnifying glass. "You were burned by some organic acid," Abe finally told him.

"I'm lucky that way," Hellboy said without bothering to look.

Abe plucked a sterile scalpel from a tray next to Hellboy's head and began to probe inside the gash. Despite himself, Hellboy grunted with pain.

"Son," Broom said quietly. "About Rasputin—"

"Don't worry," Hellboy said before Father could finish. "I'll get him soon enough."

The professor shook his head and leaned closer to Hellboy. "Listen to me. This time is *different*. There's more at stake than *ever* before."

Hellboy only looked at him out of the side of one eye. "How hard can it be? I punched the crap out of that thing he sent—*ouch!*"

Abe paused, but Hellboy's attention went back to Father and his next words. "I worry about you."

Now Hellboy turned his head toward the old man. "Me? Come on."

Father looked away. "Well, I won't be around forever, you know."

Hellboy scowled. "Oh, stop that—*damn!*" He jerked his face back toward Abe, who tried to look appropriately guilty, then bent back over the wound anyway. "Be careful there!"

But Abe wasn't interested in Hellboy's discomfort. He had other questions on his mind. "Red, how long was it latched on to you?"

Hellboy grimaced. "I dunno. Maybe five seconds—*OW!*"

Agent Myers, who had been pretty quiet since they'd gotten back to the B.P.R.D. and carted Hellboy into the infirmary, stepped up to the side of the table. "You want me to hold him down?"

Hellboy's jaw dropped open, then he snickered. "That's right, stud. Hold *me* down."

Before Myers could say anything in return, Abe said, "Professor."

Something about the tone of his voice made Hellboy forget the next crack he was going to toss at Myers. As Father climbed off the stool and moved around to the other side of the table, Hellboy sat up a little straighter. He'd always been right with the *this-isn't-good* intuition and it was looking like right now was no exception. He started to lift his head so he could see, but Broom's sharp voice stopped him. "Don't look—turn around!"

Hellboy let his head *thunk* back down on the table. "Is it bad?" Okay, so he'd felt pretty crappy back at the hospital, and maybe he'd lost his footing in the hospital garden. And sure, the ride back to the B.P.R.D. was pretty hazy. But now that he was lying down, things were back on target.

Weren't they?

Okay, this was one of those cases where no news *was* bad news, and Hellboy just couldn't handle that. Despite Father's command, he picked his head back up and peered at the slice in his arm that Abe had now spread wide with a scalpel and a pair of medical tweezers. His angle was bad, his neck was bent, but he could just see what the big deal was.

Three eggs, nestled like ugly translucent ticks, just inside the flesh of his forearm.

Hellboy jumped as Abe plucked out the first one and held it up so they could all see it, then dropped it into a waiting glass container. "Touched you five seconds," Abe said almost admiringly. "Laid three eggs."

Hellboy glowered at the egg-thing in the container, then steeled himself as Abe went after the next one buried in his arm. "Didn't even buy me a drink," he grumbled. By the time the second one had been extracted, he felt like a pincushion; if three times was the charm, he needed to have a serious talk with the idiot who'd come up with *that* stupid saying.

Still, he was feeling a lot better now that he'd had the uninvited tenants in his forearm evicted. They moved from the exam room into one of the medical bays, and in no time, Hellboy was sitting up with his arm neatly stitched and bandaged—no more leaking onto his coat and doing the bob 'n' wobble when he tried to walk. Myers had tossed his coat into the laundry and since Hellboy knew he looked lousy in white, he'd refused the agent's offer of a triple-extra-large lab coat. He was even starting to get a little of his appetite back, and life would've been A-OK if not for the annoying *beep!* from the computer a few feet away. They all crowded around the monitor to see the image that came up with the machine's analysis, and all of a sudden Hellboy just wasn't so high on life when he saw the enlarged color view of one of the throbbing eggs.

Abe, obviously, was fascinated. He pointed at the image with one of his webbed fingers, sounding awed. "The eggs are very sensitive to heat and light. They need a humid, dark environment to hatch." He brandished a new pair of tweezers and picked up one of the eggs, then passed the metal holders to Hellboy. Hellboy squinted at it and passed it back; it was probably ridiculous, but he didn't want these things anywhere near his flesh, didn't want to take the chance that they might have this DNA-level idea that Hellboy was their freebie hotel.

Myers tracked the egg as it went from Abe to Hellboy, then back again. "Down there," he finally said, "did you ever lose track of him? Of Sammael?"

Hellboy blinked. "Well, let's see . . . there was that moment when I had a train on top of my head."

Father's eyes were troubled as he caught Hellboy's gaze. "We can't risk it," he said after a long moment of thought. "You'll go back to the tracks tomorrow with a group of agents. Search the area, top to bottom."

Off to the side, Myers listened while watching the screen and its blown-up image. His mouth twisted in revulsion when on the glass, one of the eggs twitched as something small and fetuslike inside wiggled.

Back in Professor Broom's office, Myers watched the old man place a new set of books on the reading stands in front of Abe's tank. He hadn't seen that much of the B.P.R.D., but Myers thought that this office, with its soft lighting and the thousands of carefully maintained books, all overlit by the gentle, swaying glow from Abe's tank, had to be the most comfortable place in the entire complex.

Obviously Broom wasn't going to say anything, so Myers finally cleared his throat and spoke. "I'm in way over my head. I know that."

Broom didn't look up as he carefully set up a couple of new books to be Abe's reading material, opening them to the first page of the first chapter of each. The titles were interesting in light of the creature—*no*, Myers told himself, *person*—who would be reading them: a vampire novel called *AfterAge* and a zombie novel titled *Deadrush*, both by the same author. Myers would have pegged Abe for a straight facts man, hard science and maybe geology; then again, considering he was such an integral part of the B.P.R.D., reading these supernatural stories wasn't that far off from the truth.

"You're doing fine," the professor finally said as he finished. He glanced at Abe, who was still wearing his breathing apparatus and was sitting quietly on a chair in the shadows near the door.

Myers scrubbed at his face, feeling the stubble there and not remembering the last time he'd had time to shave. "No," he said. "I'm *not*. He respects Clay, not me. I don't know why you chose me, sir, but I'm not qualified." There, he'd said it, the worst part, out loud. The part he hadn't voiced was his disillusionment, the composite of shame over his own failure and his profound disappointment that he couldn't make himself into someone Hellboy would accept. And when Broom didn't argue, Myers figured there wasn't anything else to add—the professor obviously agreed with him and would find someone else for the project. Swallowing his discouragement, Myers turned and headed for the door.

"I'm dying, Agent Myers."

Shocked, the younger man stopped and looked back at Broom. His mouth worked, but he didn't know what to say. He barely knew this man, but already he liked and respected him, already he wanted to slip into denial mode—*Don't be ridiculous, if you're sick, we'll get a second opinion; whatever's wrong can be slowed or halted altogether.* All of which was ridiculous since he didn't know the details and hey, Professor Broom was more intelligent than most of the people in this building. No doubt he'd already delved into all his options . . . and found them nonexistent.

"As a father," Broom continued, "I worry about him." The old man pinned Myers in place with his gaze. "In medieval stories, Agent Myers, there's often a young knight. Inexperienced but pure of heart."

"Oh, please," Myers said automatically. "I'm not pure of heart."

Abe shifted on his chair. "Yes, you are," he said softly. Myers shifted uncomfortably, not wanting to think about how Abe would get the information needed to make a statement like that.

Broom walked carefully over to Myers until he stood directly in front of him, looking straight into his eyes. "What I ask from you," he said firmly, "is that you have the courage to stand by his side after I'm gone. Help him find himself. Who he must be." He paused, and unaccountably Myers felt the hair rise along the surface of his arms before the professor had even finished his next sentence.

"He was born a demon. You will help him become a man."

*   *   *

Myers had been at this for hours, but it felt like minutes. Somewhere in that time period, he'd eaten a sandwich—the crumbs and bits of wilted lettuce were still wadded up in the wrapping paper on the floor where he'd missed the wastebasket—but he couldn't have said what kind it had been, something premade from the B.P.R.D. cafeteria. Ditto with the thirty-two-ounce soft drink—Coke? Pepsi? Or maybe it'd been something appropriately red, like Hawaiian Punch. Myers had no clue. Had his dinner been something *good*, say a couple of peanut butter and honey sandwiches, he would have remembered it. As it was, whatever he'd eaten was sustenance, nothing more; fuel for the body so that the mind could keep going. Learning, especially something in which he was particularly interested, had always been like that for him.

He was in one of the conference rooms off the main B.P.R.D. archive. In it were dark leather chairs surrounding a mahogany table, and top-of-the-line projection equipment—all the finest things tax dollars could secretly buy. Off to the side was a computer station, and it was here that Myers had chosen to spend his time, hammering along at the keyboard while he learned not only about Hellboy, but what the next part of his own life would entail.

The images of Hellboy flashed by on the screen, everything from the tacky tabloid headlines to the

more intimate photographs taken as he'd grown up.
There he was as a kid, only seven years old, and despite the seriousness of everything in which he was in-
volved, Myers had to grin. Put a uniform on him and
he would've looked like a sturdy little red football
player . . . well, except for the horns and the tail and
that stone arm of his. The photo of Hellboy at age
twelve really made Myers chuckle—had it been
Broom or Hellboy himself who'd had the idea to dress
him up as a human for Halloween?

The next image in the group of photos on this latest disk made the agent pause a little longer as he saw
the files go into detail on someone associated with
Hellboy, rather than the red man himself. Myers had
seen the format of *The National Enquirer* a thousand
times in the supermarket checkout line, so often that
he'd stopped paying attention. Now that he was in-
volved in the B.P.R.D., Myers realized he was going to
have to give those seemingly ludicrous headlines a little more consideration.

"Arson Suspect Now Working for Secret Government Agency!"

It was a grainy black-and-white photo shot through
a telephoto lens, still clearly outside the range of the
camera's capabilities. Despite that, Liz Sherman was,
at least to the knowing eye, clearly recognizable. Head
down, dark hair shielding her eyes as she smoked a
cigarette, there was something unaccountably miser-

able about her, an aura of pain that was belied by the sensationalism of the headline. Myers would have thought he was imagining it, until the words of the next clipping sunk into his overtired brain.

This one was from a regular newspaper, buried back a couple of pages and out of the limelight of daily life; it probably would have made the front pages but for the mudslinging that had been going on at the time between two mayoral candidates. There was Liz again, this time at age eleven. In the photo, her eyes looked more like those of a haunted victim; she was crying, and a nasty dark smear on her forehead in the black-and-white photo could only be blood. "Tragic Explosion" read the caption below a picture of what was left—not much—of a row house somewhere in the uncaring city of Detroit.

Myers hit the Next key and a QuickTime window expanded onto the screen. The interview was short and concise, and the only person on which the camera focused was young Liz Sherman. Now she was in her early twenties and armed with a Polaroid camera; as a title typed itself under the film box—"Elizabeth Anne Sherman, First Interview, B.P.R.D., Pyrokinetic"—Liz raised the camera and pointed it at the person videotaping *her*. That done, she lowered her Polaroid and focused on the camera rather than the videographer and interviewer a few feet offscreen.

"*I don't like the term 'firestarter'*," she said. Myers

noted her reluctance to look into the camera, the way she seemed to be talking more to herself than the interviewer. *"I just don't. And 'pyrokinesis' sounds like psychosis or something. I don't know . . . maybe that's right. Not being able to let go . . ."* She shrugged, but still didn't take her gaze off the Polaroid resting on her knees. *"It's scary. Sometimes you hear so-and-so lost control and just . . . exploded."* She paused and for a long few seconds didn't say anything. *"They're lucky it isn't true."*

And finally, she raised her dark and tormented eyes and looked straight into the video lens.

"With me . . . it is."

"QUIET NIGHT, HUH?" BRAD NUDGED TERRENCE, HIS coworker and best buddy, in the arm, then paused and pushed open the next door in line just enough to shine his flashlight inside the room. The patient in there was sound asleep, nothing more than a covered lump on the bed. "Wanna play poker after we finish up rounds? I brought change."

Terrence shrugged, then veered to the left to check the next room on his side of the hallway. "Why? So I can end up owing you another five or six bucks until payday? You know I'm lousy at cards."

"You'll learn."

"I'll go broke before that," Terrence retorted.

Brad grinned, then pushed open the door to the last room. He shone his light around the inside, slowing as it played over several hundred photos taped to a white bulletin board. Layer upon layer, but as far as Brad could tell, they were nothing special, just scenes of everyday life, everyday people, and a lot of the patients in here. Who knew why the woman kept taking them? Like the other rooms, the night-light in the bathroom kept this one from being truly dark—that scared too many of the patients—and he could see the woman sleeping on the bed. Liz Sherman was a pretty gal with dark hair and perpetual circles under her eyes, but there was something about her that creeped Brad out and made him keep his distance. When the beam of his flashlight passed over the back of her head, it was almost like she felt it; she rolled over and faced him but thankfully didn't wake up. He hated it when they did that, always winced at the accusing glares. Hey, he and Terrence were just doing their jobs.

"Rounds are done," Terrence said, careful to keep his voice low. "Come on. I'll give you one last night of poker, just to show I'm a good sport. But first we check out one of those microwave pizzas." He spared the corridor a final glance, then motioned for Brad to follow him back up to the orderly station. "There's absolutely zero going on here tonight."

Grigori watched the two foolish men leave, his form deepening the shadows in the far corner of the room. It always amazed him that the everyday eyes of a man were so useless—take those two, for instance. Their eyes were seemingly perfect, clear and strong, and yet there they'd been, inches away, and they had seen nothing at all.

Dismissing them, he stepped from the corner and glided up to stand next to Liz Sherman's bed. *Such a lovely woman*, he thought as he gazed down at her. *And such a powerful, powerful tool.*

Slowly Grigori extended his right hand. His voice was an oily caress floating on the night drafts that passed over her face.

"The Master is calling your name now, my girl. We are all part of his plan. You must return to the child. So once again . . ." Grigori smiled and ran his forefinger gently over the scar on Liz's forehead, careful to make his touch just short of waking her. Something twisted rolled beneath the skin of his arm, momentarily rearranging his muscles into a new and hideous shape. The fingers of his hand began to glow. "Dream of fire," he whispered.

On the bed, Liz's eyelids squeezed tight and she suddenly convulsed. After a moment, a small ripple of heat began to rise from her forehead.

There were smokestacks rising above the roofs of the buildings around hers, belching puddles of darkness into the air on a daily basis. The grown-ups complained about them now and then, but like everything else, mostly they were just a part of the way life was, like the overflowing garbage cans and the litter on the streets, the rats that scurried in the alleys.

And the kids who never, ever stopped teasing her.

The smoke and the garbage and the rats—none of that mattered to her, but the kids were a different story altogether. Staring sullenly out at the street, Liz sat on the steps of her tenement house all by herself, fingering the gold crucifix around her neck. Sometimes she thought this crucifix was the only spot of color in her life. This cross was supposed to represent something hopeful, something good to come, and so she'd gotten into the habit of touching it constantly, unconsciously rubbing it like it was a genie's lamp. And why not? She certainly didn't have any friends and she probably never would; even as young as she was, she'd already accepted that her place in the world would never be a normal one. She was, through no fault or wish of her own, destined to be an outcast.

And behind her, of course, her mother, always trying to make things better for Liz, never truly understanding why things were the way they were or that she'd never be able to fix them, never be able to get Liz "in" with the other children. Adults just didn't get it.

Liz glanced up and saw her mom smiling at her above the basket of apples she carried. There was such hope in that look, enough to break Liz's young heart. "Liz!" she called. "Liz—come on, darling. Give mummy a hand!"

Liz didn't move. Her mother was headed over to the birthday party in the small, grubby courtyard at the side of the apartment building. She didn't know the kid whose birthday it was, and didn't want to; as far as she was concerned, the bright balloon archway the adults had pieced together looked crooked and out of place between the dirty, medium-income buildings. Armed with the apples, her mother hurried through the opening and headed toward the table and a waiting pot of melted caramel.

Waiting until Liz's mother had passed, the three kids hanging out below the entrance poked at each other, then pointed at Liz and laughed cruelly. Around bites of caramel-covered apples, they lost no time in starting up their taunts.

"Freak!" yelled one.

Most of the time, she could ignore them. She'd trained herself that way, done what the Bible called "hardened her heart" to their ridicule. Today, for some reason, she couldn't—she didn't want to, she really didn't, but today Liz was unable to stop herself from turning and staring at them.

One of them, an older blond kid, grinned and punched one of his friends on the shoulder. "See? She knows her name!"

Ducking her head, Liz forced herself to look away from them and stare gloomily in the other direction. Unfortunately, that wasn't enough to get them to leave her alone.

"Go home, you freak!" shouted another. "We don't want you here!"

Liz flinched as a stone bounced off the steps next to her, then got up and backed away as they threw another one; it missed, but the third try whacked her painfully in the shoulder. Frightened, Liz turned toward the party, hoping to spot her mother. Before she spotted her, the next rock, bigger than the others, caught her hard in the face, splitting her forehead and splattering the pavement with blood. Sobbing, Liz stumbled and fell down the short flight of stairs, trying to crawl away.

The threesome over by the makeshift balloon arch only giggled. The oldest boy snatched up his next stone, then sailed it high and hard, aiming again for Liz's head.

Halfway there, the rock burst into flames and turned to ash.

Liz gasped and scrambled back to her feet, forgetting about the pain in her head and the blood running down her face. A ripple of heat was working its way up her hands, finally culminating in a pale blue flame that ringed her entire arm.

"Not again," she moaned. "Please . . . not again!"

As she looked down, she saw a small dot of firelight glint off the crucifix hanging on her chest.

"Mommy!" she screamed suddenly. "Mommy!"

Across the sidewalk, her mother jerked and looked up from the pot of caramel, recognizing Liz's voice instantly. It took only that long—a second, no more—for her to train her eyesight on her daughter's small figure and see the flames outlining her body.

"Mommy, help me! I'm burning!"

Liz's mother screamed. The hot pot of caramel upended and the apples tumbled off the table as she abandoned it and ran toward Liz, pushing aside the gawking children and the horrified adults. She had to get to Liz, to her daughter—

"Help meeeeeeeeeee!"

She never made it.

Liz felt herself . . . explode, *felt everything that she was, inside and out, go white-hot and expand, the way the stars looked on the science fiction programs she sometimes watched. A rolling cloud of hot brightness engulfed her, the courtyard, her mother, the building, and everyone around her. All she could do was stand there and endure, knowing without being told that her mother's body had burned away like flash paper along with her brother, her father—who had unwisely come to visit his estranged family only for the party—the trees and birds and rats,* everything. *And at the end, after the hot* white *of it, the shockwave hit and did the rest of the job, flattening four solid blocks of buildings around ground zero—*

Liz.

Left standing and sobbing after her destruction of anything and everything that had existed in her small and unhappy world.

On the bed, Liz Sherman suddenly screamed.

The rubber bands on her wrists vaporized and her back arched as her body was completely engulfed by flames, the burning so bright that it silhouetted the organs and bones inside her skin, the orbs of her eyes within her skull, and made her ribs stark X-ray outlines visible all the way through the sheet and blanket that covered her. It was only a matter of seconds until the glow streamed out of her room—

—and into the corridor, where it lit the nighttime dim walls with a dangerous orange-yellow glow.

Safe within the guard booth, Brad and Terrence were sharing their pre-poker game pizza and listening to the radio, some disk jockey who liked to think he was big on the humor on WXRQ. The rock and roll was decent, and if nothing else, at least the two of them agreed the guy was a moke who didn't know funny when it bit him on the ass. They had the music a little too loud, high enough to drown out the tinny *beep* from the console, so it probably took four beats for Brad to realize that the faint pinging he thought was in the radio's speaker was actually a patient's alarm. The sight of the red light flashing on the board was so unexpected that for a moment they both just stared at it in amazement—nothing weird *ever* happened down here on the second floor. Then Terrence slapped a hand on the radio's Off button and the two of them grabbed their batons. As they stood, a sound, low and huge, rumbled through the floor and the furniture and everything else around them.

Brad swallowed and thought vaguely of earthquakes, then saw Terrence's eyes actually *bulge* as the other young man stared through the glass separating them from the corridor. He followed Terrence's gaze and his mouth dropped open.

Thirty feet down the corridor, a ball of fire was rushing straight toward them.

Brad gasped and turned, but there wasn't enough time to run, and there was nowhere to go, anyway. All they could do was stand and wait, surrounded by a suddenly eerie and almost serene silence, staring in terror at what was almost certainly their oncoming death.

Terrence finally found his vocal cords. "Oh my—"

The fireball engulfed the booth, and they dove for the floor and the dubious cover of an overhanging shelf.

The glass walls exploded in the heat and the flames roared in, drowning everything in searing orange. Moments later, every single window on the hospital's second floor shattered and the fire poured outward, showering glass and ash onto the gardens below.

And then . . .

Silence and ash and cinders.

12

HIS NERVES SINGING, MYERS TRUNDLED HELLBOY'S breakfast cart quickly forward. Even through his anxiety, the agent had to admit it smelled pretty good—three dozen steaming pancakes, a mound of hot bacon, and buttered toast. Myers hadn't eaten since his marathon learning session last night but he was much too wired to think about breakfast right now. The news of Liz Sherman's latest conflagration had spread like wildfire—pun intended—through the grapevine of those agents who, like him, for one reason or another had the need to know. Based on what Myers understood was currently going down back at Bellamie Mental Hospital, Hellboy ought to be in quite the mood right about now. Myers wasn't stupid enough to think the big guy hadn't already found out.

Almost shaking with anticipation, Myers pushed open the door to Hellboy's bachelor den.

Inside, Professor Broom was sitting on the edge of the truck bed that served as Hellboy's couch. His thin arms were folded and his expression was implacable.

Hellboy was so angry he was practically waving his

fist. "How many buildings does she have to burn?" he demanded. "She belongs *here!*"

Broom didn't so much as blink as he met Hellboy's gaze. "That's not how she feels. She may *never* feel it."

Just in case they hadn't realized he was there, Myers deliberately cleared his throat. They'd heard him, he was sure of it. Even so, both ignored him.

"It's *her* choice," Broom told Hellboy. "She's human."

Hellboy's glare became even more pronounced. "Oh," he said sarcastically, "as opposed to . . ." He didn't finish his sentence, and neither did Broom.

Hellboy spun and stomped over to where a large mirror hung on the wall above a shelf loaded with personal hygiene paraphernalia. He jerked up a handheld belt sander, flipped the On switch, and savagely began grinding away at the stumps of his horns. Sparks flew in every direction and the noise drowned out any possible conversation; after about ten seconds, he finally seemed a bit calmer. He set the sander down, then sniffed the air. "Mmmmm," he noted. "Pancakes. We're going out?"

Myers pushed his hair back with one hand. "Professor, that girl you were talking about?"

Hellboy whirled, his eyes blazing. "Hey, you think twice—"

Myers plunged on. "I read her file. She blamed herself for that explosion in Pittsburgh, the one where all those agents died when they were possessed by demons and she and Hellboy fought back." He looked from Broom to Hellboy. "I think I can help," he said. "Talk to her. I can bring her back."

Hellboy's angry expression faded into amusement. "What landed you this job pushing pancakes?" He chuckled, clearly proud of his little jab. "What was your area of expertise?"

Myers shrugged and muttered a reply, forcing Hellboy to lean forward. "What was that?"

The agent lifted his chin and looked Hellboy full in the face. "Hostage negotiations."

It was the first time Myers had seen Hellboy truly pleased with him.

Myers really hadn't been prepared for this.

Yeah, he'd had his briefing, heard the news reports, weighed the rumors quickly spreading among his fellow agents. For an agency with a taciturn reputation, he found his fellow agents never stopped talking. Only to one another, of course, but still, it seemed nearly nonstop. If the nature of their business would keep them from sharing what they did and what they knew with everyone on the outside, then they would damned well turn over every single aspect of it with one another, over and over and over. Everyone wanted to be a part of everyone else's work, the quintessential beehive, all for one and one for all, and sometimes Myers thought it was a miracle that anyone got anything done at all.

But even with all that information, no one had passed along the gory details, the *real* ones that would have warned him that Liz Sherman had damned near destroyed most of Bellamie Mental Hospital.

Yeah, the photographs in her file and the archives should have given him a heads-up, but photos, especially old ones, were . . . stagnant, unreal. This was the real thing, the icepick stab of reality right to the frontal lobe. And man, Myers was getting a serious case of brain freeze.

It was, he supposed, a small miracle that the top four floors of the hospital hadn't caved in on what was left of the bottom part. The second floor was still there, but all the windows were shattered, their metal frames twisted and torn, the safety glass with wire mesh running through it shattered despite its metal reinforcements. Each window opening looked like a large, blackened mouth; some had the scorched remains of window blinds hanging out of the opening at crooked angles, dangling in the light October breeze like teeth held in place by the last, jagged remains of fleshy tendons.

Below the semidemolished remains of the building, the gardens were filled with still-burning debris—sheets, a few mattresses and chairs, a thousand other unidentifiable bits and pieces. Repair crews rushed in every direction, trying to figure out how to get things patched back together as quickly as possible, while firemen scurried around them, aiming hoses and extinguishers at the flaming mini-masses. Myers could see figures through the lighted windows of the upper floors, staring down curiously, shoving each other out of the way to get a better view. The maximum security personnel up there were clearly having a hell of a time keeping everyone quiet and calm. The lighting wasn't that great—generators were for emergencies, not surgery—and Myers could see some of them with their palms plastered against the windows, pushing on the glass and rocking with excitement. He could only imagine how much fun things were going to be on that ward tonight.

Myers got out of his cab and paid the driver, going for the "hide-the-agent-in-plain-sight" route. No stiff FBI suit for him, at least not tonight; a nondescript sport jacket over a soft, dark shirt and a rather gaudily patterned tie, khaki pants, and Nikes made him look like someone's visitor, or maybe an office worker coming in to check on what kind of damage had been done to the computer systems.

A security guard checked his name against a clipboard, then let Myers inside, where Dr. Marsh was waiting for him at the reception desk. Everything down on the first floor smelled of smoke, although there was no visible damage, and all the nurses and maintenance personnel had this vaguely terrified visage—their eyes darted back and forth, and they jumped at noises that were just a shade louder than normal.

"Second floor?" he asked as he and the doctor headed down the hall.

The white-haired woman shot him a sideways glance. "There *is* no second floor anymore, Agent Myers. Not to any usable degree, anyway. It's burned away right down to the metal reinforcing studs—a brilliant idea implemented during the renovation done in the eighties—and the outside brick and mortar work."

"Oh," was all Myers could think of to say.

The doctor stopped at a locked set of double doors with narrow, wire-reinforced windows and motioned to the two security guards on the other side. A buzzer sounded, disengaging the lock, and Myers followed her through. Dr. Marsh led him to the second window in a row of five, and when he looked through it, Myers realized he was seeing through one-way glass. The room before him was padded heavily and, except for the silver camera high in the corner, completely white. There'd been monitors at the guard station he'd passed, so it was obvious where the feed from the camera went.

"She's been like this since it happened," Dr. Marsh

said as they looked through the window at Liz Sherman. The woman's face was lined with shock and tension. "There were no casualties, but it's put a *big* dent in our Thorazine supply." She gave him a dubious look. "Are you sure you want to go in?"

He nodded, then reached up and yanked on his tie to loosen it. A final, worried look, then Dr. Marsh inclined her head toward the guard back at the door; he must've pushed a button because a second later the door to his right clanked and opened slightly.

He pushed through, then pulled it closed behind him until he heard the lock catch. Dressed in a clean gown, Liz was sitting on a heavily upholstered chair and staring into space; she didn't acknowledge his presence or even blink as Myers knelt in front of her.

"Miss Sherman? I'm Agent Myers, FBI." Instead of responding, she purposely turned her head away. While someone else might have taken this as a rejection, Myers was heartened. *Any* response other than catatonia was a plus. "Miss Sherman, I'm Agent Myers of the FBI," he repeated. He paused, then told her something she likely already knew. "The hospital called us. They don't feel they're capable of caring for you any longer."

Silence.

"Liz," he said, then paused, trying to think of

something that might soften her up. He went for the obvious. "May I call you Liz? It's a beautiful name—"

She sighed, and he heard a hint of impatience in the sound. "Sixty percent of the women in this world are named Liz."

Myers smiled to himself. He'd actually expected a comment like that. Aloud, he said, "It's still impressive by my standards. My name's John."

She gazed at him dully and he took a chance and offered his hand. When she turned away, he shrugged and dropped it back to his knee. He was way too smart to take that as a personal insult. "Listen," he said. "Dr. Broom asked me to invite you back to the Bureau. No special precautions, no security escorts. You and me in a taxi, like regular folks."

Liz looked down at her wrists thoughtfully. "Doesn't sound like him."

Myers let her consider his words for a few moments, then told her, "Miss Sherman, he's asking you back, but it's entirely your choice."

"Choice, huh?" As Myers watched her, she seemed to be looking at something over his shoulder. Finally, he turned around and saw her staring at both their reflections in the surface of the one-way glass. In here, the image was slightly distorted because the glass was covered by a protective layer of heavy Plexiglas. "That's cute," she said softly. "I've quit the Bureau thirteen times. I always go back." She returned her gaze to the thick rubber bands encircling each wrist, then gave each of them a hard enough snap to make Myers wince. She stared at the reddening skin around each of her wrists.

"Where else would I go?"

13

THE LIGHT AND SOUND OF THE SUBWAY TRAIN SCREAM-
ing past was more like an explosion than anything
else. It roared through the tunnel with a blast of high
beams, and then it was gone, leaving behind a sudden,
teeth-jittering emptiness and a ringing in the ears.

Circles of light abruptly swept the space, revealing
walls encrusted with mildew and rusting steel columns
dripping with moisture and stains. Here and there rats
chittered and scurried through the filthy, trash-filled
puddles in the center of the tracks, their clawed feet
making erratic trails among the debris. Agent Clay
swung his own flashlight from side to side, occasionally kicking out at a rodent that dared to get too close;
another half dozen agents followed behind him with
two of them, Moss and Quarry, armed with heavy-
duty flamethrowers. Trailing to the rear and taking in
the not-so-touristy sights in companionable silence,
were Hellboy and Abe.

Finally they turned off the main subway tunnel and
filed into a side tunnel that was too narrow to let pass
more than two men at a time. After about twenty feet

it widened into a small alcove, itself ending at a couple of double metal doors hanging crookedly on what was left of rust-eaten hinges. Clay kicked the doors open and shone his light inside, then motioned for the others that it was okay to follow.

Inside was a storeroom of sorts, piled high with abandoned filing cabinets, old-fashioned typewriters, and stained school desks with thousands of names and figures carved into the humidity-soaked wood. Although the walls in here were just as moisture-damaged as the tunnels, the agents could see the remains of a hundred-year-old mural that ran the full width of the side wall. On it, happy boys were doing charitable acts—one was helping old ladies with groceries, another coaxed a cat from a tree, yet another tied a shoe for a child smaller than him. It was all very holier-than-thou, and beneath the painted Latin phrase declared *Viriliter Age*, the translation of which encouraged the viewer to act like a man.

Quarry shook out a triple-wide map, then shone his flashlight on it. "We're in the cellar of the Benjamin Institute, a turn of the century orphanage," he told the others as he pointed at a spot on the paper. "It's been closed since they moved the sewers in 1951." He refolded the map and put it away; the sound of the paper crinkling was unpleasant, magnified by the high ceiling and the air currents of the close-by tunnels. The long beams of the agents' flashlights bobbed and left tracer images as the men constantly aimed them at the lightless corners and the blacker areas beneath the junked pieces of furniture.

Next to Hellboy, Abe pulled off his gloves, set them aside, then extended one hand to test the air. He tilted his head thoughtfully, then nodded. "There's a pulse," he said. Then he knelt in front of an oily-looking puddle and lightly skimmed the top of it with his palm. Dust and tiny pieces of debris on the dark surface floated idly toward his skin. "And it's coming from . . ." Eyes glittering, he raised his other hand and pointed. "There." The agents immediately turned the beams of their lights in that direction. "There's a cistern on the other side," Abe said. "Most of the eggs are there."

Several of the men moved forward and shouldered aside a couple of filing cabinets that were in the way, but all they found was a blank concrete wall, as stained and dirty as the rest of the room. "No way in," said Agent Quarry.

Clay nodded and faced the others. "We should go back and request permission to—"

BAM!

Clay jumped back as behind him Hellboy's stone hand smashed into the wall blocking their progress. Cracks spider-webbed from the point of impact and a small chunk of concrete flew outward. Before the agent could protest, Hellboy raised his hand and beat on the wall again, then again, faster and faster until his stone hand was a jackhammer blur and the wall just couldn't stand up to the assault.

The ticking of the clocks around him was comforting. Stable, calming, exactly what he liked to hear while he was engaged in a project.

Sitting quietly at a table in the lower level furnace room of the sugar factory, Kroenen methodically worked on repairing his mechanical hand. Normally it worked fine, but the humidity and the grime down here had worked their way into a couple of the gears and made two of the finger joints stick. He wanted it to work like the scores of clocks around him—steadily, reliably, no break in the routine.

This was a good place, a private place. For a change he could loosen the leather mask that normally covered his face, not worry about keeping his deformities covered. Ilsa and Grigori were used to it and didn't care anyway, but occasionally he had to interact with others; rarely could those people handle the sight of his wet-looking eyes, bulging and lidless, the raw-gummed skull grin that was exposed by taut skin and a mouth that had no lips. Down here it was different—

Something pounded through the layers of concrete walls that separated him from the cistern and the orphanage.

Kroenen grimaced and abandoned his work on the

hand as he listened to the dull hammering. It sounded far away but sound could be deceiving down here; one moment it could seem muffled by the heavy architecture, another it could echo as though overhead. This time, though, he could go on the physical—on the tabletop the mechanical hand rattled with every blow.

Kroenen snapped the hand back into place, quickly strapped his mask back on, and rose. With quick, spiderlike movements, he retrieved an ancient leather folder and opened it. Inside, engraved on a stiff piece of papyrus, was an image of Sammael; he took it out and carefully placed it on the table, then took two torn pieces of paper from a separate envelope. Working quickly, he rolled them together and placed them in a pouch on his belt.

With a last, regretful look at his collection of faithfully ticking clocks, Kroenen turned and hurried out of the furnace room.

There was enough concrete dust in the air to choke a horse, but Hellboy waved it away and gestured toward the ragged, man-sized hole he'd beaten through the wall. "You coming or not?" he asked Clay. The agent gave him an uncertain look, watching as Hellboy pushed through the opening, his massive shoulders scraping the sides. Finally Clay followed him through, turning back to give Quarry and Moss instructions. "You two, check this dump. Then join us." They nodded and moved away.

When Abe ducked through the hole, he found Hellboy and Clay standing in the middle of an abandoned shower room. The area was finished with mildewed tiles that might have once been white but were now cracked and blackened, the stains showing patterns where water had leaked through the years. The showers formed a sort of large oval, ringed with rusting metal pipes that were still spilling water onto the floor after all this time. The floor itself was slanted down to a large metal grate in the center.

Abe studied the grate, looking at it intently as he tried to read the air around it. Eventually he glanced at Hellboy and nodded; immediately Hellboy leaned down and with a chesty "*Hmmmphf!*" yanked the grate free and spun it off to the side, where it banged loudly against the wall and wobbled to a stop. A second later, hundreds of roaches streamed out of the newly opened hole, fleeing from the unexpected intruders.

Abe made a face as they watched the bugs scurry for new hiding places. "I'm glad I'm not human," he commented. "This place would be an embarrassment."

Hellboy didn't say anything. He was too busy peering into the dark hole in the floor, trying to see into the vast cistern below. It was useless, like trying to see to the bottom of an ink well. Abe gave it a shot, then pulled two chemical flares from his belt, lit them, and dropped them into the blackness. He and Hellboy peered after them, but they could see little—a few pieces of furniture and floating paper close to the surface, but nothing else.

Readying himself, Abe pulled off the breathing apparatus that let him walk around the dry side of the world, then he activated the small locator pack on the left side of his belt. Hellboy followed suit, and with a muted *beep* the devices synchronized, their tiny lights— Abe's blue, Hellboy's red—now blinking in unison before they dimmed to normal mode. As Abe stepped forward, Hellboy held out his big hand and opened it. On his palm was an undersized receptacle containing a small bone.

"Here you go, Doctor. This should cover your tail fin—it's a bone from Saint Dionysius, on loan from the Vatican. Looks like a pinkie."

Abe nodded and took the offered gift, then tied it, bone and holder and all, to his wrist. He looked at the hole again, sitting there and waiting for him like a big, black mouth, trying not to think about all the crap he was going to be running through his gills in only a few seconds. "Remind me why I keep doing this."

Hellboy looked at him from beneath his horns. "Rotten eggs and the safety of mankind."

"Oh," Abe said. "Right."

Transparent membranes slid into place over both of

Abe's eyes, and without another word, he dove into the cistern.

Down, down, down, slicing through the water with a feeling of freedom that could never be gained in his tank. For this freedom, however, he paid a price; tension etched through his smooth muscles, every dark spot and bubble in the filthy water caught his attention and made him veer. In a wide open space like this, he could be prey just as well as predator—one of the reasons he'd dismissed the notion of a permanent life in the oceans a long time ago.

Still, Abe kept going. As always, he found it interesting that he could see so easily in dark water. He supposed he was no different from the fish in the deeper parts of the ocean; maybe without his knowledge, he was using a hidden form of sonar in addition to his psychic abilities. All in all, it was a pretty good perk that kept him from running blindly forward and bashing his head on something he hadn't seen coming.

Down here, he could tell that everything was usually a shade of dirty black-blue. At the bottom—which really wasn't all *that* far down—Abe found an entire control room, reduced to eternal silence by the suffocating water. As Abe examined his surroundings, magazines from as far back as the 1940s floated past, swaying with the currents like paper jellyfish. The chemical flares were still burning, mingling with the natural bluish color of the water and casting a sickly yellowish glow over everything that only added to the eerie, otherworldly feel of the place.

But even the best of the best cannot do everything, cannot know everything, cannot *see* everything.

And, as still and silent as the inanimate objects that camouflaged him, Sammael watched the approach of the faraway fish man, and waited for his arrival. . . .

14

HE HATED NOT KNOWING WHAT WAS GOING ON DOWN there.

Pacing around the shower room, Hellboy chewed on a Baby Ruth bar and stomped on a few roaches. The other bugs ran for cover, leaving him bored, so he stuffed the rest of the candy into his mouth, then climbed through the broken concrete hole and back into the orphanage's storage room. He poked around the rubble curiously, trying to pass the time with what he could find by the not-so-helpful beam of his flashlight. The place was full of weird stuff, like a pile of battered, mismatched children's shoes, under which Hellboy found a bunch of yellowing photo albums. These he pulled out and flipped open, and for his trouble he got a couple dozen fleeing silverfish and myriad sad-eyed faces, the orphans of a hundred years past. Strangely, some of the faces had been cut from the photos, while others had been left intact. Tucked into the back of one of the books was a yellowing, unfinished letter to Father Christmas, dated 1866, a sad testament to the unfulfilled wishes of a child abandoned by the rest of the world. Had this boy grown to be a man with those same dreams gone unrecognized? Or had he died as a child, never knowing so many of the simple things that people, Hellboy included, took for granted, like love and food and the warm and stable shelter of a home every evening.

"See? It's thicker, isn't it?" Hellboy looked up as Clay's voice interrupted his morbid reverie. The agent was standing below a grate, holding up a small hand mirror and, incredibly, admiring his hair implants. Vanity apparently knew no time constraints. "It's not that doll-hair thing."

Hellboy was about to say something sarcastic about men who carried hand mirrors when suddenly something moved just out of the range of his peripheral vision. He jerked his flashlight to the left and shone it down the darkness of an adjoining tunnel—

Kroenen was standing there, caught like potential roadkill in a car's headlights.

"Son of a—" Hellboy began, but Kroenen's whip-thin figure had already darted away. Yanking the Good Samaritan free of its holster, Hellboy tore down the corridor after the creep.

"Red—*wait!*" Agent Clay yelled.

Hellboy barely heard Clay's words and had no intention of stopping anyway. The static of Clay's radio carried to his ears on the drafts, then Clay shouted again, this time into what sounded like a pretty useless piece of radio equipment. "He's on the move! I'll cover him!" No doubt Clay had his own gun drawn and was barreling after Hellboy even as Hellboy lengthened his stride, determined to catch up with that skinny little Nazi zombie. Hellboy hoped Clay had the sense to watch for the bobbing flashlight beam when he came to the intersection of tunnels that Hellboy was passing now. The FBI man already sounded significantly far away in this labyrinth of abandoned sewer tunnels.

Silt covered everything at the far bottom of the cistern. As Abe's feet lightly touched the bottom, the silt billowed through the water, sending small, dirty clouds up to Abe's knees, the watery equivalent of blowing a century's worth of dust off a tabletop. As Abe strained to see what he was stepping on, he caught his first glimpse of what he'd been sent down here to look for: a small, translucent egg glimmering in the darkness. Pulling a thin glass canister from his belt, he plucked it from its resting place and pushed it inside. Abe reached for the next one, then jerked as he felt something dark glide past him. He turned, but there was nothing there.

His movement along the bottom had dislodged the silt and its lighter-weight contents. Now eggs were floating everywhere around him, undulating and winking in the currents like glowing, amber fireflies.

Abe swam slowly through the water, collecting them one by one. Just when he thought he'd retrieved all of them, he saw a small pile of the golden globes wedged between two rusting machines. Holding the canister in one hand, he stretched his other arm into the opening. As he reached, something tugged sharply along his belt; when he looked down, Abe saw the small reliquary Hellboy had given him had caught on a protruding lever and broken free. It was floating downward, heading for a drainage grate in the floor.

Abe stretched as far as he could and snagged the eggs, then shoved them into his canister and swam after the reliquary. It was resting on the grate, rocking back and forth. His fingers had almost closed on it when the movement of the water loosened it. It bobbed one more time, then slipped through the opening and disappeared.

Cursing to himself, Abe rose—

—and found himself unprotected and staring into the snarling face of Sammael.

Before he could get out of the way, the demon raked him deeply across the chest. Instantly the water filled with dark blue blood. Sammael blinked, surprised, and Abe razored backward through the water and into the first place of shelter he could get to, a long, jagged fissure in the concrete of a collapsing interior wall.

Sammael was after him in a heartbeat, clawing at

the concrete as he tried to cram his pallid, oversized body into the too-small opening. He wouldn't fit, but there was always his deadly tongue; again and again he jabbed it into the rupture in the concrete, barely missing Abe, leaving the demon to scream in rage. Fear and pain made Abe scream with him, sending a trail of blue-tinted blood bubbles floating upward. Adrenaline had gotten him to safety—for now—but the flight rush was gone and now the agony of his wounds was hammering viciously into his nerves.

The bubbles broke the surface of the cistern far above, where a second Sammael sat and watched them pop with keen interest.

Well, so much for his mental crack about hoping Agent Clay would be able to use common sense in tracking him.

Hellboy stopped and turned first one way, then the other, trying to reorient himself. He had no idea where he was and he'd lost Kroenen in the constant twisting and turning of these empty, useless tunnels. Every one of these corridors looked the same—dirty, dark, and full of mold and old litter. The place was like an underground tomb, silent except for the occasional dripping of disused pipes and the faint squealing of rodents.

Since he couldn't do anything visually, Hellboy raised his chin and sniffed the air, catching a faint whiff of . . . something. He wasn't exactly sure what he was picking up here, but the scent wasn't good. He turned right, following his nose, and found himself facing yet another open portal; when he stepped through, it was like he was walking into the storage room of a nightmare concentration camp.

Duct work crisscrossed the area overhead, leaving gaps of black shadows between the jumble of metal and pipes, making the ceiling too far away to see. For some strange reason, gas masks lined the bottom of metal tubs, interspersed with more masks made of leather. Some were old, some were new. There must have been half a hundred hanging from hooks everywhere; worse were the old pictures of children tacked on the walls beneath the masks—the small faces missing from the photographs Hellboy had found earlier, all with haunted eyes staring at him from every direction and giving him the willies. If each pair of eyes represented a ghost that was going to show up, he hoped they were friendly, because he was going to be badly outnumbered.

Moving cautiously, Hellboy went deeper into the room, moving around the disused furniture and side-stepping an open service shaft until he reached the small, battered table in the middle. On it was an engraved plaque, and when he shone his flashlight over it, Hellboy could just read the faint words.

"*Sammael: Seed of Destruction. Death becomes the fertile ground.*"

When Hellboy started to straighten up, a glob of drool smacked against one of his horn stumps.

He shook it off, then glared up at the ceiling. Wouldn't you know it—there, clinging to the side of a metal duct like a colorless leech, was Sammael.

"Didn't I kill you already?"

Sammael's answer was a leap, but Hellboy was ready for it. He moved with the creature as it came down, then shifted his own weight to the side, steering the demon's body toward the open shaft a few feet away. Sammael howled as he went over the edge, and Hellboy was almost rid of him.

Almost.

If it hadn't been for Hellboy's own damned tail.

He felt Sammael's clawed fingers wrap around it, and there was no time for him to free himself before Sammael dragged him into the black abyss with him.

It was a long, *long* way down.

And painful—yeah, that, too. Clinging to each other more than fighting, the two crashed through wiring, bounced against ducts, and slammed into pipes. Through his fragmented vision, Hellboy saw light and hoped it was the end of the fall, but no such luck. They slid a few more excruciating feet, then tumbled into yet another downward passageway. This one was filled with dripping water pipes and jutting, bone-bruising, steel I-beams; they ricocheted through, hitting side to side before finally dropping onto a flat surface of mesh-filled insulation—the ceiling to something below. Too light to hold their weight, it promptly collapsed.

They fell heavily—

—right into a subway station crowded with people.

Of course they came down fighting, and they landed right on top of the token booth. The steel gave way and glass and coins exploded outward, shrapneling the unfortunate people nearby. Amid the screaming and the fleeing people, one man, braver than the others, hurried forward and began grabbing at the money scattered on the ground.

The crowd gaped as the dust settled and they saw the two creatures pounding on each other in a ragged crater in the platform floor. Sammael reared back and punched Hellboy, putting all of his weight into the blow and sending Hellboy flying backward onto a line of turnstiles. His weight pulled every one of the machines out of its base, flattening most into useless rectangles.

Sammael jumped at him, unsheathing the bone scythe in his arm on his descent. Hellboy rolled out of the way as Sammael jabbed downward with it, ramming it into the floor. He tried again, missed again, this time managing to embed it firmly into the side of a concrete column. Hellboy hauled himself to his feet, but before he could go after the demon, Sammael gave him a tooth-filled grin and yanked viciously on the column. Hellboy registered the groan of stressed metal, then part of the office mezzanine level above him gave way.

People ran in every direction, trying to get away from the falling debris—chunks of concrete, steel cables, office furniture, file boxes of papers, and more. The noise escalated to panicked shrieks as Sammael shook the last of the concrete from his bone scythe, then took a purposeful step toward a clump of people trapped and cut off from the exit. He spread his vein-riddled arms wide and roared at them, getting ready for the slaughter.

CLANG!

The demon jerked around as a desk flew into the air from the pile of post-mezzanine rubble. A bright red fist thrust from the debris and waved triumphantly.

"Hey, chunk-face!"

Sammael growled and crouched as Hellboy burst from the minimountain of wreckage.

Hellboy grinned smugly and gave his overcoat a shake as he glared at Sammael and headed toward him. "You can do better than *that*. Big monster like you?" Before Sammael could react, Hellboy reached to the side without slowing, ripped one of the turnstile bars free and whacked him with it. "See?" Hellboy hit him again. "It *hurts!*" He began to beat on Sammael in earnest. "You shouldn't hit people!"

Hellboy swung again, but this time Sammael was ready; he blocked it and ducked underneath, then swept the bar out of Hellboy's grip hard enough to plant it deeply into the tile wall a few feet away. Hellboy tried to pull back but wasn't quite quick enough to avoid Sammael's hard uppercut.

The blow was powerful enough to send him soaring, right up and through the plate-glass window of the second level mezzanine above them. The people who'd been crowding up to the window and staring down now scrambled backward, their eyes wide, shock etched on their faces as they realized they weren't out of harm's way. Hellboy skidded past the staring office workers, scraping a jagged line across the linoleum with his stone hand. He still couldn't stop himself from crashing into a row of backlit subway advertisements; his progress was finally halted when he careened off the wall and, along with the glass and metal pieces from the ads, he crashed into a line of oak benches and snapped one completely in half.

Hellboy had just about enough time to shake the stars from his head when Sammael climbed onto the mezzanine with him. Ignoring the pain and the blood dribbling from the glass pieces lodged all over his back, Hellboy pushed to his feet. He and Sammael had taken all of two steps toward each other when a childish wail cut through the air between them.

"My kittens! My kittens!"

Standing by the far wall was a little girl, maybe eight years old. Her face had done the instantly-blotchy-and-streaked-with-tears thing as she pointed frantically to Hellboy's left. He jerked and his gaze tracked her extended finger to where a small, semi-crushed box sat on the bench next to the one Hellboy had just demolished. Inside, three spotted balls of black-and-white mewling fur.

"Aw, crap," Hellboy said, just as Sammael charged.

Hellboy lunged to the side and scooped up the box just before Sammael pulverized the wooden seat with his bone scythe. It didn't surprise Hellboy a bit that Sammael would be vindictive enough to attack something so small and helpless—demons had a tendency to be nasty like that. When his attack failed, Sammael turned on Hellboy, slashing at him wildly enough to scatter the few foolish onlookers still remaining. Hellboy retaliated with the Good Samaritan, but as before, his bullets did little permanent damage. He ran out of ammunition, and Sammael's tongue shot out before he could get to a new clip. Obviously firepower wasn't going to be an option.

The little girl screamed anew as Hellboy threw the kitten box high in the air, then blocked Sammael's tongue-lashing with his stone hand, jerking his wrist in a circular motion and trapping the yellow appendage within his thick, unyielding fingers.

"Second date!" Hellboy yelled gleefully. "No tongue!"

Hellboy's tail zipped forward and neatly caught the falling box of felines before they hit the ground. With the end of his tail still wrapped around the box, he jerked Sammael forward by his tongue and hurled him through the heavy glass that separated the mezzanine from the subway tracks below.

The glass shattered and the demon went through. Hellboy landed heavily on one side as Sammael's weight jerked him off his feet, then the demon must have gotten a handhold on something, because he started dragging Hellboy toward the busted window, either to take him with him or to use him as a personal ladder. *Damn*, Hellboy thought as he juggled the box with his tail and fought against the pulling. *I really thought he'd let go!*

Hellboy leaned back, digging in against Sammael's grip with his massive legs. It didn't help; the linoleum beneath his feet wrinkled and folded in front of Hellboy as he was towed forward a foot, then another. Sweat squeezed out of his skin, mixing with the blood dripping from his forehead and nose, stinging his eyes and the cuts patterned down his cheeks. He grunted and pulled back again, but he knew it was a losing struggle. He was only millimeters away from the jagged edges of the window, nearly *kissing* the waiting spikes of glass—

Woooooooohhhhh!

Hurtling around the curve below, a subway train smashed dead center into the dangling Sammael.

The creature's tongue abruptly released. Without Sammael's body as a counterbalance, Hellboy fell backward, landing awkwardly on his butt. He was back up in an instant, but when he hurried to the opening and peered down, he knew he could relax, at least for the moment. Sammael's motionless body was sprawled at the side of the tracks . . . well, except for the other pieces and parts of him that had caught the more unyielding front of the train. What remained of those were on the tunnel walls on either side of the tracks, sliding down the rounded surfaces in slow, nasty blobs.

"I hope that *hurt,*" Hellboy grunted. He turned at a noise behind him and saw the kid who'd hollered about her kittens; most of the other people had fled, but she'd worked her way up to within six or seven feet, showing a lot more courage than any of the adults. Her gaze darted between Hellboy's face and the box of kittens he still had entwined in his tail.

Hellboy gave her what he hoped was a passable smile although he knew he probably didn't look very approachable right now. He brought the box down and offered it to her. Inside, the three unharmed kittens meowed enthusiastically, tumbling over each other in the comical way that uncoordinated babies did. The girl took the box and made a show of inspecting the animals; when she saw they were fine, she nodded. "Thank you," she said solemnly.

Hellboy ducked his head. "My job," was all he said.

He left the child standing there and went back to the window just as a panicked-looking woman—probably her mother—pushed her way through the staring on-lookers. At the opening, Hellboy cleared away the broken remains of the glass with his stone hand so he could jump down to the tracks and inspect Sammael's body. There wasn't much to see; where the bulk of the demon's corpse had been was now a small pyre of black flame. There was no hiding it—not from Hellboy, and certainly not from the crowd of onlookers at the end of the platform. Another fun and fine cleanup job to which the muckety-mucks at the FBI could look forward and point backward at. He could almost hear the *I told you so!* litany from Father and Manning, and he hoped to God none of those train yuppies had been armed with a camera, or worse, a camcorder.

It was a surefire deal that cops, rescue, and maintenance and repair were on their way. Hellboy stood over the dwindling fire and watched it for as long as he dared, then finally turned to go, opting to head into the darker realms of the subway tunnels and away from the curious eyes of the rush-hour commuters.

He gave the smoking remains one last glance over his shoulder. "This time *stay* dead, will ya?" he rasped as he strode away.

As he rounded the curve and passed out of sight, behind him, the black flame of Sammael's fire flickered and finally went out.

15

IN THE DARKNESS, THE BRACKISH WATER WAS SUDDENLY disturbed by two small circles of movement. The water rippled outward, barely discernible above the two unhatched eggs. The amber tone within them was lost to a bright inner glow of purple that grew to twin halos of hellish black light. So small . . . but then their diaphanous surface began to bulge and twist, starting their fantastic metamorphosis. It was only a matter of seconds until the embryos burst free, twisting and spinning like tiny pieces of agonized flesh. The barely born creatures swelled, each one's parts distending and growing faster than the last.

Around the edge of a stack of water-eroded concrete piling, out of sight of the two hatchlings, Abe finally peered from his cramped hiding spot. There was no sign of Sammael, and Abe was badly wounded, far too much so to stay put and continue to play dead. He had to risk trying to get to the top or he was just going to stay wedged down here and bleed to death.

Sucking in water at the pain across his torso, Abe squeezed out of his crevice and made for the surface, swimming as fast as his injuries would allow, looking nervously over his shoulder every few seconds because he could *feel* something was wrong, that something was down there. He wouldn't be safe for long, but right now he didn't have much happening in the speed department and that was only going to get worse. The slashes across his chest gaped and stung with every movement of his arms, spreading more of his blue blood behind him like a trail of spilled ink.

Never in his life had Abe thought there would be a time when he'd be glad to get out of the water, but now was certainly it. He surged up from the water and broke into air, choking and flailing at the sudden change. Then he dragged himself out of the pool and onto the filthy tile floor, gagging as his lungs tried to shake off the sudden excess oxygen. But there was no time for such luxuries as lying down and dying, so Abe staggered to his feet and lurched toward the nearest thing he could see that might give him shelter: a line of crumbling shower stalls.

Abe had barely made it into one when he heard the water back in the pool begin to churn. Shaking with pain, he pulled himself up and onto a small triangular seat built into the wall of the shower stall in which he'd chosen to hide, making sure his feet weren't showing. He'd left a trail of blood, of course, but the floor was so filthy and the area so dark it was nearly impossible to notice it. Smell, however, was something different, and he had no idea whether whatever was hunting him was likely to pick up his scent; all he could do was hope the water would dilute it to irrelevance. Beyond the flimsy divider, he could hear the sloshing as the creatures—definitely two—heaved themselves out of the water. It wouldn't be long until he found out, and frankly, Abe wasn't even sure he was going to be conscious when that happened; the darkness around him was soaked with black-and-yellow sparkles, the precursors to passing out.

If that happened, it happened. In the meantime, it sure wouldn't hurt to ask for a little help.

"Find anything?"

Moss grunted and managed to force the filing cabinet he was pushing to move another foot out from the wall. He scooted forward and peered behind it before answering Quarry's question. Nothing but more solid wall. "Nah."

"Me neither." Agent Quarry grabbed a box and lifted it; there was a wet-sounding rip and the bottom gave out, sending moldering, water-stained papers to join the rest of the litter on the floor.

"Jesus," said Moss, but before he could complain further, they heard a set of simultaneous *beeps* and the blue light on each of their locator belts blinked to life. It was a double set of shockingly bright blue spots in the near darkness.

Quarry jerked. "Abe!"

Something *crunched* at the far end of the storeroom.

Both agents spun and jerked their flashlights in the direction of the noise; there was nothing to see but the moving shadows cast on the columns by their searching flashlight beams. "Moss, what the hell was that?" Quarry's voice was tight with anxiety.

Before the other agent could answer, two long shapes moved out of the blackness, each casting stretched, ominous shadows. It was impossible to get a good look at them, but their footsteps sounded like heavy thunderclaps—unrelenting and huge. Whatever the shapes were, they were headed straight for the FBI agents.

Quarry wasn't wasting any more time or words. He raised his gun and fired at the things coming toward them, round after round, until the clip was empty. The room filled with the booming noise of the gunshots and the muzzle flashes left little red streaks in front of their eyes, but it was useless—bullets weren't going to stop the creatures.

Gritting his teeth, Moss pulled the flamethrower from his shoulder and turned to face the advancing shadows, careful not to let the weight of the tanks strapped to his back throw him off balance. A quick flip of the ignition valve rewarded him with a spark at the end of the nozzle; that was followed by the oh-so-comforting sound of the ignition flame. Moss grinned.

It was time to even the odds between man and monster.

He aimed and gave the fuel release trigger a firm squeeze. The nozzle vomited a spectacular thirty-foot gout of flame at the approaching blackness.

Moss held it for five seconds, long enough to fry an elephant, then released the trigger. For a long moment as they stood there and squinted through the readjustment of their eyes, there was no noise beyond their own ragged breathing. Finally, Quarry lifted his arm and pointed his flashlight in front of them. Nothing.

"Whatever it was," Quarry began, "it's—"

He never got the chance to finish his sentence.

Sammael's tongue slapped around his face with a sound like a wet sheet snapping in the wind; the agent couldn't even scream as he was pulled into the darkness. Before it fell out of his hand, Quarry's flashlight bobbed up and down frantically, flickering like a strobe light over the nightmarish truth.

There were *two* Sammaels.

The first one had Agent Quarry solidly in its grip and, with a hideous parody of a gleeful smile, it drew the man's head into its oversized mouth and covered it with moist, fleshy lips. Quarry tried to scream but his mouth was covered; what came out was an insane, petrified grunting sound that went on way too long.

Instinctively, Moss turned to run. He made it about twenty feet, but he could *feel* the other creature right behind him, gaining, and he knew he wasn't going to make it. The fight part kicked in over the flight, and he turned clumsily, the tanks making him wobble, but at least he had his hand on the fuel trigger. The flame was just starting to spurt from the nozzle when the second Sammael came down on him from overhead. The beast landed with all his weight on Moss's left shoulder and drove his body down hard on that side, folding him in half and snapping his spine neatly in two.

As he fell into oblivion, his hand released the flamethrower's fuel trigger and the flame fizzled and ran out.

Hellboy had only been looking for Abe about five minutes when he found him, and that, Hellboy decided, was about five minutes too long. The instant Abe's light had gone off on his locator belt, Hellboy had focused on following the guidance system; when he'd gotten really close, he hadn't needed it any longer—his extrasensitive nose picked up not only the faint and not unpleasant scent of the sea that was an integral part of Abe, but the more startling and unwelcome scent of blood . . . *lots* of blood. For the first time since he'd come down into the tunnels on this mission, Hellboy actually felt a stab of fear about something, and seeing Abe crumpled against the wall in this filthy, blue-blood filled shower, wasn't doing much to make the sensation go away.

Automatically Hellboy's hand went for his own locator switch. He flipped it on but it had taken one too
many whacks in his battle with Sammael—he got one
weak spark and that was all, not even so much as a
flicker from the red light. Fine, he could be flexible
and go the person-to-person route. When he thumbed
the Talk button on his walkie-talkie, he was almost
sappily happy that the thing actually worked. "We
need medics down here!" he barked into it. "Now!
Over."

Hellboy released the button, then held it up to his
ear.

Static.

Clay was utterly lost.

He turned in the nearly complete darkness, shining
his flashlight beam all around him. He could go for his
locator belt, but did he really want to admit that the
only reason he'd flipped the panic button was because
he'd lost his sense of direction down here? That he'd
lost track of Hellboy? Yeah, some FBI sharpie he'd
look like then.

No, it was better to keep his trap shut and find his
own way out, but boy, when he got back to the
B.P.R.D., he was going to ream Hellboy out good. Red
knew he wasn't supposed to just take off like that, especially when they were in someplace like this maze.
They could be a block apart, or a mile—there was just

no way to tell. And the walkie-talkies? Half the time they wouldn't work; as if having concrete walls between everyone wasn't bad enough, the metal reinforcing rods placed in most of them completely fouled up any signal, acting as signal blockers rather than conductors.

So where was he? Clay scowled up at a grate in the ceiling through which an extremely thin light shone. Standing down here and craning his neck upward toward a metal-covered hole really ticked him off—it was way too much like being in a dungeon. Still, there were two things that dungeons and subways always had in common: you went *up* to get *out*.

Clay rubbed his hands together, then started to reach up. Suddenly Hellboy's voice sputtered through the walkie-talkie's speakers. *"Who's there? Clay? Come in—someone!"*

At the sound of Hellboy's urgent voice, the agent lowered his hands and grabbed for his radio instead. "Clay, Code 30. This is Clay. Over."

With his attention focused intently on the walkie-talkie, Clay didn't see Kroenen as the zombie Nazi let go of an overhead pipe and dropped lightly to the ground behind him. There was a *snick* as he unsheathed one of the long blades he always seemed to have secreted somewhere on his wire-thin body. Such a tiny sound, and yet something in Agent Clay's senses registered it; he yanked his gun out, turned, and fired just as Kroenen leaped forward, blade extended. The flash from the gun's dark muzzle glimmered on the silver edge of Kroenen's blade right before it sunk into Clay's body. It seemed to take twice as long for Kroenen to pull the blade out of his flesh.

The walkie-talkie squawked again, this time more loudly—Hellboy had obviously heard the sound of the gunfire. Clay had gotten off at least three shots, but incredibly, Kroenen was still standing. At least he'd retreated a few feet away, and taken that damnable sword with him. Something wet tickled beneath his nose and Clay reached up to wipe it away, trying foggily to decide what to do next; his arm felt as heavy as a log, hard to lift, and when he ran his fingers across the cleft between his upper lip and his nose, it came away heavily smeared with blood.

Clay didn't feel it when he toppled over.

Kroenen tilted his head and watched dispassionately as the FBI man fell. Dust poured out of the holes in his chest, making neat little hills at his feet. That was of no consequence—there was always more where that came from; what did annoy him was that there was no time to ensure this troublesome government man was out of the game permanently. Kroenen could hear Hellboy's footsteps reverberating off the tunnel walls. He would be here in moments and when faced with the prospect of dealing with someone of Hellboy's size and ugly temperament, Kroenen wisely decided it was best to take the silent way out.

For authenticity's sake, he gave up his weapon, placing it at a believable angle between himself and the prone FBI agent. Then he quickly stretched out on the grubby floor, choosing a spot that would make it seem credible that he had gone down under the other man's volley of shots. As an added bonus, Kroenen would be able to see everything that went on, get a nice, good look at the kid as he discovered his friend's unfortunate condition. Indeed, life was good.

As Kroenen had expected, he barely had time to arrange himself in a death pose before Hellboy's arrival. Golden eyes glittering with loathing, Hellboy barely glanced at what he thought was Kroenen's corpse before heading over to kneel by the agent's side. He felt for a pulse, then tried again. And again.

And each time the expression on Hellboy's face became bleaker, while in Kroenen's twisted mind, he listened to the sounds of a Wagner aria as he waited for his next chance to rise.

16

THE MUSIC BLARING FROM THE CAB'S RADIO WAS AT eardrum-shattering levels, Janet Jackson screaming about what someone had done or not done for her lately. In the backseat, Myers watched Liz Sherman poke her head out of the window on her side of the cab, scan the passing scenery for a moment, then bring up her Polaroid and snap off a shot. Without so much as looking at it, she passed it over to Myers to hold while it developed. "It feels good to be outside!" She had to practically shout to be heard over the singing. "It's been so long!"

Myers heard her, but just barely. This was ridiculous—Jesus, he really hated overly loud music. Leaning forward, he rapped on the bullet-proof piece of acrylic that separated the front from the backseat. The driver glanced at him in the rearview mirror and gave the agent what was proba- bly intended as a congenial smile; Myers just thought it looked sharp and full of teeth badly in need of a brushing. "Hey!" he shouted. "The music—*turn down the music!*"

The driver's head bobbed up and down enthusiastically and his grin got even wider. "Yeah, yeah—music!" He reached for the radio knob and Myers sighed in relief. That sigh turned into a wince when the driver merely changed the station; now the speakers—four of the wretched things embedded in the back dashboard, of course—were blaring techno, and Myers hated techno more than he hated loud music. The guy hadn't acquiesced to lowering it a single decibel.

Aggravated, he sat back on the seat and looked over at Liz. The sight of her—or rather, her legs—made him forget his anger, the cabdriver, even the horrid techno band yowling out of the sound system. Liz had hoisted herself up and out of the open window, and now she was sitting with her feet inside the cab and the rest of her outside and blowing in the wind.

"Jesus!" he managed. "That's not—that's not safe, Miss Sherman!" He tried again, louder, desperate to be heard over the music. "Miss Sherman?"

She couldn't hear him, of course. Hell, he couldn't hear himself thanks to all this racket. Before he could decide what to do, her hand snaked back through the window and offered him another slowly developing Polaroid picture. He twisted around and placed it next to the other one on the back dashboard, then smiled in spite of himself. He was supposed to escort her, right? Keep an eye on her? So what the hell . . . why not?

Myers turned sideways on the seat, then pulled himself up and out of the window on his side.

When she saw him over the roof of the car, she masked it quickly, but he saw a flicker of surprise dance across her eyes. "Nice view," he commented. Impulsively, he waved at her, and in return, for the first time, Liz Sherman actually smiled at him.

"A smile, huh?" His own mouth turned up at the edges. Without warning, she raised the camera and snapped off yet another Polaroid, this time of him. With her dark hair blowing in the wind and the sun on her flawless skin, it was startling how beautiful she looked.

"Don't get used to it," she said, and Myers had to blink. Don't get used to what? He'd been lost in his own thoughts for a moment there, and he had to go through a mental rebriefing before he could figure out his place in the way the world was currently running. The music was thundering around his legs, and while he didn't like it, Myers found himself inadvertently tapping along with the main beat of it. Right now, he couldn't take his eyes off Liz Sherman, but that was okay—he was just doing his job, making sure she left that hospital and got safely back to the B.P.R.D. Nothing more, nothing less. He was only being loyal.

And on the heels of that, he thought, *Yeah, Myers. You just keep telling yourself that.*

In the medical lab, the unconscious Abe Sapien floated serenely inside a special tank. No normal hospital had ever seen anything like this—in fact, no normal doctor had any clue that there was a need for such a thing to exist in the first place. Affixed to the inside of the Plexiglas were LED strips that monitored the water temperature, pH level, body toxins, waste, and a hundred other top-secret things which the B.P.R.D. doctors were well paid to analyze. Abe's normally blue skin was slightly gray, and Hellboy wanted to believe that was because of the way the way light reflected through the water. He knew damned well that the truth had more to do with blood loss and how severely his friend was injured.

Wrapped all the way around Abe's torso and right arm was a biocast, a cybernetic healing unit that would, hopefully, speed Abe along the road to recovery. Hellboy had once been given a rubber ball with a couple dozen long black rubber "hairs" running out of it, some kind of movie promotion giveaway that someone had thought his cats would enjoy (they'd ignored it). Right now Abe looked like that ball: rounded out because of the biocast, with a web of tubes and hoses holding him in place, waving in the air like multicolored octopus arms or your garden variety Lovecraftian monster.

Sitting shirtless on a nearby exam table, swathed in a bunch of bandages all his own, Hellboy sat and studied his pal, not really thinking so much as . . . *concentrating*. If focus could actually *make* something happen—and wasn't that sort of what Liz was all about?—then he was going to focus Abe along a little faster.

"He'll make it," a voice said from behind him. Hellboy turned and saw Dr. Manning standing there in his GQ-quality suit. The overall impression was ruined by the sour look on the man's face. "But not everyone was so lucky." Manning's expression went even darker. "Two agents died today. Clay probably won't survive the night. You were reckless."

Hellboy's yellow eyes narrowed. "I knew those men better than you did."

Manning's eyebrows raised. "Ah, I see. That makes it all right, then." He shrugged a little too carelessly and turned to leave. It was an invitation and Hellboy knew it, knew he should leave things alone and not take the bait.

Fat chance.

He stood, muscles bunching painfully around his bruises and the stitched-up gashes beneath the bandages. "No, it doesn't make it 'all right.' But I stopped that creature, didn't I?" He didn't need vindication or support from this jerk, but for once, after all he and everyone else had been through tonight, it would be nice to hear an acknowledgment of how important their work, their *sacrifices*, were. Did this guy even have a clue? Or was he still so wrapped up in his cloak of disbelief that he couldn't see that?

Manning paused and looked back. "That's what you do," he said, and for a moment Hellboy thought the guy was actually going to wear the white hat for a change, even if only temporarily. But, of course, Manning had to keep running his mouth. "That's why we need you," he continued. "You have an insight." He paused, just long enough to build a little power for his next words. "You know monsters."

Hellboy felt his face grow thunderous, welcomed the tension riding along the curves of his muscles like static electricity. "What are you trying to say?"

This time Manning turned and faced him fully, crossing his arms and lifting his chin. "In the end, after you've killed and captured every freak out there, there's still one left. *You.*"

Hellboy could feel a double pulse beating unpleasantly in his head, one behind each horn. Manning let out a deep sigh. "I wish I could be more gracious, but—"

WHAM!

On the theory that actions really do speak louder than words, Hellboy finished his sentence by smashing a metal locker with his stone hand, then grabbing it and hefting it high above his head with only one hand, clearly aimed in the other man's direction. Manning's face paled as the sound of metal crunching reverberated around the room; he couldn't stop himself from automatically ducking when Hellboy's elbow bent in preparation for a throw. Without another word, he turned and ran out of the medical bay.

It was hard to believe that this whole area was underground, especially when all the public could see were the rather nondescript offices of a waste management company. What was in front of Liz now was, at least by government standards (which usually meant gray filing cabinets, cluttered desks, and lots of electronic equipment that didn't work but couldn't be thrown out because it was government property), blatantly decadent. They were in a large central area with the B.P.R.D. logo inset into the floor in solid brass. Evenly spaced at strategic points, guards were monitoring computer stations while others tracked blips on tactical glass boards. All very high tech and big money.

At the other edge, corridors radiated outward like the spokes of a wheel, each interspersed with glass partitions and leading to offices and God knew what else. With Myers and her suitcases at her side, Liz realized it had been some time since her last visit to the B.P.R.D., and a lot had changed. Still, some things never did.

There was Professor Broom, headed their way from one of the satellite corridors.

But on second glance, he looked . . . impossibly *old*, stooped, and thin, as if the weight of his own knowledge was beating him into the ground and sucking the meat right off his bones. He was wearing a dark shirt and slacks, and the burgundy wool vest he had on over his shirt was hanging loose on his frame; Liz couldn't ever remember having seen him in clothing that didn't fit impeccably. Nevertheless, he was, as always, completely congenial, painfully courteous. "Welcome back."

She nodded, then felt compelled to remind him, "It's only for the weekend, Professor Broom. Then I'll be on my way."

He didn't even blink. "Come and go as you please." He waved a hand at their quietly efficient surroundings. "Find your way back. We've made quite a few changes—"

The rest of what he was saying was lost in an explosion of broken glass. Myers yanked out his weapon as Liz gave a small, surprised scream; then a mangled metal locker slammed to the floor in one of the corridors, leaving behind it a rim of thick safety glass and bent aluminum studs.

A second later, Dr. Manning came hightailing it out of a door in front of where the locker had landed. He saw Broom and made a beeline for him, gasping and sputtering, jabbing a forefinger at the air in indignation. "I want that *thing* locked up, starting now! *Now!* You hear me?" He fled to parts unknown without waiting for an answer.

Liz looked in Broom's direction and raised one dark eyebrow. "Nothing's changed," she said wryly. "Home, sweet home."

Broom looked aghast at the mess in the corridor, then hurried after Manning. Amused, Liz watched him go, then turned to see Hellboy calmly stepping through the hole he'd made in the corridor's glass wall. When he saw her, he froze, but only for a moment. "Liz?" He stared, then his mouth stretched into a grin. "*Liz!*"

Oh no. She didn't want to give explanations to Hellboy right now, couldn't deal with the emotional strain of their whole relationship . . . not that that's what it actually was or had been, or even ever *would* be. Instead of staying to talk to him, she gripped her suitcases harder, turned on her heel, and strode off in the opposite direction.

Behind her, Myers slid his gun back into his holster as Hellboy skidded to a stop next to him. "You!" he chortled. "You did it, buddy!"

Not knowing what to say, Myers only nodded, then turned and followed Liz. He wasn't sure what was up with these two, but he had to make sure it didn't trip a switch in her mind and make her change her tune about staying around the research facility for the weekend.

Behind them, Hellboy was left standing all alone in the center of the B.P.R.D. logo. He didn't seem to mind as he grinned toward anyone who happened to be passing by or coming in to do yet another Hellboy-created cleanup.

"Whoo hoo!"

Been here, done this.

Yeah, Liz thought. *Nothing's changed.*

The same fourteen-by-fourteen room—although the black, back part of her mind wanted to call it a *cell*—with the same supposedly mentally calming cream paint and the thinly disguised fireproof insulation covering the walls. The same furniture, also fireproof, in pastel colors that she found more hospital-like than comforting. There were fresh white sheets on the bed and an oversized pillow, and while someone *had* placed a small glass bowl of pistachios on the night stand, there were no pictures on the walls, no sense of permanence or home. The B.P.R.D. could hardly be blamed for that; she had abandoned the organization so many times that Dr. Broom had finally given up on keeping a place for her here; his female child, so to speak, had left the nest and was unlikely to return.

Or so he had thought.

She tossed her bags on the end of the bed, then turned and flounced down on it. The mattress felt good. Myers was lingering in the doorway, watching her, doing his agently duty in getting her settled. Most of the time, she preferred being alone; for right now, though, Liz felt like him being there was an okay thing. Who knew how long *that* feeling would last.

He didn't say anything so she felt compelled to fill in the silence. Reflexively she pulled on one of the heavy rubber bands on one wrist, then let it snap back against the skin. "A little something I learned in therapy," she said. He winced, but she ignored that. "I'm depressed, one rubber band." She added another rubber band to the layer over her fingers, pulled back, then released them. "I'm impatient, two rubber bands."

When she'd started talking, Myers had come in and sat next to her on the edge of the bed, careful not to touch her. He watched solemnly as she pulled on the bands, then released them. Finally, he said, "I'll get you a fresh pack."

Hellboy watched one of the cats, a big, formerly muscular tabby that was now running toward pudgy, bat playfully at Hellboy's latest failure, a wad of paper on which only two words were visible—*Dear Liz*. Morosely, Hellboy scooped up the crumpled paper with his tail and dropped it into a wastebasket already brimming with more of the same; it was only a matter of time before one of cats realized the potential in the trash bin and upended it. Not that it made any difference—the floor around Hellboy's stainless steel desk was littered with yet more botched attempts at letter writing.

As the projector played *Duck Soup* in the background, Hellboy pulled out another piece of paper and started fresh. *Dear Liz.* There were so many things he wanted to say to her, but he'd never been good with the writing part. Hell, he'd never been good with the saying part, either. Still, he had to try. He couldn't let a little thing like communication bring a big red guy like him down.

He'd gotten a few more words scrawled out when he heard the door open and the squeaky wheels of the food cart. Hellboy bent lower, trying to ignore it, then Myers's voice cut into his concentration. "Where do you—"

"Shhh! Just a second."

The agent obligingly lapsed into silence and chose his own spot, hefting the tray loaded with chili and slices of bread onto the dining table on the other side of the room. After a moment, Hellboy said, "Myers, you're a talker. What's a good word—a *solid* word—for 'need'?"

Myers thought about it. "Need *is* a good, solid word."

Hellboy scowled at the paper in front of him. "Nah. Sounds too needy."

Myers shrugged, then inclined his head at the waiting chili. "Start in. You've got nachos coming."

He started out the door, then moved to the side as Liz came through. Hellboy's eyes widened as he saw her, but he didn't say anything—hell, he *couldn't* say anything—as she surveyed the room and all his cats.

"Oh, my God," she said with a grin. "Look at them all! Who had babies?" She knelt on the floor and several of them came running immediately. "Come here, Tiger." She petted and scratched at whichever one came within range as they twined about her, rubbing against her knees and soaking up the attention.

Hellboy screwed up his courage. "Uh . . . Liz? I, uh, there's something I'd like you to . . . something I *need* you to hear."

Liz was still scratching Tiger on the head. "Well, is it long? I'm going out, but—"

Hellboy sat up straight. "Out? Out *out?*"

Liz stopped fooling with the cat and looked at him quizzically. "For a cup of coffee. But go ahead—read."

Suspicion bloomed in his head and suddenly his letter confession didn't seem so important. "You're going alone?"

Liz stood, smiling a little as the four or five cats that had been gathered around her mewled plaintively. "No. Myers is taking me."

Hellboy was on his feet and headed toward her instantly, and never mind that he felt like she'd slapped him across the face. "Him? Why him? Why not me?"

Whatever she was going to say in response was cut off by the sound of the food cart's wheels again—*squeak! squeak! squeak!* Hellboy jerked toward the sound, then his shoulders slumped as Myers came in with the promised nachos.

"Hey," Myers said, frowning at the still-untouched tray on the table. "Your chili's getting cold."

Hellboy sucked in air, then slowly lowered himself back onto his chair. He had a brief vision of what the chili and nachos might look like thrown against the wall, but even he knew that would score him really high on the petulant child scale. "Not hungry."

Liz glanced at Myers, then back at Hellboy. "What did you want me to hear?"

Swallowing, Hellboy folded his piece of paper in half, then in quarters. He could feel his emotions starting a slow burn, but it wouldn't take long to go to high heat. It would be best if they both left before his thermostat went to red. "It's nothing. Just a list. It's . . . not finished."

Liz nodded, apparently oblivious to the turmoil Hellboy was enduring. Wasn't that always the way? "Oh, okay." She gave him a little good-bye wave. "Maybe later then."

And then she was out the door, leaving Hellboy to

stare at Agent Myers. The guy had the nerve to smile at him. "Anything else you—"

"Not from you," Hellboy snapped.

Myers blinked. "Well, good ni—"

"Good *night*." Hellboy intentionally swiveled his chair so that his back was to Myers, signaling a definitive end to any more of the man's chitchat.

It seemed Agent Myers had turned into the competition.

17

BACK IN ONE OF THE MEDICAL BAYS, PROFESSOR BROOM stood in front of the stainless steel autopsy table on which lay Kroenen's cold, naked body.

Eyeing the corpse impassively, Broom raised a tape recorder and depressed the Record button. "The subject, Karl Ruprecht Kroenen." The old man stopped for a moment and scanned the body critically. Except for a neatly folded sheet across the hip and genital area, Kroenen was naked. It was anything but an attractive sight, but it was certainly intriguing.

Broom depressed the button and spoke again as he examined the intricate silver hand and harness lying on a smaller table off to the side. "The subject suffered a masochistic compulsion known as surgical addiction. Both eyelids were surgically removed along with his upper and lower lips, making it difficult for him to speak and even more challenging for others to understand him. I would presume he stopped talking shortly after the surgery was performed. The blood in his veins dried up decades ago. Only dust remains."

The professor left the body and crossed the room to

where he could study a set of X-rays hanging against a light board. "Four pulverized vertebrae," he continued. "A steel rod inserted into his pelvis held him up." He paused to shake his head as he turned back to stare at the dead man. There was a video camera at each corner of the room, recording the autopsy from all four points of view, and Broom couldn't help but wonder if the agents who'd pulled safety monitoring duty had the answer to his next question. "What horrible willpower could keep a thing like this alive?"

Glancing back to Kroenen's hand, Broom noticed the belt and pouch on the table. Curious, he set down his recorder and slipped his fingers into the pouch.

And pulled out two small, strange pieces of paper.

Agent Lime checked his watch. Time to go pick up Hellboy's dishes and take them back to the kitchen. Myers was supposed to be the big guy's new babysitter, but he was out with that firestarter woman, Liz Sherman, so Lime had pulled backup duty. Actually, he didn't mind so much. Hellboy could be a handful, but he was a pretty good sport—a good thing considering he could probably smash them all to a pulp if he got pissed. Visiting him was always interesting; he might be watching *Dumb and Dumber* or some Bruce Willis flick—*Die Hard* was always a good bet, and Lime could settle in and relax for a while under the guise of keeping the big red guy company. He wasn't so high on all those cats, but he also wasn't stupid enough to say that out loud. At least he wasn't allergic, like some of the other agents.

Whistling, Lime went through the security door that led into Hellboy's living quarters. Pushing the cart in front of him, the agent took all of three steps inside before he jerked to a stop. What he saw across the room was enough to make his jaw drop open.

At the far end of the space, a couple of the heavier pieces of furniture had been shoved aside. Where there had once been a wall, there was now only a huge, ragged hole; rimmed with rebar and broken concrete. Lime knew instantly that it was more than large enough for Hellboy to squeeze into.

"Jesus!"

The agent shoved the cart out of the way and ran to the opening. Beyond it was—scratch that—had *been* the outer wall of a metal service shaft. The metal separator had been peeled open like a sardine can, and he could see all the way into the shaft. It went farther down, but it also went up . . . all the way to ground level. Lime was betting that was the direction Hellboy had headed. He twisted around so he could see upward, but the only thing in sight was darkness.

Hellboy was long gone.

Although it was the largest city in New Jersey, there wasn't much that was impressive about Newark's skyline. At around 270,000 people, it was fairly crowded but still a small city; Myers didn't want to think about what Newark had been like at its peak in the 1930s, when the census had recorded its population at over 440,000. For some reason the numbers had gone steadily downward since then; even so, there was precious little room to breathe around here. It wasn't Myers's favorite city . . . but then he'd always seen it from the perspective of an FBI agent, always on the run, going somewhere, checking or tracking someone—office buildings, dark rooms, dirty alleyways, smoke- and booze-filled bars.

Tonight was giving him an entirely different point of view.

He and Liz came out of Starbucks to discover that a two-person jazz band had set up right there at the corner. They'd just started playing and hadn't yet drawn a crowd—a good thing, because Liz had confessed that she hated crowds almost as much as she detested strangers who were gutsy enough to look her in the eye. Myers handed Liz her coffee as he unchained the moped, enjoying the background music but knowing they'd be better off heading away from the busier streets. She followed along, occasionally raising her ever-present Polaroid to take a snapshot of something that caught her eye; she'd hang on to it for a few minutes while it finished developing, then most of the time tuck it into her coat pocket without ever looking at it; he had the feeling she'd go over all the photographs very carefully later, once she was alone in her room. It wasn't hard to make her laugh now that she was away from the B.P.R.D. and all the people who had already, as she put it, "tried and condemned me with their eyes."

He balanced his coffee cup in the circle of his thumb and forefinger and pushed the moped down the sidewalk, letting the machine force the people coming toward them to swerve around. Most of the shops they passed were closing down, especially as they headed toward a more residential neighborhood. Waiting for a stoplight, he and Liz continued the conversation started all the way back at Starbucks, a sort of back and forth, pros and cons about—who else?—Hellboy.

"I admire him," Myers said. He tried not to sound too stubborn. "He's a force of nature."

Liz snickered. "He's just pushy."

Myers shook his head. "No. He's determined—unstoppable."

"Cocky."

"Strong."

"A brute." Liz raised an eyebrow, as if daring him to find a comeback for that one.

But Myers wasn't giving up. "My uncle used to say that we *like* people for their qualities but *love* them for their defects."

A small, half smile worked its way across Liz's

mouth as she sipped her coffee, but she didn't say anything.

"He loves you," Myers said bluntly.

"I know."

"What about you?" Myers watched her carefully.

She tilted her head and considered his question. "I don't know. Really, I grew up with him." She hesitated. "I've missed him, too, but now every time I see him, I get confused. Hardly a day goes by that he's not on my mind. Even now, I feel like he's here."

Following them was easy, so much so that Hellboy didn't even think about it as he leaped from roof to roof along their path, always keeping either them or Myers's moped within easy view. His stomach was churning as he watched them, and it sure wasn't because he'd skipped dinner. With all the special abilities he had, why couldn't he have super hearing? Like that *Bionic Woman* character . . . what had been her name? Jamie Somers, that's right, played by Lindsay Wagner. Boy, she'd been able to hear everything. What he wouldn't give to be a fly on the moped's front fender right about now.

They were talking back and forth, and while Hellboy couldn't hear a thing, it seemed rapid fire to him, witty repartee. He'd *never* been able to do that. "What are you two talking about?" Frustrated, he found himself asking the question of empty air, waving a fist futilely in front of his own face. "What's so fascinating? So *important?*"

There was no answer, of course—good thing—and he got up and hopped to the next roof as they moved on down the sidewalk, clearly bent on leaving the crowds behind. Liz didn't like crowds, no sir. As he watched, Myers reached into his pocket and pulled out a couple of those little plastic creamers, along with two sugar packets. "No cream and sugar," Hellboy told him, even though the other man was obviously out of earshot. "She takes it black." As Hellboy knew she would, Liz held up a hand and shook her head. "Told ya," Hellboy muttered with a scowl. *He* was the one who knew Liz, not Myers. So why wasn't it Myers instead of him playing hopscotch along the rooftops?

Yeah, Hellboy thought as he paced them from above. *I could teach this guy a thing or two about the likes and dislikes of Liz Sherman.* He was actually starting to feel a little superior when he saw Liz's hands cut through the air, a gesture too harsh for calm conversation. Was she upset? No, it didn't seem so. What, then?

Damn, he wished he knew what they were talking about.

Myers watched with concern as Liz shook first one hand, then her other. "It's freezing, isn't it?"

But Liz's answer surprised him. "The coffee's warming me up." She turned one palm up and he could see where the skin had pinkened from the heat of the cup.

Now everything was closed up. They walked on, passing the darkened windows of the storefronts, not bothering to look in any of them. After another block or so, they came to a park; it was small and the grass was still green beneath trees that were dropping brightly colored leaves onto the well-manicured lawn. Not far away was a train station, so it wasn't hard to imagine this park as a little lunchtime oasis, or even a place where friends and lovers might meet after work.

Myers cleared his throat. "What do we do now?" he asked, then grinned. What he was about to say had no doubt been said about every small town in the U.S. of A., but it certainly fit the moment. "Newark, New Jersey. Entertainment capital of the world."

Liz didn't seem to mind the cliché. She picked a bench, then ran her hand over the surface to sweep off the wet leaves and grit. "You offered me a cup of coffee. I've got one, so just sit down."

She was pretty good with orders, Myers thought. Well, she was good with just about everything—the way she looked, the way she moved, the nonpretentious way she had of holding up her end of a conversation.

Myers grinned and did what he was he told. As far

as he was concerned, Liz Sherman was just good all the way around.

Hellboy hit the side of the building rather than landing on its roof.

His face smashed up against the brickwork and he barely got his hands up there in time to grab the edge of the parapet. He grunted, hanging for a few seconds to get his bearings and let the sting fade out of his nose, then hauled himself up. "Damn it," he growled as he hooked his tail along the edge to help pull his weight over the wall, then rolled to a sitting position. What if someone had seen—

Oops.

Not ten feet away was a kid feeding a bunch of pigeons in a coop.

Hellboy's mouth worked. "Uh . . . hi." *Lame*, he thought. *Very lame*.

Maybe nine years old, dressed in dirty jeans and a shirt with an *X-Men* logo on it, at first the boy did nothing but stare at him. Smart kid; it was only a matter of seconds until the light of recognition blazed in his eyes. "You're Hellboy!"

For a moment, Hellboy didn't know what to say, then he raised one red finger to his lips. "Shhhhhh," he said in a stage whisper. He inclined his head over the edge, indicating where Myers and Liz sat comfortably—*too* comfortably—on a bench in the

tiny park across the street. "I'm . . . on a mission."
Yeah, that was good. Kids loved that spy stuff. "Don't
tell anyone, huh?"

He knew by the look on the boy's face that he
wouldn't say a word.

At least for an hour or two.

Running a hand over the thinning hair on his
scalp, Professor Broom thoughtfully examined the
ragged hole in the wall. Hellboy had certainly done
some damage to his quarters this time, although that
could hardly have been avoided because of the size
needed to accommodate his huge frame. Broom had
no idea how Hellboy could have known about that
service shaft; maybe Hellboy's hearing was more acute
than he'd let on, and he'd lain awake nights listening
to voices drifting down it, clothes being dropped, God
alone knew what else. Or maybe he'd picked up those
same sounds unconsciously, then simply picked this
spot as the starting point for his escape based on that
subliminal knowledge.

And when Broom turned, there it was, of course—
Hellboy's locator belt, hanging on the wall where he'd
left it. That meant the big red guy was out there,
somewhere, and completely untrackable.

Agent Lime stood behind him, a worried look on
his face. He was clearly blaming himself for Hellboy's
escape, but Broom didn't know what else he could say

to set Lime's mind at ease. It was, perhaps, a lesson they should all learn: if Hellboy wanted to go, there was nothing in this building that was capable of stopping him. "Should we send out some scouts?"

"No," Broom said, knowing they wouldn't find Hellboy until he wanted to be found, or until he returned on his own. And Hellboy always returned. The professor sighed. "Enough—he will never change. Always a child . . . always."

The old man turned and resolutely made his way toward his office, leaving the repairs to those who would know how to do such things and who would, no doubt uselessly, try yet another method of reinforcing the walls in Hellboy's living area.

18

WHITE WALLS, WHITE CABINETS, WHITE LIGHTS, A white tile floor; sterility and silence, except for the faint ticking of the industrial clock on the wall over the door. Not a bit of warmth or movement in the room, and the gray-skinned, lipless, lidless cadaver of Kroenen on the table went right along with everything else.

Until his chest began a slow, rhythmic rise and fall, air filling dried-up lung cavities and sending oxygen to the desiccated limbs.

Until he sat up.

Kroenen turned his head, bulging eyes searching until he spotted the object he wanted on the table a few feet away. Ah, yes . . . there it was. He stood and made his way over to the table, letting the sheet fall carelessly to the floor. He shoved his arm stump into place against the prosthetic hand; there was a *click* as the mechanical parts automatically tightened around the scarred end of his arm, making it throb with delightful pain. He flexed the shiny fingers, watching each of them work perfectly. Yes, that was much, *much* better.

Kroenen glanced around until he spotted his clothes, which had been carelessly folded and dropped into a plastic medical tub at the end of the longest counter. He retrieved them and spread them out on the examining table, dressing with care in the leather outfit and making sure to fasten all the shiny buckles as tightly as possible and with the same precision as he had worked on his silver hand.

The last thing he put on was his mask, and Kroenen drew the zipper closed with a mixture of reluctance and relief. He wore the mask only because his appearance made others . . . *uncomfortable*. On the other hand, he'd become so accustomed to the feel and smell of leather against the mummified flesh of his face that the tickle of air against his skin—or what was left of it—was no longer pleasant, or even desirable. Something was always wrong with the stuff—it was too cold, too hot, too moist. Yes, he was definitely glad to put the mask back on.

That done, he found his Ragnarok knives on the bottom surface of the tub and held them up for inspection. Good—everything was as it should be. He'd been afraid that idiotic Professor Broom would clean them with acetone, then assign one of his agents to take the knives to the B.P.R.D.'s machine shop and have the edges dulled, perhaps permanently ruining them. But they were nice and sharp, and they had, at least, done a passable job of cleaning Agent Clay's blood off the one without damaging it. As he turned one over, it reflected the bright overhead lights, then the flat of the blade picked up a shadow. When Kroenen held it just so, he could see the clear reflection of the room's other occupant standing behind him.

Grigori.

Hellboy smelled the chocolate chip cookies before he saw them. He'd did know how long he'd been staring morosely down at Myers and Liz; one moment his mind would be blank, the next it would be filled with a hundred, a *thousand* possibilities about those two, and none of them were good. The smell of the warm chocolate brought him out of his reverie and reminded him that he'd skipped dinner; his stomach was grumbling and unhappy, although it was nothing compared to what his heart was going through. When he turned and looked at the boy, the kid was holding a tray with two glasses of milk and a plate sporting a nice half dozen of the chewy and gooey kind.

"My mom baked 'em," he said proudly. He set the tray carefully on the wall next to Hellboy, then climbed up and sat on the other side of it.

Hellboy's head swiveled back to the view below and his mouth turned down. "That's it. She's laughing—I'm done." He grabbed three cookies and scarfed them down, barely registering the smooth chocolate taste, the crunchy walnuts. Their goodness came to him more in the sweet aftertaste that spread through his taste buds.

The boy looked from Hellboy to the two on the bench below. "They don't *look* like spies," he said doubtfully.

"Come on!" Hellboy exclaimed. "Look at him—those shifty eyes. That phony grin." His stomach rumbled and he glanced at the last cookie on the plate. "You gonna eat that?" When the boy shook his head, Hellboy started to pick it up, then froze. He squinted, making sure he was seeing what he was seeing—was Myers yawning?

He was.

Hellboy slapped his forehead. "Oh, the *yawning* trick. That's so nineteen-fifties!" He poked the boy in the side and pointed at the duo below. "Watch his arm," he instructed. Before things went any further, Hellboy turned and quickly scanned the rooftop behind them. There—a good-sized pebble. It was just what he needed.

Sure enough, Myers was saying something to Liz and doing the old stretch-the-arms-up-and-over trick. When he was through stretching, one arm came down behind her and rested on her shoulders. Hellboy eyed the pebble, judged the distance, then let her fly.

Thunk!

Hellboy snickered and both he and the boy rolled backward and ducked behind the parapet as Myers jerked his arm away and rubbed at the top of his head, then stood and looked around. The agent's annoyed "Hey—what the hell?" was loud enough to be carried on the breeze—both Hellboy and the boy heard it. As the boy giggled, Hellboy stuffed the last cookie into his mouth and he and the kid gave each other a sturdy high five.

Beneath the lens of his micro-scanner, the two pieces of paper Broom had taken from Kroenen's pouch were being meticulously aligned by the computer's document regeneration program. The professor sat and watched patiently, not letting himself think about how much he despised computers, and he didn't give a damn how much easier they supposedly made things. Anyone with a quarter of a brain could understand that computers also made the world harder and more complex. More *dangerous*. He was sure he could make a list—handwritten, of course—that would stretch all the way across New Jersey and contain all the things that now had to be done and watched over and protected, and all *those* because of the invention of the computer. The idea that nowadays nearly every home had at least one sometimes frightened him almost as much as the occult and its endlessly dark possibilities.

There—at last the program was finished filling in a couple of missing areas and he could finally read the

Cyrillic letters. "Hmmmm," the professor murmured to himself. "Sebastian Plackba #16, Moscow." He turned away from the damnable machine and dug around in his filing cabinet until he came up with a folder full of photographs; he extracted several and spread them on the desktop, treating the older ones with care while he mulled over the shots of Grigori, standing tall and proud in a German uniform. He lifted a book from a nearby shelf and flipped through it until he found what he was looking for: another picture of Grigori, this time decked out in an Orthodox priest's black cassock. The man had certainly gone from one end of the spectrum to the other, hadn't he?

Still, these photographs were telling him nothing truly important, nothing he didn't already know. He had one last place to try, tucked away in the locked bottom drawer of his desk. It had been some time since he'd taken this particular tome from its old wooden box, and when he did so now, Broom had to blow the dust aside to see the hand-tooled leather cover. He opened it with extreme care, mindful of the creakiness in the book's spine, the dryness of its pages. His fingers ran across the text delicately, picking out Rasputin's date of birth, his date of death, and finally, the line he had somehow known would be included:

His mausoleum is at SEBASTIAN PLACKBA #16.

Broom nodded to himself. "It's Rasputin's mausoleum."

Tchkkk.

Broom jerked around in time to see, of all people, Kroenen descending the spiral staircase in the corner. The dead man—how could he be anything but?—was fully masked and dressed, gripping his blade with a sickening familiarity. Broom had seen a lot of things in his time—spells, demons, men who could breathe underwater, and women who could walk through fire and come out the other side unscathed—but this was . . . *unspeakable*. A man of dust and metal, with no blood or heartbeat or, likely, *soul*. There were few things in this life that had truly terrified him, yet this . . .

But he'd be damned before he'd show it.

Broom forced himself to look steadily at the zombified Kroenen as he came toward him. "I see the puppet," he said blandly. "But where is the puppet *master?*"

"*Very good, Professor Broom.*"

Broom ground his teeth and willed his old body not to flinch at the hissing voice behind him. Loath to turn his back on Kroenen, it seemed he had no choice if he was to face Grigori. As Broom swiveled to meet him, Grigori stepped from the shadows next to Abe's unoccupied tank.

Broom studied Grigori with false composure. "It *was* you—the scraps of paper, Liz's sudden relapse and return—"

"Bread crumbs on the trail, like in a fable." Grigori smiled darkly and folded his hands in front of him in a gesture that almost made him seem about to give benediction. "They both distract and guide him exactly where I need him."

"Moscow," Broom said, knowing Grigori was talking about Hellboy.

"His destiny." With his hands still folded primly, Grigori glided forward until he stood directly in front of Broom. "You raised the child. Nurtured him. So in return, would you permit me? A brief, *brief* glimpse of the future." Before Broom could pull back, Grigori stretched out one thin-fingered hand and lightly touched the center of the Professor's forehead.

There was nothing left of New York.

Everything from horizon to horizon was charred and smoldering, once-tall buildings reduced to rubble and metal supports twisted in upright positions like plastic bag ties. Bodies and body parts were everywhere in the streets, hanging from tree limbs, draped across the spiky tops of the few remaining fences like a tribute to Vlad Tepes. In the not-too-far distance marched an apocalyptic army of monstrous beasts; huge and lumbering and unstoppable, their deformed bodies were silhouetted against a blood-red sky.

And lording over it all, sitting on a throne mounted atop a mountain of rotting skeletons and festering skulls, was

Hellboy, the version of his son that Broom had never seen nor hoped to see. Huge, muscular, and unearthly—his horns had grown back longer and stronger and their tips were dripping with the scarlet blood of mankind, while from his mouth and eyes spilled a never-ending flood of unearthly fire.

Broom yanked himself out of the hideous vision and stumbled backward, too shaken to hide the effect of the horrible prophecy.

Grigori's finely manicured hand dropped back to the front of his robe and once again folded with his other one. "If only you'd had him destroyed sixty years ago," he said with false sympathy. "None of this would have come to pass. But then, how could you have known?"

Broom's mouth worked, but God help him, he could think of absolutely nothing to say.

A corner of Grigori's mouth turned up, as if he knew exactly what was going on in the professor's head. "Your God chooses to remain silent," he said. "Mine lives within me."

Grigori stepped back a little, and it took more will than he'd exercised at any other time in his life for Broom to suppress a shudder—he would *not* show fear to this creature—as Grigori's neck and shoulders visibly heaved and twitched beneath the thin layer of clothing he wore. "In the frozen waters of the Malaya

Nevka," Grigori told him, "in the darkness of the void, every time I died and crossed over, a little more of the Master came back with me. He disclosed to me the child's true name." Grigori paused and looked questioningly at Broom. "Would you like to know it?"

"I know what to call him," Broom said tersely. "Nothing you can say or do will change that. I call him *son*." While he was speaking, the professor discreetly pulled his rosary from his pocket and placed it on top of the book he'd retrieved from his desk. Broom couldn't see Kroenen as he took a position behind his back, but he could *feel* the man—Kroenen was like a monster, a walking vat of poison in dead human skin.

"I'm ready," Broom said simply.

Grigori's night-filled smile reappeared. "Good. Now I'll add two more crumbs." He watched appreciatively as Kroenen unsheathed his knives, not realizing that Broom could see them, too, reflected in the glass of Abe's tank. "Grief," said Grigori softly. "And . . . revenge."

Professor Broom gasped as Kroenen's knives went in, and in, and in . . .

Without warning, a dozen pigeons sprang into the air and flew erratically in every direction.

Hellboy jumped at the sudden movement, then refocused on Myers and Liz, ready to return to his brooding. They were still sitting down there on the park bench, talking about who knew what, but at least Myers's arm was where it should be and not across Liz's shoulders. No more of *that* funny business.

"Just go down there and tell her how you feel," the boy said impatiently. When Hellboy shook his head, the kid rolled his eyes. "My mom says—"

Hellboy's eyes flashed. "It's not that easy, okay?" He took a deep breath, then reminded himself—and the boy—of something else. "Plus, you're *nine*. You're not old enough to give me advice."

The boy opened his mouth to argue, then instead gave Hellboy a shrug that clearly meant he was giving up. Hellboy was still watching him when the boy looked down at the street and frowned. "Who are those guys?"

When Hellboy turned his attention back to the park, he felt every muscle in his body tense. Rolling to a stop in front of the spot where Myers and Liz sat were two black sedans, clearly B.P.R.D. vehicles.

"Something's wrong," Hellboy whispered. By the time he saw the door on the first of the cars fling open and Agent Lime bound out of the passenger side, Hellboy was on his feet and leaning forward, desperately wishing he could hear what was being said. But all he could do was watch helplessly as Lime grabbed Myers by the arm and began talking rapidly and gesturing. Then he saw Liz clap her hands over her ears.

Her scream just about ripped his heart out.

19

THERE WERE AT LEAST TWENTY PEOPLE BETWEEN HIM and Broom's office, but Hellboy didn't notice; he shouldered roughly through the crowd, making no apologies, meeting no resistance.

The B.P.R.D. cars had beat him back to headquarters, of course, so it hadn't been until he'd arrived a full twenty minutes later that Hellboy had found out what the big deal was. Now his mind and heart were all jumbled up with self-loathing, guilt, grief, regret, and anger—how stupid of him to be out there following Liz around and worried about his own emotions when he should have been back here, should have *stayed* here where Father had put him, should have been protecting his *own*. If he'd done that, maybe Father would still be alive and his attacker might be a very small pile of broken bone fragments.

But recrimination was free and hindsight was just as cheap; right now Hellboy had plenty of both and no doubt there would be more to come.

The old man's office was wall-to-wall people, and to Hellboy's eyes, it all seemed particularly harsh and

heartless. The person he loved most in the world—
Father—was slumped on his chair. Tilted slightly to
one side with his chin resting on his chest and his eyes
closed, Broom looked so fragile and still, as if he'd
only fallen asleep while working. Lately, that hadn't
been uncommon, so it was disconcerting to see him in
that position now, yet know the pose meant something entirely different. If Hellboy had had any doubt,
there were plenty of nasty reality reminders in the
form of camera flashes as the B.P.R.D.'s on-staff foren-
sics investigators worked the room inch by inch. Oh,
and let's not forget the scarlet pool of blood that had
gathered around Father's feet, soaking into the fine,
soft leather of his favorite oxfords.

Tom Manning was there, but he respectfully
stepped aside as he saw Hellboy come through. Even
though she'd been in the building, Liz had waited
until Hellboy's arrival to go in; now she was right on
his heels, and he heard her whimper as she saw the
professor. Hellboy's face was contorted with grief as he
knelt at the side of the chair, and when he looked at
Liz, there were tears of disbelief streaming down his
face. No one in the room dared to stop him as Hellboy
reached out and tenderly pulled Broom close to his
chest. The old man's head lolled against his shoulder
and his arms hung limp. So many times as a child
Hellboy had sat on this man's lap and rested his head
against his chest, heard Broom's strong and steady

heartbeat through the familiar woolen vest. Even though he expected it now, when nothing but silence came through to his ears, Hellboy just cried harder. "Father, I-I'm back," he managed to say. "I'm back. I'm back."

Even Manning couldn't bear to see Hellboy like this. As unobtrusively as possible, he herded everyone out. Liz hung back, staying at the doorway and blinking back tears as Hellboy hung his head and touched the forever-stilled hand. His voice was low and utterly heartbroken.

"I wasn't here. You died alone. . . ."

It seemed fitting that it was pouring rain for Trevor Bruttenholm's funeral. The old man had liked rainy days and the weather matched Hellboy's mood—dark and brooding, a storm brewing just out of sight.

He wished he could go to the funeral, be a pallbearer or even just carry Father's coffin all by himself. But no, he was stuck here, squatting on the edge of this damned roof like a gargoyle, helpless, forbidden to follow and attend as Broom was lowered into his final resting place. He watched as the pallbearers, Manning and Myers among them, carried the mahogany casket between two rows of B.P.R.D. agents, then loaded it into the hearse. His golden gaze followed the men as they climbed into the waiting sedans, then tracked the procession as it wound toward the main gate and finally went out of sight. Rain sheeted down from the heavy gray sky and soaked through Hellboy's overcoat, but he didn't feel it, wouldn't have cared if he had. When the cars were out of sight, he stayed where he was and stared at absolutely nothing.

While from the shelter of a doorway across the rooftop, Liz Sherman hung in the shadows and watched him.

"He hasn't spoken to anyone in three days," Liz said worriedly. "Not a word. He doesn't eat, he doesn't sleep." She paced the floor in front of the tank in the med lab, her face lit by the blue-green sheen of the gently moving water beyond the glass. Inside it, Abe floated upside down, conscious but still in his biocast, still with a ways to go on the road to being healed. Like most hospital patients, he was thoroughly bored at his confinement, and he'd been playing with a Rubik's Cube, trying in vain to get the colored squares to line up where they should go. "I've never seen him like this. *Never.*" She stopped her pacing and looked at Abe. "Should I stay? With him, I mean?" A faint smile crossed her face.

"Listen," Abe said. Coming through the speaker, his voice was bubbly and slightly hollow-sounding, like the transmission from a scuba suit microphone. "I'm not much of a problem solver." He held up the cube for Liz so she could get a better view of it and gave her his own slightly disgusted grin. "Three decades and I've only gotten two sides." He frowned at the cube, then twisted it once or twice, succeeding only in screwing up what he'd managed to accomplish so far. He sighed and put his attention back on her. "But I know this much. If there's trouble, all we have is each other. And I'm stuck here, so . . ." He let that sink in for a moment, then raised a webbed hand and pressed it against the tank's glass. "Take care of the big monkey for me, will you?"

She nodded solemnly, then slid her hand over his, only separated by the glass.

It was dusk outside, but in the underground conference room at the B.P.R.D., there was no way to tell that . . . except that Myers could feel it in his muscles, the way they wouldn't relax despite an undercutting of constant fatigue brought on by the stress of recent events. Manning had the projection screen warmed up, and now he hit a button on the remote and the darkened room filled with light from the screen, the tan color of an old piece of paper filled with black Cyrillic writing. The image washed the room in a sort of sepia tone that was reminiscent of 1930s photographs, making the faces of the agents seated around the table look sallow and unhealthy, painting deep-set shadows beneath their eyes and in the hollows of their cheeks.

"We've collected and destroyed thousands of eggs," Manning was saying. "There's no trace of this Sammael or this Rasputin character. But we have this address." He used a laser pointer to draw multiple circles around part of the writing displayed on the screen. "Sebastian Plackba #16. Volokolamsk Fields, fifty miles from Moscow. We leave as soon as we get clearance and equipment."

Manning turned and faced the men listening attentively to him, then folded his arms. Backlit by the tan lighting, Myers couldn't see Manning's face, but the hard tone of his voice covered it all. "Hellboy's coming, but *I'll* be in charge this time. Either we wrap this up or I'm closing this freak show for good."

An awkward silence fell over the room as he snapped off the projector. Manning's way of finally dismissing them was to start gathering up his papers and shoving them jerkily into his briefcase. Out of the corner of his eye, Myers saw Liz pass by the open conference room door, but he dared not get up and follow her.

Liz found Hellboy standing in front of Professor Broom's desk, staring pensively at the knickknacks arranged on its surface. His massive chest was bare except for the bandages still covering the wounds he'd received in the recent battle with Sammael. She watched him from across the room and didn't say anything, wanting to leave him undisturbed in his grief, but at the same time wanting to somehow comfort him. But how? After all that had happened to her and in her life, she wasn't sure she had comfort left in her for anyone, even herself. And certainly there were others in the world more qualified to offer it.

Waiting, she saw Hellboy pluck something from the desk's surface and hold it up. The item—Broom's black rosary—gleamed in the low light of the office, and Hellboy swung it back and forth a couple of times, but gently, as though he were afraid he'd offend a higher power if he were too rough with it. He stopped and leaned forward, reading something on one of the opened pages; even from where she stood, Liz could see that a portion of the contents had been underlined.

"Hi," she finally ventured.

He straightened and turned to face her as she slowly came forward. "Hi."

She rubbed her fingers together absently, then made herself stop when she felt a small burn start to build in the tips. "I've . . . changed my mind. I'll come to Moscow. If you're still going."

Hellboy nodded, then cleared his throat. "I am." He hesitated, then looked as though he had to force his next words to come out. "But I have something to say, too. I . . . never had the guts before." He'd been looking at his hands, at the floor, at anything else, but

now he raised his gaze to her face and looked Liz
squarely in the eye. "I understand what you don't like
about me," he said. "I do. What I am makes you feel
out of place out *there*." He gestured vaguely toward
the ceiling, and Liz knew exactly what he meant.

Liz inhaled. "Red, I—"

"Listen," Hellboy cut in. "I'm not like Myers. He
makes you feel like you belong. And that's good, it
really is. I wish I could do something about *this*,"—he
pointed at his own face—"but I can't." He looked
down at the floor for a moment, then gave her a faint
grin. "I can promise you only two things. One, I'll always look this good. Two, I won't give up on you.
Ever."

For a long moment, she didn't respond at all. Then,
very softly, she said, "I like that."

Hellboy nodded firmly. "Good."

20

MOVING SLOWLY, THE LIMO AND MOTORCYCLE CARA-van wound its way through the wasteland of rust and decay that was all that remained of the Topockba Steel Mills. Times were hard and had been for a very long time. Likewise, money was—at least to the average man—scarce, and political favoritism was reserved for the select few. The economics of it all could be seen in the rotting warehouses that lined the litter-filled streets like dead, steel watchdogs, black-windowed buildings with twisted metal supports and broken-out glass. The only movement in this land of frigid desolation was a few lonely and heavily dressed sentries who, until they saw the limo, stood miserable and shivering in the cold and were clearly less than enthused about their lot in life.

The limo pulled up in front of a warehouse no more or less significant-looking than any other, easing to a halt like a predatory black snake. A tiny guardhouse stood to the left of its heavy metal door, and the noise of the car and the motorcycles made a guard poke his head out of a window; his annoyed look quickly evaporated into a smart salute and a moment later the scarred door trundled open so they could steer their vehicles inside.

When the limo was stopped, the back door opened and a fleshy Russian military man, General Lapikov, struggled out, waving away the chauffeur who offered to assist him. A moment later, Grigori and Ilsa slid from the backseat with a lot more grace than their escort.

"I have accumulated many objects of great interest," General Lapikov told them proudly. He puffed his chest out, stretching the already well-tested buttons on his heavily decorated uniform. "All in the interest of preserving our heritage, of course."

As the general led them through the storehouse, Grigori and Ilsa looked at each other, communicating their disdain with eye contact while carefully maintaining poker expressions. The place was damp and badly taken care of, full of spider webs, rat droppings, and puddles of moisture in the low spots on the floor. It was also a repository of bric-a-brac—to their left was a towering, unattractive marble sculpture of Lenin's head, to their right a line of old master paintings which might or might not have been authentic. Other more questionable objets d'art included battered tanks, warheads, missiles, and a jumble of unidentifiable weapons.

"Many," continued the general in his heavy Russian accent, "believe Mother Russia to be very close to an historic rebirth." He'd led Grigori and Ilsa down several aisles, and now he stopped in front of a cargo container and gestured for one of the soldiers following them to come forward. He obeyed, unshouldering a small butane torch. It took only a few seconds to melt away the lead Kremlin seal that ran across the two main boards, then he pulled them open and exposed the contents for their inspection.

"Rebirth," Grigori mused. "I like that." He and Ilsa stepped closer and gazed at the opening. Inside was a massive stone monolith, probably of polished marble.

"Twenty tons of stone," Lapikov said. "This thing fell from the sky into Tunguska Forest."

Grigori nodded. "June 30, 1908. It burned hundreds of square miles of forest. The Romanovs took possession of it immediately, and the czar guarded it jealously. I've wanted it for ages." His long fingers brushed over the smooth, perfectly white surface, then stopped at an imprint in the center: two circular engravings that matched Hellboy's four-fingered stone hand. He smiled "Now, finally, it's mine."

General Lapikov arched one heavy eyebrow, and it was the first time he'd looked worried since exiting the limo outside the warehouse. "You are aware, of course, there is no way you'll get it out of Russian territory."

"He is aware," Ilsa said curtly. She reached into the shoulder bag and pulled out a small, heavy chrome box. The general relaxed when she flipped open the lid and revealed a healthy-sized pile of gold coins. They gleamed in the poor overhead light.

The general smiled happily and quickly took it from her. "It's a pleasure doing business with you. Perhaps you have . . . *other* interests?"

"Enjoy the bright metal you've earned," Grigori said laconically. He didn't take his gaze from the cold marble. "There will be no further transactions. Only . . . closure."

RUSSIAN AIRSPACE OVER THE BLACK SEA

Hellboy watched the white eye of a full moon out of the tiny, round window as their oversized cargo plane sliced through the air. On a map tacked up to a plastic divider a few feet away, one of the airmen had drawn a red line indicating their flight path and its progress— they were close, very close. Turning away from the window and trying unsuccessfully to shut out the ceaseless drone of the engine, Hellboy forced his attention back to the brightly lit worktable in the center of the cargo hold. Off to one side, Myers was keeping a large cargo crate steady as Agents Lime and Stone stenciled the words Fragile! Live Cargo! across its front.

Leaning against the worktable, Hellboy pointed out

the medieval illustration of Sammael on its surface to Liz and Manning. " 'One falls, two shall arise.' So you pop one, two come out. You kill two, you get four. You kill four, you're in trouble." He looked at Manning through narrowed eyes. "We have to nail 'em all at once. *And* the eggs."

Manning's mouth twisted in distaste. "When we do, no mumbo-jumbo. Double-core Vulcan-65 grenades." He held up a set of heavy grenade belts. "We've installed a very handy timer. Set, and walk away. The cable pulls the safety pins—*kaboom!* Easy to clean, easy to use."

Hellboy stared from Manning to the grenade belts in amazement. "Those things never work—*never!*"

"Each of us gets a belt," Manning said, pointedly ignoring him. He pushed a couple toward Hellboy.

"I won't take 'em." Hellboy set his jaw stubbornly. "They never work," he repeated.

Manning scowled at Hellboy, but before he could say anything more, Agent Myers came forward. "I'll carry his."

"Boy Scout," Hellboy muttered. Dismissing the grenade belt, he opted instead for wrapping Professor Broom's rosary around his wrist.

VOLOKOLAMSK FIELDS, MOSCOW

They had two gleaming black vans and a black truck, and they probably stood out like bull's eye targets against the stark white, snow-covered roads of pre-winter Moscow. Inside the truck's cab, Liz and Myers struggled with a map of Moscow, trying unsuccessfully to pinpoint their own location and where they were headed. Giving up, Liz picked up her radio. "Sparky to Big Red," she said, then rolled down her window and stuck her head outside so she could look back at the truck. The air whipping through her hair was frigid and damp, brutally cold; it would be pouring through the breathing holes drilled into Hellboy's crate, and she hoped Hellboy was okay back there. She worried about him, sitting in the back like that, in the dark and the cold. Was it really a good idea to pen him up like this right now, and leave him with only his memories and regrets?

But his voice came back instantly. *"Sparky? Who came up with that—Myers?"*

Liz snickered but didn't bother to answer. Next to her, Myers said, "We're almost there."

Myers slowed, then turned off the pavement onto a dirt road. Liz lifted the radio to her mouth again. "We're leaving the main road, so hang on."

The truck hit a series of bumps, banging and rattling along a road whose dirt and rock-riddled surface was hidden by the soft-packed snow. Liz could hear the crate shifting, feel the truck lurch over a bump, then rattle again as the crate bounced in the back. She hoped Hellboy was holding on or he was going to

have more than horns for bumps on his head. As if he
could hear her thoughts, the radio crackled to life.
"This better be the place or I'll puke."

Myers braked and pulled over as the van he'd been
following stopped. Before he had the chance to shut
off the engine, Liz hopped out of the front and trudged
to the back of the truck, shifting from foot to foot impatiently until a couple of the other agents pried open
the crate. "Come out and see," she suggested as Hellboy squinted in the suddenly bright light.

He clambered out and shaded his eyes against the
painful white of the snow. "Sebastian Plackba #16,"
he said, when he could finally get a clear view of the
nineteenth-century cemetery in which they'd parked.
He let his gaze roam over their surroundings, taking in
everything from the broken, spiked fences covered in
rust and dead vines to the rows of crypts and tomb-
stones that meandered through the deeply piled snow
and the wild, winter-dormant foliage. There were
thick-branched trees everywhere, their limbs spidery
and leafless, like twisted fingers grasping for something out of reach in the cold sky.

Beside them, Agents Lime and Stone geared up,
strapping on their backpacks and grenade belts, then
equipping themselves with a flashlight in one hand
and a weapon in the other. With determined expressions on their faces, they picked one of the lanes leading into the labyrinthine lanes of the dead and headed

into it, trudging gamely through the deep snow. After a moment, Hellboy, Liz, Myers, and Manning followed, letting the rest of the agents bring up the rear.

Was it only an hour later that they stopped searching? No, it had to be three hours, or a day, or maybe it was a damned week. Who knew? They were all frustrated, irritated, and incredibly cold, stomping around in circles and crossing their own tracks, and they were probably lucky to find their way back to where they'd started before they all froze to death.

Exhaling slowly, Myers looked around again, trying to get some kind of clue as to how the addresses of the dead worked in this place. Even loaded down with two grenade belts—his own and Hellboy's—he was game for going back and trying again, but clearly Manning had reached his limit.

"Forget it," Manning said. His mouth was a thin, aggravated slash against skin gone red from the cold and a nose that was as wet and runny as a sled dog's. He'd been stomping through the snow and rubbing his hands together in an effort to stay warm for the last half hour. "This is practically a city. It stinks, and it's muddy. We'll go back, check into a hotel, and regroup after breakfast. We'll have to make a grid, go by quadrants. Maybe satellite photography." He gestured toward the vehicles and the other agents turned to go.

Hellboy folded his arms. "Let me ask for directions."

Manning and most of the others looked at Hellboy in amazement as he strode away, watching as he picked one of the nearby crypt entrances, peered at the writing for no particular reason, then shoved the stone top of it to the side. He waited patiently for the others to join him so they could see the rotting coffin about ten feet below, then dropped into the crypt. He landed to the side of the coffin and the already crumbling top broke away and exposed its contents—a mummified corpse dressed in a miserably tattered and mildew-stained suit.

Hellboy bowed his head for a moment, giving the body at his feet a modicum of respect. Then he dug around in one of his deep overcoat pockets until he found and pulled out a carved metal amulet. With precise movements, he leaned over and pressed the odd-shaped piece of metal hard to the cadaver's forehead as he whispered, "*Animan edere, animus corpus.*"

For a long moment, nothing happened. Then, just as Manning was about to remind Hellboy and the rest of them that he'd prohibited supernatural crap like this, the body spasmed and twisted. Incredibly, the jaw opened and the sunken, dried-out cheeks sucked in air to fill the dead thing's decayed lungs. One inhalation, then two, and the tongueless corpse managed to mutter a low string of Russian words:

"*Shto khochesh?*" ("*What do you want?*")

Manning gasped and stepped back from the opening as Hellboy lifted the body from its resting place and swung it up and onto his shoulders like it was nothing more out of the ordinary than a camping bag. He climbed out of the crypt, proudly showing off the prize to the rest of the gawking team. When he spoke, he sounded absurdly cheerful, considering he was toting around a dead man as baggage. "Sixty feet farther, comrades, and three rows in."

Liz's hand went to her mouth and her eyes widened as the corpse Hellboy was carrying twitched, then fought to briefly raise one weak hand. "This here is Ivan Klimentovich," Hellboy announced. "Say 'hi,' Ivan."

Once again, the corpse mumbled something in Russian. "*Idti tuda, krasnaya obizyanka.*" ("*Go that way, red monkey.*")

Hellboy obeyed, heading off easily through the drifting snow while the others followed with more difficulty. He went the requisite thirty yards, then turned left. One row, two, then three, and there it was.

Grigori Yefimovich Rasputin's mausoleum was impossible to miss . . . provided, of course, you'd been able to find it in the first place. Flashy in life, Rasputin had gone the same route in death. Marking the entrance to his final resting place—or at least to what the general populace *thought* was such—was a miniature black marble castle, complete with turrets and parapets, spires and fancy stonework around the entrance and the small, fake windows. It was pretty unbelievable that they'd missed it, but then the cold could do weird things to your sense of direction and time, not to mention body thermometer.

Hellboy stood back and let Myers go after the sealed entrance with a crowbar, and for all its postmortem pomp and glory, the agent was able to beat off the lock on the old steel door and get it open in less than a minute. Hellboy, still carrying the desiccated corpse of Ivan Klimentovich, led the way inside.

And, as such things always seemed to be, the inside of Rasputin's tomb was a hell of a lot bigger than the outside.

21

MANNING HAD ASSIGNED A COUPLE OF THE LARGER-framed agents to stand guard at the entrance to the mausoleum while Hellboy and the rest of the group carefully descended a narrow flight of wet, curving stone steps. It was an eerie and unsettling place, where the damp walls were lined with yellowed skulls and a sort of dim under-lighting that wasn't quite enough to let them actually see where they were going without their flashlights—even their feet were shrouded in blackness. The rest of them didn't notice, but Liz had slipped off her gloves and was enjoying running her fingers along the stone walls, relishing the feel of the icy moisture that coated her always-hot fingertips. She disliked the darkness in here—it was too much like perpetual nightfall—but the slick stonework smelled like wet concrete sidewalks after a good rain, and that was always high on her list of favorites. As long it didn't end up mixed with the scent of decomposing corpses, they'd be in good shape.

A few feet in front of Liz, Myers wasn't nearly so happy. He'd never had anything in particular against

cold, damp, dark places—well, other than they reminded him of tombs, which was exactly what this
was—but so far, every time he'd ended up somewhere
underground with Hellboy things had gone rapidly
to hell. Apparently this was becoming a habit, because now his damned flashlight was acting wonky,
flickering in and out, and he *knew* the thing had
fresh batteries, he had put them in himself. The
beam would flicker and he would shake the flashlight
and then it would be fine . . . then twenty seconds
later he'd have to do it all over again. By the fourth
time, he was ready to start banging the thing against
the stone wall.

Finally reaching the bottom of the staircase, they
all paused. What had looked like a small tomb at
ground level had turned into an underground
labyrinth—now three corridors branched off in different directions, and of course, none of them were particularly well lit. As Hellboy carefully deposited the
talking corpse amid a pile of moldering coffins against
the wall, the rest of the group stopped and looked
around uncertainly. "We'll be all right as long as we
don't separate," Hellboy began. "We—"

Wham!

With a clang of locking metal, a line of heavy steel
plates shot upward from the floor. Each was covered in
long spikes sharpened to a razor point, and in the
space of only a heartbeat the staircase behind them

was demolished and Hellboy, Manning, and Agent Stone were cut off from Myers and Liz.

And Agent Stone, who hadn't even had time to grunt in surprise, was dead.

For a long moment, Stone's corpse simply stood there, eyes blank and seeing an eternity that the others had yet to visit. Then blood gushed out of his mouth and eyes and he fell forward, exposing the shoulder-to-hip slashes along his back, wounds that went all the way through to the bone. When he flashed his light downward, Hellboy saw a scarlet puddle had surrounded the agent almost instantly, leaking between the barrier of metal plates. Hellboy heard Liz gasp and jerked his light back up, hoping she hadn't seen what was had happened to the man before the plates had come up.

Hellboy hammered on the plates, his blows barely falling in the dubious safety zone between the wicked, spike-studded surface. It was no good—the plates separating them had to be steel and were at least six inches thick. Surrendering, Hellboy thumbed the speaker on his walkie-talkie. "Okay, someone's expecting us," he said. "Turn on your locators. If anyone sees anything—"

"*Marco,*" Liz's voice came back.

Hellboy smiled a little. "Polo."

There was a static-filled pause, then Myers's voice came over the speaker. "*Are you sure about this?*"

Hellboy hesitated. "On a scale of one to ten? Two." He glanced at the steel wall again, just to reaffirm that he couldn't break through. Given the choice, he'd go it alone; rehashing that choice with Liz along as company, he'd turn back. This time, however, their path had been predetermined. "But she'll take care of you, Myers. She's a tough one."

Myers didn't answer, but as Hellboy listened, he could hear their footsteps fading on the other side. Turning away reluctantly, Hellboy swung the beam of his flashlight, and headed down the tunnel on the left. Manning followed as Agent Lime dubiously eyed Ivan's corpse reclining on the pile of coffins. After a moment, he picked it up and brought up the rear, trying not to break any of the dead man's fragile bones or breathe in the dust of the thing's disintegrating burial suit.

It felt like it took forever to get down this tunnel. No one talked, even though the going was pretty easy: a downward slope but not enough so that they stumbled, more skulls on the walls but by now they'd become used to that sight. Then the tunnel curved and ended abruptly, widening into a vast, underground chamber. Slavic motifs were etched into the archways spaced throughout, as well as around the rugged stone pillars that ran from the ground up to the faraway ceiling. Water, probably snowmelt, trickled down the rough walls and pooled on the uneven floor.

A few feet in front of them was a small, stone bridge, the only access from their location to a small hexagonal structure from which light poured. Hellboy glanced at it, then at Manning; without another word, the three of them stepped onto the bridge.

Something clanged, and they all jerked and looked upward. They could barely see the source, a heavy door far overhead that had released and dropped open. Now it was just hanging up there, like a big, hungry mouth.

Instinctively they surged forward on the bridge.

And from somewhere else . . .

Tick tick tick tick tick tick . . .

The sound of a massive clock? Unsure, Manning asked, "What's that?"

Hellboy gestured sharply for silence, trying to figure it out. Even so, the corpse muttered, *"Eto shto-to bol'shoye."* (*"It's something big."*)

Straining uselessly, they stared into the darkness that spread beyond the feeble beams of their flashlights. "We should go back," Manning said finally. "You," he nodded in Hellboy's direction, "you could tear that door apart."

Tick tick tick tick tick tick . . .

Hellboy stood where he was, still listening, his immense frame stopping them from going any farther. "Don't move," he said. "We—"

"—should go back," Manning finished for him. *"Now."*

But Hellboy wasn't moving. "No," he said stubbornly. "Don't—"

"*I'm* in charge," Manning snapped. "We go *back*."

Before he could continue, Hellboy reached out and yanked Manning forward. Manning squawked in surprise, then—

Sssssshhhhhhssssssssshhhhh

—wheezed as a gigantic metal pendulum swung right through the space in which he'd been standing only a second before. The honed bottom edge of it sliced through the stone bridge as though the structure were made of butter, demolishing nearly everything on the other side of it. The deceptively fragile stonework crumbled into oblivion, taking Agent Lime and Ivan's corpse with it; the corpse went silently, but Agent Lime's scream as he fell into the darkness seemed like it would last forever. Maybe, in their memories, it would.

Except for one minor thing.

On the far end of the bridge in front of them, something else clanged in the darkness. The faintest glimmer of movement caught their eye—another overhead steel door, this one shuddering downward on a direct line to block their escape.

Hellboy grimaced. "Son of a—"

Sssssshhhhhhssssssssshhhhh

The two of them heard the pendulum start its reverse swing. They sprinted toward the lowering door, barely managing to get out of the way of the slightly altered arc of the massive blade. More of the crude stone bridge shattered, and there sure wasn't a whole lot left to stand on. Hellboy gave Manning a little bit of a shove to send him in front and Manning took advantage of the momentum to launch himself on all fours through the rapidly shrinking entryway. Hellboy followed, then tripped and nearly went down as the stone pathway fell apart beneath each of his heavy footfalls.

Ssssshhhhhhsssssssshhhhh

The pendulum's final swing took out the last bit of bridge on which Hellboy was standing—

—but he was in midair by then, leaping as hard and long as he could—

—and just making it through the opening into the hexagonal building.

For a few tense moments, all Hellboy and Manning could do was stand in the nearly complete darkness and hold their breath. They had left behind certain death, but what waited for them now? Ultimately, they had no choice but to go forward and find out.

Wary of any more ambushes, Hellboy let the beam of his flashlight dance around them, thwacking his hand on both sides when he swung too wide. Apparently they were in some kind of an extremely narrow, arched corridor constructed of the same stone material as the bridge outside had been. The

light they'd seen while on the bridge must have
been some kind of an illusion, a lure to get them in
here, because now it was gone. Instead of the seemingly endless nothing that had surrounded them out
there, this section's walls were lined with endless
rows of rusty steel blades. While not very well taken
care of, this was obviously the compilation of a very
serious collector.

From somewhere past the dark tunnel came the
faintest traces of music—Wagner, "Liebestod" from
Tristan und Isolde. Stepping cautiously, they moved
toward the sound, listening to the notes getting louder
and louder as they progressed, at last getting a glimpse
at the growing source of illumination farther down the
line. Finally, they could just make out Kroenen,
bathed in yellow gaslight and nodding attentively to
the music while above him a series of deadly-looking
ropes, hooks, and pulleys swayed to an underground
breeze. The sight of Kroenen made Hellboy's jaw
grind. He remembered the last time he'd seen the
guy—lying dead, or so he'd assumed, in the tunnel
next to the badly injured Agent Clay. He should've
made sure then, should've rearranged the dust-filled
body into so many pieces that it couldn't be put back
together.

They crept forward, with Hellboy leading the way.
It was hard to see, and the darkness at their feet made
it all the more treacherous, making it seem as if they

were losing their balance at any given time. Every time they looked at the spot of brightness, it would blind them for a moment, leave them with nothing in front of their eyes but dancing nightspots. As luck would have it, at one point, Manning *did* stumble; instinctively, he threw out a hand to catch himself and his fingers found the wall . . . and the sharp edge of one of the blades hanging there.

"Ouch!"

The word—that single, small utterance—bounced through the narrow tunnel as though Manning had brayed it into a megaphone. They were still hidden by the darkness of the tunnel, but up ahead they both saw Kroenen sit up, his skeletal, mask-covered head swiveling as he tried to pinpoint the location of the noise. Without moving any other part of his body, he lifted a hand and quietly began to wind up the gears on his chest.

Great.

They were almost to the end of the tunnel and Hellboy shot Manning a dirty look. Manning at least had the good grace to look sheepish, but when Hellboy looked back—

Kroenen was gone.

"Crap," Hellboy muttered over his shoulder. "This guy moves like a cockroach."

Just to be ready, Hellboy drew his gun and crept forward with Manning close on his heels. They left the tunnel behind almost reluctantly; at least in there they'd had an overhead surface providing cover; out here they were in a sort of lab, with lots of shadowy areas up by the ceiling and way too many objets d'pain that could drop onto their heads at any moment. To add to the aggravation, the floor was made of decrepit, squeaky, wooden planks—masking their footsteps was damned near impossible. The Wagner piece stopped as the needle ran to the end of the old vinyl record and the room dropped into sudden, unnerving silence.

Both Hellboy and Manning jerked at the sound of blades slicing through the air. They tried to dodge, but Manning simply didn't make it in time; he cried out as one of Kroenen's short swords ripped deeply into the meat of his arm. Manning staggered backward as blood swelled from the wound and he automatically clutched at it, too shocked to try to block Kroenen's next strike. The skeletal man went in for the kill—

And Hellboy thrust his stone hand between the blade and Manning's throat.

Sparks danced off the edge of the sword, and Kroenen struck again, and then again. Each time Hellboy blocked, moving forward until he was a protective shield for Manning, forcing Kroenen backward. There was no way to tell what was going on behind Kroenen's mask, but finally the zombie-Nazi tossed his two short swords aside in frustration, then unsheathed the longer, more vicious-looking one strapped at his waist.

"Screw that!" Hellboy snapped. As fast as Kroenen was, he didn't get the sword out of range before Hellboy reached out and yanked it from his grip. Snarling, Hellboy brought it up and bent it until it snapped, then flung the pieces away. Kroenen started to backpedal and Hellboy hit him brutally, right in the center of the man's leather-and-steel mask. The metal crumpled and the two lenses covering Kroenen's eyes disintegrated into starred glass.

"You killed my father!" Hellboy said furiously, then hit him again, and again. Kroenen staggered backward with each blow, but he still wouldn't *fall*. Hellboy punched him a final time and the remains of the mask went flying, revealing Kroenen's hideously scarred face. "Give your soul to God," Hellboy hissed at him. "Your ass is *mine!*"

Incredibly, Kroenen erupted into laughter. The sound was like a series of asthmatic wheezes, short, sharp, and completely unexpected.

Hellboy had maybe a half second to register that something was wrong, then the floor fell out from under him.

A trapdoor! Manning went down with him, followed by the clunky antique phonograph. Hellboy's stone hand shot out and closed around a rope just as his other hand found Manning's wrist and locked around it. The rope slid downward, feeding through a copper pulley somewhere overhead; then it stopped with a bone-rattling wrench as a knot in its length lodged in the pulley. Hellboy's backpack jerked free and dropped away, following the phonograph into the darkness somewhere below.

Silence . . . then a couple of seconds later, the phonograph hit the ground below them with a resounding crash. Hellboy and Manning hung there, and Hellboy could hear Manning panting below him. "Well," Manning managed to whisper, "it's not *that* big a fall—"

Before Hellboy could reply, a harsh series of clangs reverberated below their feet. More metal—that stuff seemed to be a habit around Kroenen and his creepy buddies—and when the two of them stretched their necks so they could see the ground, it was bristling with sparkling steel spikes that were at least six feet tall.

Wonderful.

Dangling in the darkness, Hellboy waited.

It wasn't long before his patience paid off. Oh yeah—there was Kroenen, peering over the edge of the trapdoor like an ugly-eyed spider, trying to see what he could see, listening for any kind of a sound. *Come on*, Hellboy thought. *Just a little more . . .*

With Manning now hanging off the back of his

utility belt like a heavy monkey, Hellboy threw the
length of rope that had been dangling below him up
and over Kroenen's head, catching the monster man
in a nice, tidy loop. Hellboy yanked him forward as
hard as he could, but Kroenen wasn't going to be as
easy as Hellboy had assumed; before he'd gone three
inches, Kroenen had a blade in each hand and he
drove them into the floor, giving himself a good, solid
anchor. But Hellboy had alternate plans, too, and that
hold was just what Hellboy needed; keeping a die-
hard hold on the lasso around Kroenen's neck, Hellboy pulled himself up the rope, hand over hand,
heading up and out of the pit.

With his lipless mouth pulled back into a grotesque
slash across the lower half of his skull, Kroenen
brought up one of his blades and swung the sharp end
toward the rope.

"Oh, no you don't," Hellboy growled. With a fast
double-loop of the rope around the wrist of his stone
fist, he pulled down as hard as he could. His remaining
knife-anchor just wasn't enough to hold him there,
and Kroenen gagged and fell forward, tumbling over
the edge of the trapdoor.

He screamed all the way down and landed headfirst
on the spikes, wriggling like a fish caught on a hook.
But every movement only made it worse and sent him
sliding farther down the blades. He was thoroughly
and completely stuck.

Hellboy turned his attention to the hatch in the floor above him and began hauling himself and Manning upward. Finally catching the edge, he dragged himself and his cargo over, then sat for a moment as Manning let go of his utility belt and rolled away. Hellboy's gaze fastened on something off to the side— one of Kroenen's blades, firmly embedded in the floor. At its back end was Kroenen's prosthetic hand, still ticking and twitching away. It could mean only one thing.

The fiend was still alive.

Peering over the edge of the trapdoor, Hellboy could just see Kroenen. He'd already freed one arm by slicing through his own bicep—strands of dried-out muscle hung from the stump like dirty pieces of rope. The monster would probably free himself by chopping off half his body, then sewing himself together out of someone else's parts.

Not this time.

Hellboy got to his feet and glared down at the struggling Kroenen. "You like playing possum, you Nazi pinhead?" he growled. Hellboy took two strides to the right, where a massive cogwheel had been pushed out of the way. He got a solid grip on the piece of machinery's edge and with a grunt, hauled it over to the opening in the floor. With a cry of satisfaction, he forced it over the edge. "Then try playing *dead*."

Kroenen had just enough time for a blood-freezing scream before he was crushed completely.

Hellboy watched as Manning tore pieces off the bottom of his custom-made dress shirt and carefully bandaged his gashed arm. He had to admit that it looked pretty painful—cut to the bone, blood soaked through the covering almost immediately and it was definitely going to need a whole bunch of stitches. Even so, the guy seemed to be taking it like a trooper.

"Are you okay?" Hellboy finally asked. When Manning gave him a weak but stubborn nod, Hellboy dug in his belt and found a cigar stump, stuck it between his lips, and fired up his Zippo. "You'd better stay here," he decided. "I'll find a way out, and we'll come back for you."

For a moment, Manning only watched him. Finally he asked, "You call that thing a cigar?" He seemed to have found a little strength to put into his voice.

Hellboy's eyebrows raised and he chewed on the stump a little for good measure. "Yup."

Manning shook his head, disgusted. "You never, *ever* light a cigar that way." As Hellboy watched, Manning pulled out one of his own fine cigars, snipped off the end with a clipper he dug out of his pants pocket, then held it out. "Use a wooden match," he said. "It preserves the flavor."

Hellboy took the offered cigar and ground out his stump. When Manning held out a lit match, he was more than willing to take him up on the offer. The smoothness of the tobacco gift was a definite pleasure, and he grinned.

"Thank you," Manning said solemnly.

But Hellboy only grinned. "My job."

22

LIZ AND MYERS PICKED THEIR WAY FORWARD IN AN-
other narrow, stone-and-earth-walled tunnel in a different part of the underground tomb. Littered with
rocks and bits of the crumbling stone walls, this one
wasn't nearly as smooth-sailing as the one that Hellboy and Manning had headed off in. To make sure
that things stayed on the challenging side, it wasn't
long before the two of them came face-to-face with a
cave-in that made them eye the ceiling and walls
nervously, then compare it with the bits of ceiling,
rocks, timber, coffins, and corpses that formed the
chaotic barrier that now blocked their way. After a
moment of hesitation, they decided to squeeze past
the debris, taking advantage of a thin opening on one
side of the pile.

"So," Myers said as he led the way, "he thinks that
you and I . . ." He hesitated, then decided to skip
over the details. He rushed on. "That's why he's mad
at me."

Moving sideways, Myers slid a few inches farther
through the space next to the cave-in. Liz was right

next to him, moving in tandem. A few small bones rolled down the debris in front of her and wet earth trickled down and over their shoulders. Both drew their arms tightly against their body, pointing their beams at the ground. For some reason, Myers thought it felt oddly intimate, and it gave him the courage to blurt out his next question.

"But . . . it's not true, is it?"

He couldn't see her face in the darkness, but Myers could hear the surprise in Liz's voice, feel it in the blank silence that fell before she finally asked, "What?"

He took a deep breath. "That you feel the same way about me."

There was a second of dead silence, then she asked, "You want to know that? *Now?*" He sensed more than saw her shake her head in disbelief, heard her impatient exhalation. "Red, white . . . whatever. Guys are *all* the same."

Myers clamped his mouth shut, feeling like an idiot. Finally getting past the cave-in, he and Liz could turn and walk normally. He heard her behind him, but embarrassment kept him from saying anything more about the subject of him and her . . . if there *was* a subject at all, and he certainly didn't have the guts to turn and look at her right now.

Abruptly the tunnel widened and unpleasantly cold water filled their shoes. Myers found his footing but it wasn't good; he turned and shined his light down on the water to light Liz's way as she angled her foot toward a large stone. "Watch out," he said. "It's slippery."

Damn—there went his light again, shorting out. He shook it, then banged it against his leg, but this time it did no good. Without being asked, Liz stepped around him and aimed her flashlight beam into the darkness.

"Oh, my *God*," she breathed.

Myers jerked around, his flashlight banging hard against the wall. Suddenly the beam came on, spilling a good, solid cone of light into a large, natural cavern circling out from the tunnel entrance they'd just exited. Facing them, glittering in the double line of light like a curtain of amber beads, was an entire wall of translucent eggs.

A movement to the right drew their attention and Liz and Myers automatically turned their flashlights that way. What they saw made them freeze: Sammael, pallid and slimy, squatted in the water like a filthy, feral dog, gnawing ambitiously on a human arm bone. At the end of the bone jiggled a ragged human hand, still seeping blood. Sammael's milky pupils constricted when the glow of the lights crossed his eyes; clutching the dismembered arm in one clawed hand, he snarled at them with a red-soaked mouth.

The sound brought more company—another Sammael rose from the brackish water, shaking its marble-white skin like a wet animal. Then a third one lifted its blue-veined head, presenting Myers and Liz with a trio of impending death.

They didn't need a discussion to know they had to get the hell out of there, but when Liz and Myers turned to run—

Clank!

Too late. The rusted hulk of a previously unseen metal door surged up from beneath the water, cutting off any hope of escape. Trapped, they had no choice but to stand and fight.

Myers whirled and grabbed for a pair of the explosive grenades, but before he could set the timer on one, a handful of claws raked them from his grasp, cutting deeply into his flesh in more than one place. He cried out and clutched at the bloodied, torn fabric across his midsection, then toppled into the groundwater and rolled away, sputtering and coughing.

Heart hammering, Liz jammed her finger against the Talk button on her walkie-talkie. "Marco! Marco!" she said urgently. The triple Sammaels were tracking her and Myers, their albino eyes narrowing hungrily. Didn't these things *ever* stop eating?

"Get your Big Red butt over here *now!*"

He'd left the injured Manning behind, and now Hellboy was in a steep tunnel, the only other way out of the hexagonal room. The ground had gradually inclined until he'd ended up on enough of an upward slope that he had to labor to climb it, pulling himself along on the more sturdy rocks and roots. Finally it leveled out enough for him to catch his breath.

Except he was at a dead end.

Wait . . . *there*. On the ground a few inches to his right. It was a crack, thin but still wide enough to let Hellboy see the vaguest hint of light. Was that voices? Curious, he pressed one ear to the ground. Yes, definitely—Liz and Myers, and they were right below him. Suddenly the radio on his belt squealed to life, and he was hearing Liz's panicked cry from both directions at once—through the ground below him *and* through the puny speaker in the walkie-talkie.

"Marco! Marco! Get your Big Red butt over here now!"

He couldn't see anything through the crack, but there was no mistaking the urgency in her voice. With the dead-end wall in front of him and the way back to absolutely nothing behind him, Hellboy chose the only way that would get him to Liz. He leaned over and began to pound furiously on the floor with his stone hand. "Hang on, kid—I'm coming for you!"

Wham Wham Wham!

Three tremendous strikes later, the rocks began to crumble. Two more—

Wham Wham!

—and he could see Liz and Myers below, and the sight didn't bring him any comfort. They were caught in a circle of Sammaels, four of them, and there was no way they were getting out alive without some Hellboy help. For a second, Hellboy was mesmerized as Myers yanked out his gun and shot the one that had crept the closest. Three shots, three hits, all in the head . . . and although the creature backed up a few feet, it shook off the bullets as though the agent had pelted it with pebbles.

The Sammael to that one's left sprang for Myers at the same Hellboy put his full weight into a mighty stomp on the already weakened floor. It gave way and crashed down, dumping a good ton or two of stone onto the creature in midair, with Hellboy adding his own not insubstantial weight to the mix. He landed hard but unhurt, then bounded to his feet with his fists up and ready, but the creature was crushed.

Hellboy saw Liz jerk at something behind him and realized that two of the eggs on the wall were glowing, already pulsing with life and metamorphosing into new Sammaels at terrifying speed. In a matter of seconds, where there had been three Sammaels left, now there were five.

As the one nearest Liz turned its sickly gaze on her, Hellboy gestured at her to flee. She followed his lead instantly, dashing to safety before the creature could start in her direction. Hellboy whirled and caught

Myers's eye. "Sorry," he couldn't help quipping. "Just couldn't leave you two alone!" Before Myers could retort, Hellboy scooped him up and sprinted to where Liz crouched, dropping him in what he hoped was a safe place . . . for now.

As he started to turn back, he saw Myers's eyes widen when the man's flashlight beam caught something behind Hellboy. He had time only to grunt before one of the Sammaels leaped onto his back and another clamped its sharp, pointed teeth around his leg. The damned thing bit down and *chewed*, making Hellboy howl in surprise and pain. As the third one joined the fray and the fourth looked for a way into the pile, Hellboy felt like a zebra being brought down by a pride of lions.

But this time, the zebra was going to fight back.

Somewhere between the punching and the biting, he got his hand free and dragged out his gun. A squeeze of the trigger put a round dead center into the chest of the one gnawing on his leg and its teeth fell away with the rest of its dead body . . . but barely five seconds later, two took the place of the one that had fallen.

His torso covered with blood, Hellboy pounded and snarled and fought for all he was worth. But when the two newly born Sammaels sprang on top of him, even he knew he was in a world of trouble way too deep for him to get free.

* * *

Liz's own fear was paralyzing her.

She watched in frozen horror as Hellboy was covered by the Sammael creatures, as they beat him and clawed him, as their teeth tore into his red-tinted flesh and coated it with the darker liquid of his lifeblood. He had done this for her—taken their attack onto himself—and he would die to protect her.

And all she could do was stand here, with her heart jackhammering in her chest and her breath coming in short gasps, her eyes bulging but with only the barest ripple of heat shimmering over her body. Why? *Why,* damn it? She wasn't positive—hell, she wasn't even thinking *clearly*—but she had an inkling of the answer: fear wasn't the trigger.

Anger was.

Myers had managed to claw his way upright again. Now, dripping and bleeding and badly hurt, he was all but helpless to do anything to assist Hellboy. Without taking her gaze from the battle raging in front of her, Liz swatted Myers on the arm to pull his attention away from the losing battle going on a few yards away. "Hit me," she ordered.

Despite his injuries and his pale, pain-soaked face, Myers still gaped at her. *"What?"*

"Hit me," she repeated. When he still only stared, she said, "All my life I've run away from it. Now I *want* it to happen—*do it!"*

They both jerked as Hellboy screamed beneath the pile of attacking creatures. Water exploded from underneath the writhing bodies, and suddenly two of the Sammaels turned their attention toward Liz and Myers.

Even so, Myers shook his head. "I-I *can't*. I—"

Liz slapped him, and Myers gasped in shock. "I know now," she told him in a nearly singsong voice. "I love *him*. I've always loved *him*."

Myers swallowed and stared at her. Liz could see in his face that her words had stung, but she knew it still wouldn't be enough to make him strike her. *Nothing* she said or did would *ever* be enough—he was that kind of man. But she could also see that he would do what she asked because it was the only thing that would save Hellboy, and her, and only as a side part of it, himself.

She saw the muscle in his jaw tense, then he pulled back his hand and smacked her hard across the face.

There was a sudden . . . *pulse* around the both of them, a rise in heat that was enough to make the air shimmer in a circle like a desert mirage at the high heat of summer. She wasn't *really* angry, but the effect she'd wanted was there—her body was going to react as though she was. The air around Liz actually vibrated and abruptly her pupils glowed and reflected red light, the crimson eyes of an animal caught by the flash of a camera. Amazingly, she even managed to send a faint smile in Myers's direction. "Go now," she instructed him in a deceptively gentle voice.

He didn't need to be told twice.

Myers found himself a spot in the hollow of the ground and behind an oversized rock just as Liz's arm suddenly blazed with fire. The two Sammaels that had abandoned the attack on Hellboy were almost upon her, and she faced them fearlessly and calmly, with her lips pulled back in a hellish expression that might have been grin or grimace. Somewhere in the mist of her vision she saw one of the Sammaels that was on top of Hellboy pause and raise its head. The movement might have been curiosity or fear, like prey hearing the hunter's first gunshot.

Despite the weight of the creatures trying to keep him down, Hellboy managed to stagger to his feet and turn toward her, just in time to see her body shake in a surge of white-hot energy. The best he could manage was a weak, "Liz—"

The water at her feet blasted outward as a concave shockwave of fire exploded outward and devoured every single thing in its path.

Something was ringing in his ears.

No, wait—it was a pulse, a . . . something. A heartbeat, that was it. His own heartbeat.

Hellboy sucked in air painfully, then nearly retched at the stench of smoke and cooked flesh. It felt like it took every bit of strength he had left just to throw off the weight of the two dead Sammaels still draped over him like an unwanted blanket; the sight of their half-charred bodies made Hellboy gag and crawl away, but when he struggled to his feet and staggered forward, he crashed into a pile of blackened bones, yet another Sammael corpse, this one grilled almost beyond recognition. His mouth was cracked and dry, coated inside and out with ash—water would have been a great and wonderful thing, but it was a sure bet he wouldn't find any around here. There was a faint orange-and-red glow left over from the conflagration, and for as far as he could see, nearly everything was half-buried in a cracked, bone-dry bed of mud.

He spied Liz a few feet away and headed toward her, intending to move faster than he found he actually could. Hellboy's legs felt like toasted petrified logs, but at least he was alive, at least *she* was alive, too. On the far side of the room he caught a glimpse of Myers, okay but a little singed around the edges as he clawed his way out from behind a rock, and too groggy to acknowledge anything. Hellboy shook his head, but he still couldn't hear anything—Liz's firestorm had knocked out his hearing. Hopefully it would come back, but in the meantime . . .

He turned around, his eyes widening. Only a few feet away was Grigori, bare-chested and resplendent in his black robes. Amazingly, the man was *laughing;*

Hellboy couldn't hear it, but he could see Grigori's face working, watch his wide-stretched smile expose teeth and his thin body shake with mirth, as though the dark man was witnessing some absurd comedy.

Something, instinct perhaps, made Hellboy twist around and look to the side.

Just in time to see the coldly beautiful Ilsa raise her hammer and, in a simple and brutal move, whack him solidly on top of the head.

23

Hellboy lifted his head—

Headache.

—slowly. His skull felt like a big old piece of lead balanced on his neck, and there was a certain spot right in the top center that was throbbing worse than the rest of it. What the hell had happened? Oh yeah . . . that walking blond iceberg had smacked him with something hard. A hammer, that was it. Being hit with a hammer . . . now *that* ticked him off.

Hellboy started to raise a hand to his head, then found he couldn't. He moved his head a little too quickly as he tried to see why and got a significant stab of discomfort across the crown of his scalp; painful but not debilitating, and it was lessening as the seconds passed. But why couldn't he move?

His eyes were still squeezed shut and he forced them open and tried to blink away the double dose of grogginess caused by Liz's firestorm and Ilsa's blow. Man, he was learning he really had to watch out for the women in his life.

A few more seconds and feeling was coming back

to his limbs. Until now he hadn't realized he wasn't actually sitting; rather, he was standing and chained firmly to some kind of massive wooden yoke. He tested the chains but they held, and besides, he wasn't at full strength yet. But when he got there . . .

In the meantime, Hellboy studied his surroundings. More chambers, more space—Rasputin's tomb must be full of catacombs and secret places. This latest one was large and churchlike, surrounded by dozens of funeral niches; in each alcove stood a shadowy, crumbling statue holding a sword aloft, and no doubt every single stiff statue had some great and secret meaning. Spaced evenly around the room were tall stone and marble columns, several of which flanked a number of huge mechanical gears. Hellboy would have chalked the machinery up to being more leftovers from Kroenen's crazed preoccupations except that in the center of everything, where in a normal church an altar might be, was some kind of huge solar system model. It glittered and shimmered in the oil lamps set around the space's high ceiling.

A noise bled into his eardrums as his hearing returned, small, rhythmic thuds undercut with the sounds of delicate glass breaking. Still blinking, Hellboy followed the sound and saw Ilsa; she'd set out all the grenade belts and was methodically working on destroying the timer on each grenade with that nasty hammer of hers. So much for the grenades as an artillery option.

Hellboy's vision was clearing and his thinking process was rapidly doing the same. His searching gaze eventually found Myers, tied to a stone pillar next to the main nave. Although the front of him was heavily stained with blood, the agent didn't look that badly hurt—at least not much more than he'd been back in the egg chamber—but Hellboy had doubts about what the future held for the guy; beneath Myers's feet was a channel clearly meant for blood, and it led to an immense slab that looked like it was made of polished white marble. Slabs were never a good thing, and big slabs were even worse.

But where the hell was Liz?

Over there, and didn't it just figure that the man standing over her was the gloomy guy himself, Grigori. Lying at his feet, Liz was clearly unconscious. Dressed in black ceremonial robes, Grigori had his back to Hellboy, but Hellboy could still see that the man was reading from an open, ancient leather book. Splayed across the wall in front of him in cracked paint was a mural of the angel Abbadon. In the mural, the figure had lots of dark, curly hair, spiky wings and proudly held a key aloft.

Grigori lifted his chin and spoke in a booming voice. "And I looked and beheld an angel, and in his hand was the key to the bottomless pit!"

What was this—a sacrifice? Of *Liz*? Hellboy tensed, his headache forgotten along with the hundreds of Sammael injuries along the rest of his body. He could feel fury building inside him, heating up his insides, making his blood pound in his veins.

A few feet away, Grigori waved grandly at the huge piece of marble, and for the first time, Hellboy realized that even though Grigori wasn't facing him, the guy knew very well that he was conscious. "These were the words I heard as a peasant boy in Tobolsk," Grigori said. "And now, that door . . ." He stopped for a moment and inclined his head respectfully toward the marble slab. "Sent by the Ogdru Jahad so that they might at long last enter our world."

Finished with the grenade belts, Ilsa put away her hammer and strode up to where Hellboy was chained. She stared at him with an expression that was almost adoration. "*You* are the key!" she told him excitedly. "The right hand of doom!"

Hellboy scowled at her, but his gaze was drawn inexorably back to the marble slab. For the first time, he noticed the engravings on it, the three hand imprints.

"What did you think it was made for?" Ilsa demanded triumphantly. She gestured at it jerkily. "Go on—open the locks!"

Hellboy stared first at her, then at his own huge right arm. Was he seeing what he thought he was seeing? Was this really what this part of his own body had been made for? He knew he shouldn't but at the same time, there was that continuous curiosity, that itch that screamed to be scratched. What exactly would happen if he did?

Myers's voice momentarily cut into Hellboy's thoughts. "Don't do it!" Myers yelled. "Don't do it!" The agent pulled frantically at the ropes holding him and scrambled his feet along the floor, but it was useless—he couldn't get free.

Ilsa took two long steps and kicked the agent hard in the face. "Silence!" she snarled. Myers's head snapped back against the pillar and blood sprayed from his nose and lips, but he didn't pass out. Still full of fight, Myers spat a mouthful of blood at her in retaliation, but Ilsa had already moved out of range.

Far above them, a metal dome slid open, revealing the huge, bloated-looking moon. As Hellboy twisted his neck and stared up at it, the moon's lower left edge suddenly grayed out—the start of a full lunar eclipse. The solar system panel monitored the eclipse's progress, ticking along as the bright surface of the moon was slowly consumed by darkness.

Ilsa sidled up to Hellboy and gave him a radiant, sinister smile. "Imagine it," she cooed. "An Eden for you and—" She pointed at the still unconscious Liz. "*Her.*"

Hellboy ground his teeth. "No."

Surprised, Grigori turned to face Hellboy at last.

"No?" He tilted his head, then gestured at Liz with his palm up, like a benevolent saint pardoning a sinner. His voice was calm, utterly reasonable. "In exchange for her life, then," he told Hellboy. "Open the door."

Her life? For a stupid *door*? No—that couldn't be. Things couldn't come to that, this couldn't actually be happening. Was it? But he couldn't open that door, he *wouldn't*. It was a tormenting thing to have to do, but Hellboy shook his head. *No.*

Instead of looking angry, Grigori's expression was one of infinite patience. "As you wish." His voice was almost sad. He crouched next to Liz, then leaned forward until his face was directly over hers. A slight tilt to the side and Grigori whispered something in Liz's ear that Hellboy couldn't hear.

Liz's body suddenly arched high enough to see the space between the small of her back and the ground. When her mouth opened, a bright plume of energy, red and delicate, wafted from her lips and Grigori pulled back and greedily inhaled it. A flash between her mouth and his, and as quickly as it had tensed, Liz's body went limp.

"She'd dead," Grigori said simply.

For a moment, Hellboy lost everything—his thoughts, his air, his heartbeat. Then he found it all again . . . and screamed. "*No! Noooooooooo—*" He surged against the chains that held him, but only one gave way. Ilsa, with her cold, evil smile, was a little too close; Hellboy gave her a swat that sent her stumbling backward and clutching at her face.

While Hellboy fought to free his other hand, Grigori stood and watched the eclipse, seemingly indifferent to Hellboy's torment. Without taking his gaze from the disappearing moon, Grigori told Hellboy, "Her soul awaits you on the other side. If you want her back . . ." Finally his eyes grazed Hellboy's struggling figure. "Open the door and claim her."

No matter what he tried or how hard he pulled, the chain around Hellboy's other wrist still held him fast—they must have put a spell on it, strengthened it with something that Hellboy couldn't fight. Grigori's words reverberated in his brain, each repetition becoming louder than the last.

"Open the door and claim her."

But then, what about the rest of the world? What about Myers, and the B.P.R.D., and all the innocent blood that would be spilled at the hands of something unnameable that might be set free? Did he even *know* what that was?

Not a clue.

But if he didn't do what Grigori wanted, then Liz was gone forever. Irretrievable. *Dead.*

Still tugging futilely at the chain, Hellboy tried just as hard to find an answer to his dilemma . . . but he couldn't. Abruptly the room darkened, and when he looked up, he realized the moon was almost totally eclipsed. There was no more time left for decision making.

It was now or never.

Liz . . .

Hellboy dropped his gaze back to Liz's still, silent form. When he spoke, his voice was a hoarse whisper. *"For her."*

Grigori looked away from the moon, then stepped over Liz and moved close to Hellboy. His mouth twisted as he saw Broom's rosary wrapped around Hellboy's wrist, and with a sneer he ripped it free and tossed it behind him; it slid to within a few feet of where Myers was still bound to one of the stone pillars.

Grigori's dark eyes were shining like pits of oil as he studied Hellboy. "Names hold the power and nature of things," he told Hellboy solemnly. "Mine, for example—Rasputin. *The crossroads.*" He smiled thinly. "And the crossroads I have become." He glanced up at the moon, then turned back to Hellboy. The tone of his voice dropped to a deep bass rumble. "Your true name," he intoned. "*Anung-un-Rama.* Repeat it. Become the key!"

Hellboy swallowed and glanced at Myers. The agent was shaking his head violently—

No no no no no!

—but Hellboy couldn't help him now, he couldn't help anyone but Liz. He didn't *want* to. The best he could do was hope that once he'd done what he had to in order to let Liz live again, he could somehow *undo* it on the other end.

He closed his eyes and took a deep breath.

"*Anun-un-Rama* . . ."

And then everything changed.

Suddenly, his stone hand went kiln-red and a line of ancient symbols of fire burned themselves around the heavy stone. For a short, stunning moment, as flames engulfed his entire body, he knew exactly what Liz felt like in her moments of supreme glory.

Hellboy roared as power and heat coursed through his body and huge, majestic horns, larger than any he'd ever had or imagined he would, burst from the nubs he'd kept so carefully shaven all these years. His voice was loud enough to shake the walls of the cavernous room and clouds of light and energy boiled out of his mouth.

Myers's jaw dropped open as he cringed back against his post and stared at Hellboy. No, not Hellboy, but someone . . . some*thing* different—

The new Prince of Hell.

Inebriated with power, unstoppable, Hellboy freed his other chained arm with barely a thought. Consumed with arrogance and fire, he smiled as he strode forth and looked down on everyone else in the room. His shadow fell across the edge of the ancient white marble slab, then crept across the marble's surface on its own accord and stayed, until it had completely covered the surface and turned it as black as obsidian.

"No—don't do it!" Myers screamed from where he was imprisoned. *"Listen to me!"*

Smiling widely, the new Hellboy ignored the FBI agent and instead jammed his enormous hand into the first imprint on the slab, seated it firmly—

Clack!

—and twisted it.

A beam of light, crimson and thick, shot from the slab into the sky. Strong enough to be visible all over Moscow, strong enough to reach all the way to the darkened side of the moon, it bathed everything in a red, dirty glow. Symbols began to flicker in and out of view on each side of it, etching fire-tinged symbols into the very air. The red column of light spread, crawling outward to cut into the universe itself, rippling everything around it and haloing anything that was its own source of light. The sky was a vast ocean of stars beyond the ruby pillar of brightness, where something darker and unseen began to stir from a long-uninterrupted slumber.

Hellboy reborn watched with glee as the first imprint on the slab sizzled, then reformed into a strange, twisted glyph burned into the stone in scarlet. Overhead, far out of range of sight or reason but still *sensed*, the unspeakably enormous creature called Ogdru Jahad—the Seven Gods of Chaos—shifted and broke free, uncurling its gelatinous limbs, expanding and reaching . . .

With his face split into a wide, hellish grin, Hellboy thrust his stone hand into the second imprint—

Clack!

—and turned.

Watching in horror and disbelief, Myers refused to surrender to the idea that this was it, this was the end of . . . well, the end of *everything*. It took all of his strength and more flexibility than he'd ever dreamed he possessed, but Myers finally got one arm free of the flesh-grating ropes wound around him. Looking frantically, his gaze stopped on the rosary a foot or so away; people always says good things come in small packages, and size-wise, this sure wasn't much . . . but it was going to have to do it *all*.

Up at the altar's solar control panel, Grigori lifted his arms toward the wide expanse of sky visible through the open door. Lightning crackled across the heavens, skirting around the streaming scarlet light and sending flashes of electricity onto the impossibly gargantuan tentacles that were just beginning their reach into the earthly plane. Reveling in the first signs of the otherworldly arrival, Grigori sucked in air and began to laugh manically. *"The final seal!"* he shrieked. *"OPEN IT!"*

Myers wasn't sure if Hellboy heard Grigori's command or if he was just acting on his own volition.

The diabolic smile that had grown with the turning of each portion of the slab had widened so much that it now looked as though the top and bottom of Hellboy's skull might split; his horns were huge and sharp, glistening blood-red in the light. Just as Myers closed his hand around the rosary, Hellboy shoved his stone hand forward and fit it into the last engraving—

Clank!

When Ilsa saw Myers lift the holy necklace, she lunged at him. Without pausing, he slugged her full in the face, hard enough to send her staggering backward until she went down. He held up the rosary triumphantly, then, hoping he was in time, flung it at Hellboy with all his might, screaming, *"Remember who you ARE!"*

Caught in the millisecond pause before the final turn, the reborn Hellboy snagged it instinctively out of midair with his free hand. When his red fingers folded around it, smoke poured from between his fingers and he automatically tossed it away, not noticing that it landed next to the grenade belts with the destroyed timers.

Instead of turning the final imprint, Hellboy opened his palm and stared at the charred imprint in the center of it: the cross, surrounded by beads. For a long, strange second, the demonic Hellboy blinked at his injury with a half-puzzled, half-hurt expression.

Then he looked over at Grigori, who was waiting expectantly for the completion of his precious ritual.

With a blood-curdling scream, Hellboy yanked his stone hand out of the slab's depression, reached up with both hands, and savagely broke off his horns. Blinding light and energy spilled from the stumps, making everyone throw their hands up to protect their eyes. Spinning around with one horn still clutched in his big hand, Hellboy thrust it forward—

—deeply into Grigori's abdomen.

With a strangled cry, Grigori dropped to his knees, clutching his stomach as Hellboy towered over him. Hellboy tossed the bloodstained horn aside as the marble slab made a cracking nose; when he looked over at it, the third imprint was sinking into the surface of the stone, spreading and melding with it until it finally disappeared. The wildly flickering lights around them abruptly winked out as the connection between the slab and the moon was broken.

The sudden absence of sound and scarlet light paralyzed them all for a long moment, then from where she lay in the dirt, Ilsa lifted her face to the silent, clearing sky and pulled her bloodied lips back in a silent snarl. The building thunderclouds were gone, the eclipse had ended, and a few feet away, Grigori was crumpled on his side in agony.

Hellboy held up his stone hand and watched the burning glyphs etched in the stone dim and finally die away altogether. He ground his teeth and endured the pain as his features and body smoothed out and resumed their shape, shrinking down from huge to their normally oversized form. Around them, the church room was, at last, quiet, and filled with nothing more than the soft glow of the scattered oil lamps.

Grigori twisted on the ground and turned his face to Hellboy. "You will never fulfill your destiny," he gasped. Blood dribbled from the corners of his mouth and his fine ceremonial robe was soaked with red grit. "You will never understand the power inside you!"

Hellboy stared down at him dispassionately. "I can live with that." Stepping over to where Myers was still stranded, a two-fisted yank pulled apart the thick ropes that held the agent. Finally the man was free and he clawed his way up the post until he was standing at Hellboy's side.

His heart breaking, Hellboy turned and gingerly lifted Liz's limp body into his arms. He lowered his face to hers and kissed her forehead, then ran his fingers through her hair and breathed in the familiar scent of her—fire and cinders—as he carried her down the steps. Myers followed silently, his insides churning in sympathy for Hellboy, for Liz, for himself. Three steps later, his foot came down on something hard and round, and he looked down.

A glass eye. For some reason, having it there on the

ground, *looking* at them, sent a ripple of dread up the agent's spine.

Both Hellboy and Myers froze at the sound of a whisper coming from out of the dark behind them.

"Child . . ."

With Liz still limp in his arms, Hellboy turned stiffly toward the voice. There he was—Grigori, on his knees and sending Hellboy a one-eyed, blood-filled smile. Hellboy grimaced. First of all, Grigori was supposed to be dead; secondly, it was never a good thing when a man-beast like him gazed at you with a smile on his face.

"Look what you've done." Grigori lifted his head a little more, until the top half of his face slid into a shaft of warm light. There was something soft and fleshy wriggling in his empty eye socket, shifting like lazy worms. "You've killed *me*," Grigori told him with difficulty. "An insignificant man. But you have brought forth a *god*."

With that, Grigori spread his blood-soaked hands wide, revealing the deep puncture wound that Hellboy had inflicted with his broken horn. The ends of it had widened into a gaping cavity in the man's stomach; the instant Grigori let go of his skin, a tangle of long, pale appendages spilled from the opening like pulsing, wet intestines. They undulated frantically on the ground, falling over themselves as more and more of the same poured from Grigori's abdomen. "Behold!"

he wheezed. "My master, Behemoth! Guardian of Thresholds . . . *Destroyer of Worlds!*"

Hellboy and Myers stumbled backward as a steamy, slime-covered seven-foot-high tower of flesh with too many tentacles to count erupted from what had come from Grigori's body. It surged forward and landed greasily on the obsidian slab, squirming and growing, doubling its size as each second ticked past, leaving its once great host to die, disregarded, on the dirt- and rock-strewn floor of the cavern.

Ilsa darted around the infant Behemoth with barely a glance at it, dropping to her knees next to Grigori's splayed corpse. Crying, she pulled him upright and cradled him tenderly, then bent and kissed him full on his bloody mouth. A shadow suddenly covered her— one of the Behemoth's gigantic appendages—but she only glanced at it disdainfully before turning her cold, withering gaze to Hellboy and Myers. "Hell will hold no surprises for us," she said flatly.

And died as the monstrous column of flesh fell and crushed her along with the sad remains of her long-time lover.

Hellboy and Myers had managed to retreat as far as the entrance to a passageway that Hellboy hoped would eventually lead back to Manning and, just maybe, the cemetery itself. Shooting a glance back toward the church room, Hellboy carefully handed Liz's body over to Agent Myers. He was too injured to get far with her, but anything was better than being in this cavern with that creature. "Keep her safe," he said hoarsely. "No matter *what*. I'll deal with whatever that thing is back there."

Myers's eyes widened. "Alone?"

Hellboy gave him a shrug that looked a lot more careless than he actually felt. "How big can it be?" he asked with a caustic little smile. Before Myers could reply, something huge, *really* huge, completely filled the tunnel behind them. Hellboy inhaled and started to turn and confront it, then the end of it—cold, wet and disgustingly slippery—wrapped around his waist and yanked him back and out of the tunnel at breakneck speed, scraping him high along the ceiling and smashing half of the oil lamps up there on his head. It whipped him around and forward, and finally Hellboy saw what he was up against.

Gah!

The creature was the size of a house, and to make matters worse, Hellboy's head was drenched in hot oil, his horn stumps smoking where they'd run against the stone ceiling. He squirmed in its grip, but the thing was way too strong for—

Wham!

Suddenly it threw him at the ceiling. Hellboy had time to wonder testily if it thought he was a tennis ball, then he hit hard—and crashed harder to the floor. The floor cracked beneath him, sending a wide split several feet in each direction. He blinked and tried to clear his head, then saw the rosary and the grenade belts, only inches away from his outstretched hand. He lunged for them but didn't make it; instead, one of the beast's tremendous tentacles slammed down, cutting off his attempt. With hundreds of those things and only one of him, he was *way* outnumbered.

The weight of the massive appendage sent a shock-wave through the floor, bouncing both of the grenade belts that Hellboy had been aiming for right into the widening fissure. As the tentacle pulled up and prepared to strike again, Hellboy rolled close enough to the ground crack to see the belts; they were maybe four feet down, balanced on a dangerously crumbling ledge. Below that and barely visible through the narrowing heart of the fractured stonework was a mesh of turning gears and cogs, some still-running piece of the machinery that Grigori and Kroenen had set in motion.

A splatter of moisture against his face warned Hellboy that the dripping tentacle was coming for him again. He skipped out of the way, doing a tight double-spin that let him yank a heavy, rusted broadsword from the petrified grip of the nearest stone statue. It came free with the statue's hand still attached. No matter; Hellboy covered that with his own and came back around, swinging the sword with every bit of muscle he could put into it. *Bull's-eye!* As old and decrepit as the blade was, centrifugal force and Hellboy's own weight was on his side; he sliced clean through the thick, fleshy thing grabbing for him, sending the disembodied piece of it rolling aside and into the crack in the floor.

But Hellboy's victory was pathetically short-lived. The stump of the Behemoth's appendage pulsed out a disgusting white goo, then a mass of wriggling mini-limbs, like small, rapidly growing fingers pushed out from its wet end. The fingers grabbed for his face as Hellboy raised the sword, slashing again and again, desperately trying to gain some ground, all the while knowing the creature was growing larger with every piece that he chopped off.

But he would not give up, he would not lie down and call this a lost battle. There was way too much at stake here—the world, for instance. Another cut, and another, and suddenly there was the fissure, finally within reach. Holding off the jabbing, gasping attack with the sword in one hand, Hellboy slid down on his side and leaned into the crack, struggling to reach the belt. Stretching . . . almost . . .

No matter how he tried, Hellboy was still a few inches too far. He wasn't gonna make it.

Screw this.

With a final wild slash, he rolled bodily into the crack, righting himself at the last second so that he landed on the ledge with both feet. And wouldn't you know, the damned thing crumbled beneath him.

Fighting for balance as a few of the stones buried in the walls of the crack tumbled into the gears below, ducking under the searching tentacles rolling over the edge above him, Hellboy tried to grab the belts as the stones were pulverized to dust in the massive machinery only a few yards beneath him. No good—the collapsing earth and stones sent the belts sliding even farther away. If he didn't do something fast, soon they'd be toast.

Something cold and nasty slid under his arm and around one shoulder and pulled him upward. Fighting against the tentacle, Hellboy had an instant—just that—while he was airborne to reach out with his tail and snag two of those belts, holding on to them with everything he had as he was swung around like the bucket seat on a cheap carnival ride. And while that was bad enough, what was coming was a whole lot worse.

The Behemoth lifted him high into the air. Hellboy squirmed and pounded on the tentacle, but he'd lost the sword on the way up and this beast wasn't feeling anything . . . except hungry. Directly below and opening wide was an orifice that couldn't be anything but its mouth: way too big, multilayered, ringed with teeth and more moving parts in one place than anything organic had a right to possess, it was a vague cross between an octopus's beak and the mouth of a spider on nuclear steroids.

And Hellboy was definitely on the menu for dinner.

But he'd be damned if he'd go down without a fight.

He jerked his tail up and grabbed the two grenade belts, but the timers were crushed and useless. He got a tiny spark, but that was all. "They *never* work," he grumbled, then gasped and gripped the belts tighter as the tentacle swung him hard in the other direction. His stomach turned one way, then righted itself, throwing a flash memory of going over the bars on a swing set when he'd been a child. Now there wasn't much time left, so he wrapped the belts around his stone arm and gritted his teeth as the Behemoth's mouth loomed in front of him.

"Ugh!" Instinct made him try to jerk away, but he was held fast. He sucked in a final lungful of air. "Now this is gonna *hurt!*"

Squeezing his eyes shut, Hellboy pulled the pins on all the grenades at once right before the monster dropped him into its open mouth and swallowed him whole.

24

DARK.

Wet.

Burning.

And then—

Noise filled Hellboy's ears, a massive, strange gurgle. Like Jonah in the belly of the whale, he was surrounded, smothered, and enveloped.

But even that wasn't as consuming as the white-orange light that abruptly boiled through the Behemoth's body system when the grenades began to ignite in a marvelously hot chain reaction.

It lit up the creature from the inside, silhouetting internal organs that until a millisecond ago had still been growing. Alien body parts and twisted structures, a massive, shuddering throat, the huge, hanging sack that functioned as its gut, swinging free within its body cavity with Hellboy's form, curled like a fetus, silhouetted within it and looking small and insignificant in relation to what had eaten him.

The Behemoth burned from the inside out, screaming hellishly and thrashing as explosion after explosion pounded its center, and section by painful section completely and utterly ripped it apart. The final trio sent fire, stinking pieces of burned flesh, and white body fluids in every direction, and out of the middle of it—

Hellboy, landing with a sickening, bone-bruising *thud*, just as the Behemoth gave a final, mighty bellow and toppled sideways. Hellboy saw the mass of dead-weight tentacles falling straight for him, but he was too dazed to move, too shocked and incapacitated by the creature's digestive fluids to get his limbs to respond to his mental commands. His eyes had been pulled open with the final explosion and now he wanted to squeeze them shut again, didn't want to see the things that were destined to pulverize him, but even that tiny movement was impossible—his eyelids simply wouldn't obey.

Eyes wide, Hellboy stared at the oncoming appendages—

—as a foot away from his face they disintegrated in a blaze of sparkling energy, leaving nothing to drift down on him but a few leftover flesh-colored cinders.

Liz.

Myers.

Hellboy rolled to the side and groaned, then forced his arms to push him up, his wobbly legs to curl under and lift. Two more heavy shockwaves of light rolled across him, the beast's final death song; then there was nothing in the church room but empty, blessed silence; even the gears in the cavern below had at last stopped their grinding and ticking and turning. When Hellboy made it to his feet at last, he was covered in the slimy white sludge that had been the Behemoth's lifeblood, every pore of his body marinated in the ugly stuff. He cleared his throat, then spit out a wad of ash and goo. *Yuck.*

"Ouch," he croaked. "It *did* hurt."

—there were still working vocal cords in there. In fact, it seemed that everything was good and in working condition, even if on the surface he was slightly well done.

Finding his balance was tricky but not impossible. Hellboy lurched away from the smelly remains of Grigori's monster and headed for the passageway in which he'd left Myers and Liz. Her body was on the floor and the agent was still there, crouching protectively over her, his face full of shadows and shock. Relief shone in his eyes when Myers lifted his face and saw that it was Hellboy dragging himself painfully toward them.

Uneven footsteps from the other direction made Hellboy and Myers freeze, then Manning limped into view. Apparently he'd gotten tired of waiting and found his way to where the noise and action was. Hellboy was glad the man hadn't found them before now—he'd had all the people to take care of that he could handle.

Myers scooted aside to make room for Hellboy, and he crawled over to Liz's body, then delicately lifted her head in one big hand. He pulled her to his chest and held her there; wherever she was, she had to be able to hear his heartbeat, to know that it beat only for her. He wasn't ready to let her go, not yet.

Not *ever*.

Hellboy bent his head and put his lips next to her ear, then whispered something that the other two men couldn't hear.

But he wasn't really talking to Liz.

He raised his head and stared at her face.

And waited.

Five heartbeats, then ten.

Liz moaned softly, then opened her eyes.

He wanted to jump, run, bellow with joy, but there would be time for things like that later. Because now there would *be* a later. Instead, Hellboy smiled down at her, running his fingers ever so lightly through her hair.

Liz blinked at him, confusion filming her eyes. "In the dark . . ." she said. Her words were so weak they could barely be heard. "I heard your voice. What did you say?"

Hellboy kept stroking, marveling at the silky feeling of her hair despite the dust ground into it, the softness of her skin when his big fingers brushed against her cheek. Finally, he answered. "You, on the other side," he told her. "Let her go. Because for her, *for her*, I'll die. I'll cross over."

Hellboy looked away for a moment and when he finished, there was a shade of the emotion that must have been evident to whoever, or *whatever*, had been listening to his message.

"And you'll be sorry I did."

At his side, Myers couldn't help but smile. Liz's eyes cleared a bit more and she smiled up at Hellboy. The expression on her face said it all—everything Hellboy had ever waited for and wanted to see when she looked at him. She didn't have to say it, now or ever; he could see it in the way her eyes sparkled when she gazed at his face, in the firm, loving set of her mouth when she smiled.

And, of course, there was the gentle ring of yellow-orange fire that rimmed her body.

Manning watched without saying anything, but Myers looked away, half embarrassed, half saddened, his dusty face illuminated by the flames.

Liz found her strength and pushed up to her elbows, then slipped a hand around Hellboy's neck and drew his face to hers. As their lips met and they finally kissed, Liz's fire haloed them both, making the two of them the only ones in the world. . . .

. . . who mattered.